TAKEN BY A BEAST

THE WHITEHAVEN SHIFTERS

KELLY LORD

Copyright 2022 © Kelly Lord

All rights reserved.

No part of this publication may be reproduced, distributed, or transmitted in any form or by any means, including photocopying, recording, or other electronic or mechanical methods, without prior written permission of the publisher, except in the case of brief quotations embodied in critical reviews and certain other non-commercial uses permitted by copyright law.

Contact: kellylord23@gmail.com
Cover Design: www.miblart.com
Formatted by www.phoenixbookpromo.com

TRIGGER WARNING

This book contains sex, mature language, forced proximity, mentions of gender stereotypes, mentions of class stereotypes, a scene of moderate violence. There is no domestic abuse in this story. All sex is consensual. There is no cheating.

CHAPTER ONE

Riley Roth

Shortcuts are only a good idea if they cut the traveling time by half. Not if it means getting lost in the middle of Hillbilly Hick-Ville with nowhere to turn around. I was lost. Having driven for miles and miles in the wrong direction, admitting to myself that I was royally screwed. I should have taken my mom's advice and let the chauffeur drive me, but after the fight we had about me acting like a spoiled, entitled bitch, and me yelling in her face that I hated her guts and wished that she'd drop dead, I thought it would be best to leave before we said something we might later regret. Not about her cussing me out, or me wishing her dead, but before either of us brought up the sensitive subject of Dad. So, I left things sour between us. All the hurtful things I wanted to say kept bobbing to the surface, and now I was cursing myself for not coming up with an epic one-liner. It would have given her something to think about. How dare she call me spoiled when she and Dad indulged me? She helped to create the monster in me, and I intend to make her rue the day she ever crossed me. The condescending bitch.

With my music cranked up high, I cruised along the dark woodland road with my favorite song blasting through the speakers. I focused hard on the meandering way ahead, refusing to look from left to right at the surrounding forest. Dark looming trees wanted to keep me hostage, but I wanted out. I hated the woods, and the sooner I found a way out of here, the better. I will take that stupid intern job and prove to Mom I'm not lazy. She'll choke on her words when I have Mr. Wade eating out of the palm of my hand. I smiled to myself smugly.

A huge dark mass darted out from the trees and blocked the road.

"Oh shit!" I screamed, swerving around it with only a second to spare.

I slammed my foot hard on the brake, forcing an emergency stop. What the fuck was that? In the red glow of my backlight, I saw the furry blob move and realized it was a bear.

I almost hit a bear!

That would have made a dent the size of a crater in my bumper. I could have been killed. Docile beast. Didn't it hear my engine noise? I was miles from Viper City. The radio signal was shit, which was why I played a CD. And if my radio struggled to get a signal, that probably meant my phone would too. Stupid fucking unlit hillbilly hick road. The dark dense woodland was closing in on me, threatening to swallow me whole. I remember reading a road sign five miles back the other way, but the name 'Whitevale' didn't ring any bells. And without any internet signal, I couldn't use Google maps. This was just fucking perfect. Now I was trapped here, in a forest crawling with bears. Teddy Ruxpin, and his huge hairy meatballs, turned to look at me, sniffing the air. My backlight bathed his fur in red and it reflected in his eyes, making him look like an angry demon. He blew out a sharp blast of white condensation through his nostrils, and then he shook his head like he smelled something nasty, probably getting a lungful of burned rubber. Then he dropped onto all fours and loped closer to the car.

Shit! What do you even do when you're confronted with a bear?

In a quick attempt to armor myself inside my shiny red Bugatti Chiron, which undoubtedly attracted it like a red rag to a bull, I closed the window, killed the engine, and remained still. In the Jurassic Park movies, the T-Rex couldn't see people if they stayed still. So, I didn't move a muscle. My heart pounded inside my chest like a jackhammer as the bear peered through the window, tapping its claw against the glass. I side-eyed it, trying to figure out if it was knocking to get my attention, or whether it had seen its reflection and thought it was another bear. I was pretty sure it scratched its chin as it thought about that. I hoped the bear would continue on its merry way, but it seemed more interested in me than going home. I let out a terrified sob as it pushed the car and made it wobble. It peered right at me as if it expected me to acknowledge it, then gave the car another forceful shove. What did it want? All I had was a packet of breath mints and a bottle of water. I didn't have any food.

"Shoo!" I swatted my hand. "Go find your friend, Boo Boo, and steal a picnic basket, or something."

The bear began to claw at the door handle as if it was trying to get in. As my eyes darted down to where its claw was, I saw his huge bear-sized balls beneath an almighty protrusion. He was aroused. And he was trying to get the goddamned door open so he could break in and attack me with his grizzly appendage.

"Grr!" it growled, and it shook the entire fucking forest, sending bats fluttering from the treetops.

"Go away!" I screamed. "Leave me alone!"

He — who was hung like the world's most endowed grizzly — dipped his head low and nudged the side of the car, causing it to rock from side to side. I screamed again, my fingers shaking as I started the engine, then sped off down the road, turning the corner on two wheels. It was lucky I didn't crash because I could hardly control such a powerful vehicle. It was new. I was still getting used to it.

"Fuck! Oh, shit! That was so close!" I rushed my words, panic-stricken.

The scary encounter left me feeling shaken and spooked. There were no street lamps to light the way ahead. I had to rely on my headlights to illuminate the bends in the road. Anything could have jumped out of the woods at me. Someone should put up signs to warn people about this.

I drove for three miles until I reached a town called Lakewell. My car had taken quite a blow, and I needed to find somewhere safe to pull over and assess the damage. I whimpered, hitting my palms on the steering wheel. There was likely to be a huge paw-sized dent in my door.

Great! This was just fucking perfect. Mom is going to laugh her ass off when she hears about this.

The farther away I got, the more relaxed I became. I blew out a huge sigh of relief the minute I reached civilization. The woods creeped me out, especially at night. There was something sinister about being lost in a dark forest. And I should know because it happened to me once when I was little.

CHAPTER TWO

Riley

Lucky for me, I noticed the sign for a guest house — Anderson Retreats. The overgrown bushes were blocking part of the sign, so I almost drove straight past it.

I pulled into a free parking space and cut the engine. After three attempts to open my door, I resorted to slamming my body weight against it to get it to open. Just as I feared, the door suffered substantial damage, and that would mean a call to my insurance company. It was late. There was no way I would make it to the hotel in Viper City tonight, which meant I would be late for my meeting with Mr. Wade tomorrow. I grabbed my phone from the holder to call him and ask if we could reschedule, only to notice my battery was dead. Cursing myself for not having charged it before I left the house, I stormed out of the car, making my way over to the main entrance of the guest house. Once inside the modern building, a gray-haired man in his late fifties greeted me at the reception desk.

"Hi there, do you have a reservation, Miss?" he asked politely.

"No," I reply, waving my hand in dismissal. Can I please use your phone? Mine's out of battery."

He pointed to the phone on the desk. "Sure, it's right here. But be sure to press the hash key before you dial an external number," he replied, returning a kind smile.

"Thank you so much," I replied, sighing dramatically.

I snatched up the handset, dialing the number to Wade Internationals. The billionaire CEO, Mr. Thomas Wade, was an old childhood friend of my mom's. I either worked for him, or I had to choose between my parents' companies. That was like asking me to choose which parent I loved the most. There was no right answer. I felt torn between the two, I could practically feel myself splitting down the middle they tugged on me so hard.

Mr. Wade's secretary answered in a polite, "Hello. Wade Internationals. You've reached Mr. Wade's office; how may I help you?"

All I had to do was make my excuse, and I would be home and dry.

"It's Riley Roth. put me through to Mr. Wade. He's expecting me," I replied bossily.

The secretary stammered at my abruptness, and then put me on hold while she transferred the call. After a twenty-second pause, Mr. Wade's deep baritone rumbled through the speaker.

"Riley . . . are you all set for our meeting tomorrow?" he asked, seeming enthusiastic about my arrival. "I hope you're not calling to wriggle out of it. Sasha warned me you might." His tone was playful, sounding nothing like how he spoke to his workforce.

"Um, about that . . . I had a little bump on the way," I informed him.

"That's terrible. I hope you're not hurt?" he replied, showing concern for my welfare. "Call a recovery company, if need be, and let us take care of the costs."

"I'm fine, Sir. I can handle it," I replied, wanting to show some initiative because I knew for a fact, he would report this back to my mother.

We exchanged brief pleasantries before I hung up the call.

"Thanks." I flashed the reception guy a chaste smile.

"That's quite all right, Miss. You don't have to thank me. Have a safe journey now," he replied curtly, swatting the air as if it was no big deal.

I walked back to my car, blowing out a forced breath at the state of the battered door. But as I climbed inside and started the engine, the only sound it made was a concerning splutter.

"C'mon," I muttered, frustrated.

Nothing was happening. The engine wasn't firing up. That fucking bear had killed my car.

"Shit!" I yelled, hitting the wheel with the palm of my hand.

I bumped my head on the wheel repeatedly, cursing my idiotic decision to come through this way. Honestly, I could've just sat there and cried. Today wasn't my day. I wished I could erase everything and start over from scratch. My life was all about glitter and glamor. The tabloids loved me.

They loved to hate me.

Some stories they wrote about me were true. I was a cold-hearted bitch who didn't care about anyone other than herself. No one would miss me. It was safe to say, I was going nowhere. Karma was paying me back for all my dastardly deeds of ruthlessness. There were too many to count. I toyed with people's affections and then I ripped their hearts out of their chests, then stomped on them with my designer stilettos. Not literally, but I hurt them all the same. Without an ounce of remorse. Not even shedding a tear. Then I moved on to my next victim to wreak havoc again. I often ask myself why I do it, but the answer remains the same. I don't know.

Tapping my finger against the wheel, I weighed up my limited options. Rather than stay here in a roadside guesthouse, I preferred to call a recovery company and have them take me to the luxury hotel I booked in Viper City. They had a spa where I could decompress with a cold glass of champagne. My poor abused pores had suffered nothing but road dust and engine fumes for miles. So, hoping the kind old reception guy would take pity on me a second time, I went back inside to ask if I could use the phone again.

"Excuse me," I announced. "You're not going to believe this but my car won't start. Do you mind if I call a recovery company?" I explained.

A sympathetic look creased the corners of his eyes. "You'll be lucky. Your best bet is to wait until morning. We have a spare room if you need it," he offered, bursting my last bubble of hope.

But what was the alternative? To sleep in my car. *I don't think so.*

"Fine," I replied exhaustedly. "It's been a long day, and I'm pretty tired," I confessed. All I wanted to do was take a hot shower and crawl into bed.

As a rule, I didn't carry cash on me. So, I paid for the room using my debit card. All I had to do was sign my name in the guest book, and he gave me a white plastic key card.

"Well, my name is Carl. Call me if you need anything. I hope you enjoy your stay here . . ." He eyed the name in the guest book and his pupils enlarged. "Miss Roth. Breakfast is at seven-thirty." He gulped nervously as if it dawned on him who I was.

"Thanks . . . oh, wait!" I said, remembering I left my belongings in the car.

"I'm just going to go grab my things, and I'll be right back," I told him as I rushed back outside to get my overnight bag and laptop.

I hurried to my car, opened the door, and grabbed my belongings from the passenger seat. I had a strange feeling that eyes were following me, watching every move I made. I slung the carry-on over my shoulder, glancing around to see if anyone was around. It was like the forest had eyes, which was spooky as fuck. I squinted at the tree line, but it was way too dark to see anything moving out there.

A cold wind blew around me, lifting my hair off my shoulders, and causing me to shudder. I hated the woods during the day, let alone at night.

CHAPTER THREE

Riley

I slammed the door shut and hurried back into the warmth of the guest house. Carl was busy sorting through tourist pamphlets as I darted back inside. The door closed with a soft rattle, making him glance up at me, flashing a friendly smile.

"It's creepy being so close to the forest," I muttered, hating how scared I felt.

He raised his brows at my comment as if this news unnerved him.

"Oh, you don't want to go into the woods

around here, Miss Roth. It's not safe. It's teaming with rogues," he replied solemnly as if I ought to heed his warning.

"There are plenty of rogues in California too," I replied, making a joke. "The only difference is they have Botox and a suntan."

I readjusted my grip on my overnight bag, balancing my laptop on my hip so I could carry everything. Carl's confused frown made things awkward. I returned a polite smile as I turned to leave.

"Don't worry, I'll stay well away from the woods," I replied, walking away.

My phobia of the woods started when I got lost in them during a school trip when I was seven. I remembered Dad's words, "Riley, if you ever get lost, stay where you are, and help will come." So, I sat on the ground and cried for hours. Eventually, much, much later, I was rescued, but not before it went dark. The atmosphere of the woods completely changed under the moonlight. My mom had to pay for me to have therapy because of it.

I shuffled to my room, hungry and fatigued. As I stepped through the door, I dumped down all my belongings and began peeling off my clothes as I headed to the bathroom. The green fluffy bath mat felt soft under my feet, and I glanced around at the clean, modern bathroom suite with surprise because I half-expected it to be a rat-infested hell hole. I turned the shower on and waited for the water to heat. When it was warm enough, I stepped into the tub and drew the plain white shower curtain across. Uh, what a day. Standing under the steamy water jets, I released an exhausted sigh, allowing the pressure to massage my aching muscles. It wasn't a spa, but it sufficed. Mom was going to kill me for screwing things up. She would find some way to make it my fault – for the bear on the road, my damaged car, not making it to Mr. Wade's office on time, the whole shebang. I finished washing, then dried and dressed quickly. Then completed my nightly regimen of applying body lotions, facial serums, and creams.

My weary eyes analyzed the crisp white bedroom, drinking it all in with appreciation. It was clean and modern with plain cotton bed sheets and red accessories. Not too shabby. It would be a great retreat if I needed to escape from reality. No fucker would know I'm here. I could go off the grid and vanish for a while.

Mom would be blowing up my phone right now. What a crying shame. Not.

Thank fuck my phone was dead. I rummaged through my bag for my charger. Then after a few minutes of charge, ignoring all the notifications that came beeping through, I was able to set the alarm for seven o'clock. My eyes trailed across the long, varnished countertop, noticing a coffee machine with a variety of pods, sugar sachets, and long-life milk pots.

Gah, how do people live like this?

It wasn't a difficult decision to make; I would rather die than drink instant coffee. So, I flicked through the channels trying to find something worthwhile to watch and came across a soap opera called Shifter Valley. It was the most ridiculous show I'd ever seen, but at least the guys were cute. I'm not even sure when I went to sleep; my eyelids started drooping, and the TV must have turned itself off. I dreamed I was in that fucking show. Everyone in town was a shapeshifting freak, but because it was a dream sequence, I was more focused on the fact that all the guys walked around shirtless. I'm not even sure I remember the ending because my dream melted away as I started to wake. "Mm," I mumbled, reaching out for my phone so I could check what time it was.

It felt as if I slept for longer than usual because

of the strong light pooling into the room, and I wondered if I had forgotten to set the alarm correctly. My hand felt around, seeking out the nightstand, but found nothing but air.

I cracked an eye open to see what I was doing wrong . . . only, something seemed different. A lot different.

I could've sworn the décor was all crisp white with the odd red accessory. I didn't remember the room having threadbare blue curtains, a wicker linen basket in the corner, a rickety wooden chair, or a cowboy hat dangling from the corner of it.

Oh, God. Is this some freaky weird dream?

The second I realized this wasn't a dream, and that something was amiss, my whole body stiffened with fright. I held my breath and heard the distinct sound of someone else breathing in the room. Long, languid, nasal respirations as if someone was sound asleep beside me.

As if right on cue, a large muscular arm draped over me, pulling me back against a rock-solid chest, and my eyes bulged wide with terror. It was how my Sunday mornings started after I drank too many cocktails on a Saturday night. Waking up in some random dude's house, and prayed that when I rolled over, he was hot, and not as butt-ugly as the back end of a raccoon. But I didn't go out last night. I went to bed sober — in another room — in a strange-ass town. For all I knew, he could be a serial killer. His hand brushed against my left breast, and he gave it a gentle squeeze.

"Argh!" I raised the roof with a glass-shattering scream.

CHAPTER FOUR

Riley

"Oh my god, I'm still dreaming!" I panicked, then tried pinching myself. "Wake up!" I slapped my face and made it sting. "Ow! Stupid Shifter Valley."

"Calm down, I can explain." The large naked guy held his palms up as if I was the one over-fucking-reacting.

They've gone from being shirtless to full-on nude!

"Get away from me, creep!" I yelled frantically, sidestepping away from him.

With each attempt he made to try and grab

hold of my arms, I spun mine in circles. It looked like some freakishly weird dance moves.

"I think we've finally established that this is not a dream," he patronized me.

"That just makes this ten times worse!" I shrieked, looking around for something to throw.

He held out his palm as if calming a wild animal. "Hey, I'm not going to hurt you. You're not in Shifter Valley. I know this seems a little weird but this is not how this is supposed to go down." He drove his fingers through his hair, muttering to himself like a lunatic. "I thought you'd be pleased."

And he had the audacity to look at me as if I was the one stark-raving mad.

"What?" *Was he for real?*

"You kidnapped me from the guest house. You need to let me go, or else you're going to be in serious trouble, buddy," I warned, pointing a finger at him.

He dragged his hand down his face, clearly frustrated. My eyes flew south and saw evidence of his excitement.

"Oh my God! Cover yourself!" I screamed, slapping a hand over my eyes.

I heard him move, and I quickly ran farther away around the room. When I looked again, I saw that he'd pulled on a pair of jeans. I could still make out his manhood straining against the denim, and I couldn't help but notice how well-endowed he was too.

"You slept next to me naked, and you don't think that's just a teeny-tiny bit creepy?!" I held up my forefinger and thumb to measure an inch gap.

His brows raised with amusement, his chest heaving and lips slightly parted.

He thinks I'm making fun of him, size-wise, and now he's standing there all cock-sure of himself.

Of course, it wasn't small — at all! If I had to admit it, he looked like the epitome of every female fantasy. Over six feet tall and built like a house. He was insanely handsome, with rugged good looks, dark blond hair, deep, piercing blue eyes, with a massive . . . *ugh! I'm not even going to think about that.*

Oh fuck, what am I saying? Let's not forget he's a friggin' psycho.

"Are you done checking me out now? It's my turn to talk," he said, pointing to his chest.

I flung my hands up exasperatedly. "Humor me, asshole. I've had a night from hell, and this better be part of the nightmare," I retorted.

"Interesting choice of words," he muttered to himself. His face scrunched into a scowl. "You were trespassing on a private road and almost mowed me down." He pointed at me accusingly.

"You and your careless driving, and terrible music by the way. My Chemical Romance, seriously?" He canted his head to one side, narrowing his eyes at me in mock pity.

I stared open-mouthed, struggling to believe the temerity of the arrogant asshole. I opened my mouth to speak, but he cut me off.

"Wait. I'm not done here." His voice held an indignant tone as if *he* felt like the injured party. "And to top it off. It turns out *you're my* mate. The woman who almost flattened me like a rug turns out to be my fuckin' mate. I could scent it all over you. I ran to that guest house and pulled all the thingymebobs out of your sports car." He produced the glow plugs from inside the pocket of his jeans. "Here, you want them back?" he offered, then threw them onto the bed. "Where did you get those from anyway, NASA? Real cars have spark plugs. Those look like uranium rods." His tone oozed with sarcasm.

Nobody had ever spoken to me like this before. How dare he! The arrogance. The downright disrespect.

He sabotaged my fucking car on purpose!

My clenched fists shook at my sides. I was ready to punch this guy. What if he was an escaped patient from a mental institution? It was possible. The guy was nuts. I glanced around for a phone to call 911.

"It's okay," I said, keeping my voice level. "I'm going to call someone who can help you because you need professional help." I raised my palms as I edged toward the door. "I promise I won't press charges. Do you have anyone I can call? A family member, a social worker, psychologist?" I asked, desperately trying to maintain a calm façade.

He ran his fingers through his hair and blew out a forced breath. "Har, fucking har har, very funny! Are you done?" His patience began to wane.

Shit! I've made him mad.

I cringed. "Look, maybe we just got off on the wrong foot. Just point me in the direction of the road, and I'll be out of your way. I'll send you compensation for the trauma I caused. My family is loaded, so just name your price," I tried to resolve the situation the only way I knew how — with money.

He glared back at me looking livid as he scrunched his face. "I don't want your money. I want your company. You're my mate. You're supposed to be made for me. Don't you feel it?" he asked, searching my eyes for a flicker of truth.

I shrugged. "I'm not blind. You're attractive and all. I'll give you that much. But as for feeling it . . . the only thing I'm feeling right now is creeped the fuck out. Now, if you'll excuse me . . . I have a job interview to get to."

I didn't know what else he expected me to say, but the more time I took to fully appreciate him, the more I wanted to unravel the mystery surrounding the hunky dork. Be it my oversexed hormones or genuine curiosity. He intrigued me.

"Forget about the interview for a sec and just give me a chance. Let me explain what I am. All I'm asking for is a month. That's long enough to get to know me and decide whether you like me or not. Then if you think it's not working out, you can leave, and I promise to let you. With no hard feelings, of course," he begged, his throat bobbing nervously.

"Uh, you don't get it. If I don't show up for my interview, my mom will kill me. She's been riding my ass about being more self-sufficient. If I screw this up, she'll disinherit me for sure." I sighed. "Don't take this the wrong way, but there are dating apps for shit like this."

I saw the world come to an end in his eyes, forcing him to do what he did next.

Beg.

"Please," he asked again. "My kind gets one true soulmate. No one else even comes close. Please, give me a chance to prove I'm worth it. I promise I'll treat you like a fucking queen."

I pinched the bridge of my nose and squeezed my eyes shut, giving it some thought. The things he said were cute, but the entire situation was completely fucking crazy. Scratch that, this was insane. Unthinkable. Not to mention seriously sketchy. For all I knew, he could've been an axe murderer. Then again, would a mentally deranged psychopath beg me to date him for a month and promise to treat me like a queen?

How many mentally deranged psychopaths have you actually met, Riley? Yeah, that's right, none.

My gut twisted in knots, worrying about ifs, buts, and maybes.

Do I run along home to where my dull, boring life awaits me, or do I take a chance for once and do something reckless?

"I can't believe I'm saying this. I must be as insane as you are. But fine. You got a month," I replied.

I didn't want to work in a stuffy office anyway.

His face filled with shock, having expected me to turn him down flatly.

"Really?" he stumbled back with surprise.

I crossed my arms defensively and studied his body language in a silent analysis. There was still the opportunity to run if he turned out to be a nut job. He had ten seconds left to prove me wrong, then I was out of there.

"So, what are you, Amish or something? You said *my kind*," I quizzed, using my fingers to make air quotes.

"What's Amish?" he asked bemusedly.

My eyes flinched at his confusion. "You really are a recluse, huh?" I replied, wondering if he knew anything about the outside world.

His posture relaxed. "My name is Austin Rayne, and I'm a bear shifter from Forest Hills originally. Now I'm stationed here, in Lakewell."

My eyes rounded, setting firmly in a hardened glare. "S'cuse me, you're a what?" I spluttered. "I don't think I heard you right."

"I'm a bear shifter from Forest Hills," he repeated slower.

He seemed so matter of fact as he spoke, not even the hint of a smirk danced across his lips.

Either he had the perfect poker face, or he believed in what he was saying.

"Do you work for animal control, shifting bears around or something?" I asked, making sense of what he said.

He laughed heartily. "Not even close, sweetheart. It means I can turn into a bear at will. It was me you almost turned to roadkill with your fancy car," he explained.

I scrunched my face, eyeing him with skepticism. "Are you telling me you're a bear. Like an actual bear?"

Warning bells started ringing in my head, and I began edging closer and closer toward the bedroom door. This guy thought he was a bear. This was textbook clinical lycanthropy. I had heard about this. It was when people believed they could transform into animals like werewolves and shit like that. And this dude thought I was his mate.

Oh, fuck, fuckety fuck! It's just my luck to get stuck with a hot nut job.

He exhaled exasperatedly. "*No* – I'm a fucking unicorn. Of course, I'm a bear. Do you need me to prove it?"

I nodded, calling his bluff. He could've been in the same place at the same time for all I knew, running away from whatever institution he escaped from.

He pulled open the top button of his jeans and shucked them off. I may have had a sly look at his cock. It was pretty large and damn hard to miss.

The sound of snapping bones startled me. I then watched with horror as his body transformed into something large, brown, and grizzly.

CHAPTER FIVE

Riley

My jaw practically hit the floor as Austin transformed. He went from a hot looking man, into a big, furry, not so cute bear, bashing against the chest of drawers and knocking off a few framed pictures.

"You weren't kidding. Oh my God! It was you. You dented my fucking car!" I yelled, pointing an accusing finger, feeling my temper surging.

He had transformed into a huge, mean-looking grizzly bear, and in any normal circumstances, I wouldn't be yelling at him. But this was the same guy who dented my door, removed the glow plugs from my car, insulted my favorite band, and to top it all off, stole me like a creep in the dead of night.

He canted his head to one side, observing my reaction as if to say *"Seriously? You're bringing this up, now?"*

Even in bear form, he was still an annoying jerk. But a handsome annoying jerk at that. And from looking at his childhood photos, his family looked fairly fucking decent. There was nothing about them that screamed *psycho* at all.

If I had to admit it, I'd been bored for as long as I could remember. I hated the way my mom controlled me, forcing me to work for Mr. Wade, and making me take a boring office job she knew I would hate. So maybe I wanted to get back at her a little. Maybe she would panic if I was reported missing.

It served her right. And anyway, if she did disinherit me, there was always Dad to fall back on. They were always playing against each other, point-scoring, tit-for-tat. I would call her bluff for a change. I was an only child. What was she going to do? Leave all her fortune to some cat sanctuary? I didn't think so.

I would just run to my dad and flutter my

eyelashes until he coughed up some cash like he always did; then Mom would soon cave in, because at the end of the day, she was a kick-ass businesswoman, and she would rather slit her own throat than let her cheating rat of an ex-husband win.

"Change back," I ordered.

Seconds later, a very nude Austin stood before me making my cheeks blush.

Don't look . . . don't . . . look. Damn . . . too late.

"So, Riley, do you have any questions?" he asked casually.

"Yes, actually, I do. How do you know my name? I haven't told you," I asked, narrowing my eyes suspiciously.

"It was written on your luggage label and on your bumper sticker. It reads "Living the life of Riley". It wasn't rocket science to work it out," he muttered sarcastically, giving a slight shrug of his shoulders. The sudden action caused his manhood to move, thus catching my attention once again.

"The bumper sticker was a lucky guess because it's a phrase people say when they're living their best life. Put some pants on," I muttered, embarrassed I'd been caught staring at it twice.

"I'm used to being in a bear's form most of the time, but if my nudity bothers you, I'll cover my assets just for you, angel," Austin mumbled, throwing a cheeky smirk my way.

I knew I'd been busted. "So, where are we?" I asked out of curiosity, trying to change the subject. "You said Lakewell, but where's that?"

"Whitehaven. Surely you know where you are. Regular people don't come through here. My humble abode is the last ranger station before Forest Hills; that's where I grew up — obviously." The way he flared his eyes suggested he thought I was nuts.

No way was I going to admit not remembering the road signs. I couldn't even remember my phone number by heart. That was the whole point of carrying business cards in my purse.

"Forest Hills," I repeated the name of where he said he was from, my eyes rounding with mockery. "How original. A forest on a hill. Whoever named it must be a genius."

He countered my snarky attitude with a fake smile.

"Honey, you are miles from any human town, so no one will hear you scream. I mean, you could try," he shrugged, gesturing around with both hands. "The only people within a five-mile radius are four wolf shifter brothers. Maybe you could visit their mate, Isobelle. She's all right, I guess. English, and a little dramatic, but nice all the same," he spoke in a lazy country drawl.

"Wait, what?! You brought me out into the woods?" I started to hyperventilate.

His expression morphed into a concerned frown. "What's wrong with the woods?"

I was shaking. "I hate them. I mean I really, really fucking hate the woods. Oh my God. I'm gonna die," I exaggerated.

He stalked towards me; his *thing* dangled between his thighs like a swinging pendulum. I didn't get time to react before he crushed me against his chest, face first. The warm musky scent of masculine man with earthy undertones filled my lungs, making my downtown flutter like a traitorous bitch.

His strong embrace really did remind me of a bear hug. A girl could feel safe in those big, strong arms. Then I felt *it* twitching. His huge cock was squashed against me, jerking at my midriff like a horny jumbo wiener. God had blessed him down under. There was no doubt about that. It moved against me like it had a mind of its own and wanted to get under my nightdress.

I tried to mumble, but my lips and nose were squashed against Austin's torso. "Austin, get off me. Can't breathe." I slapped my palms against the back of his shoulders.

If I wasn't mistaken, I'd say he lingered for a few seconds too long, rubbing himself against me. What was he doing? Marking me with his scent? Then I felt his large hands squeeze my ass, and my eyes bulged wide.

Nope, he's just being perverse.

"Whoa! I always hoped my mate would have an ass I could grab hold of." He chuckled while grasping a cheek in each hand.

"Hey!" I slapped his back hard, and he let go.

His eyes were dark with lust, but he didn't try to kiss me. When I pushed away, he let me go.

"Sorry, been alone for way too long," he excused his feral behavior.

I walked over to the window and drew back the threadbare curtains, letting the early morning light spill into the room. My mouth hung agape as I glanced out into the wilderness, seeing nothing but forest for miles.

"How come you're afraid of the woods?" he asked in a more reverent tone, acting like he cared.

I swallowed thickly before turning around to face him. "Brew some coffee and I'll tell you, and you can tell me why you're out here all on your lonesome in Hillbilly Hicksville," I replied, trying to cut him a bargain.

He shot me a strained smile, and his huge muscular shoulders relaxed.

"Deal," he responded, the corners of his eyes creasing with fondness.

Austin pulled on a pair of faded jeans, not bothering to put on a shirt. He was so easy on the eye. I didn't mind having something worthwhile to look at. I followed him down the creaky wooden staircase and into a basic kitchen. It was small, but it had a stove, a sink, a small countertop to prepare food, and a battered table in the middle with four mismatched chairs. Old spider webs clung to the corners of the room and above the top cupboards. Either he didn't like to clean, or he didn't spend much time indoors. I sat down at the table while he made coffee and foraged for something we could eat. Minutes later, he placed down a steaming hot mug of coffee and plate of buttered toast on the table in front of me.

"So, what does a bear shifter ranger's job entail?" I asked, making casual conversation.

"It's my job to patrol the border to make sure no one gets in who doesn't belong here," he answered, sitting opposite me. "Present company excluded."

"Thanks," I replied with a breathy smile. "So, that means you don't consider me a threat?"

"Only to me," Austin commented, his eyes fixed on mine.

My blush spread across my face. He made me so nervous. Usually, I was the one to make people nervous.

"Are you out here alone or are there others like you?" I asked.

"One or two others close by," he replied. "My closest neighbors are the wolf brothers I told you about. I can't wait to tell them I met my fated mate. They share Isobelle between them. I'm glad I got you all to myself."

Shared mate? Sheesh!

"You think fate brought me to you?" I asked.

My heart fluttered. It was the sweetest thing that anyone had ever said to me.

"Yes, I do. You and your shitty taste in music," he replied with sass.

And he's back to being an ass.

"Shitty taste? All right then, what's your favorite type of music?" I asked him.

"Elvis Presley," he replied, then did the goofiest Elvis impersonation.

I almost sprayed my coffee everywhere as I snorted with laughter.

How can someone who looks like that be such a dork?

"So, what's your story?" he asked, his wild grin spread across his lips.

I relaxed, taking a moment to compose my breathing. I hated talking about my phobia, but a deal was a deal.

"I got lost in the woods when I was little," I started to share. "It was dark by the time the rangers found me. The night before, I stayed up all night to watch the *Blair Witch Project,* and it scared the living shit out of me. I couldn't tell my mom or the therapist that though. Mom would've freaked out," I confessed.

Austin let out a roar of laughter. "Jeez, the Blair fuckin' Witch!"

"Hey, I was seven, and it was right up there next to *The Grudge,* you insensitive asshole!" I yelled, swatting his chest with the back of my hand.

He grinned, shaking his head from side-to-side.

I couldn't help but notice how hot he looked as the early morning sunlight streaked across his face. My eyes may have lingered on his lips because the next thing I knew, he leaned forward and cupped my face in his large hands. I stared back into his oceanic gaze as if I could happily drown there, feeling my heart skipping in my chest.

I wanted him to be the one to kiss me. I didn't want to make the first move because that would make me seem too keen. A man usually loved it when a woman drew him in using her feminine wiles; it maintained a shroud of mystery and kept him interested.

"I'm sorry," Austin apologized. "I shouldn't have laughed."

"It's okay," I replied, meaning it. "I'll let it go this once." I gave him a small reassuring smile to let him know all was well.

Austin was nervous. I think he wanted to kiss me, but he wasn't sure whether he should ask or just do it. I could see the conflict battling behind his eyes. What to do. How to do it. Now that *was* hilarious. He had initiated something that he wasn't entirely confident in finishing, which was my cue to take charge. With all the prowess of a hungry lioness going in for the kill, I moved off the stool to kiss him, pressing myself against his granite-hard chest, hearing him gasp with shock. My dexterous fingers embarked on a voyage of their own accord, exploring every dip and groove of his gorgeous, sculpted body.

Austin's hands brushed against my arms with uncertainty, then settled either side of my waist. My fingers concluded their journey, buried deep in his hair, and anchored him right where I needed him to be. As his lips parted, my tongue swept inside his mouth, stroking and tasting his unique essence. His touch held reverence despite the plethora of strength I knew he was capable of. There was a moment's hesitation before his novice tongue began swirling in sync with mine.

The hesitancy in Austin's actions only exhibited his lack of experience. It made me want to make our first encounter more memorable, so at least I got to leave a lasting impression.

Something awakened inside me. Something primal. I was used to moving fast for sure, but this was something else. Kissing Austin felt right. Our kiss intensified, devouring one another with a ravenous hunger that only sex could sate. Again, it was nothing new for me but if I could have inhaled that hunk of a bear in one go, I would because he smelled and tasted so damned good. He was so darn addictive. Austin broke the kiss first, leaving my swollen lips thirsty for more. His hooded eyes flicked to mine languidly as if dazed with lust. A boyish smile curved his lips as he scented the air.

"Someone's turned on," he pointed out.

CHAPTER SIX

Riley

"Do you want to get down and dirty in the kitchen, or shall we go up to your room?" I asked, grabbing the bear by the fur instead of the bull by the horns.

I must have misread the signals because we were obviously not reading from the same page, or the same book for that matter. I had the Kama Sutra going through my mind while he must have been reading Bible stories.

Austin gulped and squirmed nervously on his seat.

"What? You'd really do that with me? Like now? But you don't even know me that well yet. You called me a creep five minutes ago," he mumbled, shocked by my blasé attitude when it came to sex. "I thought maybe we could cuddle or talk or something."

"Ugh, it's just sex. We're both adults. It's not like we haven't both done it with tons of people before," I nonchalantly shrugged.

Austin's Adam's apple bobbed in his throat, and his eyes flinched with disappointment.

Did what I say hurt him?

"What did I say?" I asked bemusedly.

I'd obviously struck a raw nerve. His jaw pulsed, and his lips formed a tight, thin line as he dropped his gaze to the breakfast bar.

"Just sex—" He let that hang in the air between us.

"Austin," I spoke gently, placing a hand on his forearm.

He flinched away from my touch as if he was burned by the contact, then abruptly pushed back on his stool. He stalked out of the room, leaving me sitting there dumbfounded. We'd just gone one hundred and eighty degrees in the opposite direction. One minute it was steamy hot, then the next it was like we'd been doused with ice-cold water.

Was he upset that I'd slept with other men?

He stopped in the doorway, spinning on his heel to face me. "How many?" he blurted out angrily.

"How many, what? Men?" I asked, shocked at his sudden outburst.

He dragged a hand down his face as if dreading my answer. "Yes, that's what I'm asking. How many men have you hopped into bed with without giving it a second thought?" he asked, the vehement tone in his voice commanded that I answer truthfully.

The inner conflict of needing to know but not really wanting to hear it was evident in his tortured expression. I thought for a moment, looking up at the ceiling while I mentally counted, finishing off on my fingers.

"Shit! That many, huh?" he muttered, breathing out a defeated laugh.

"I don't exactly keep a record," I replied.

Austin pinched the bridge of his nose and groaned. "I shouldn't have asked."

I fidgeted awkwardly, feeling hurt and embarrassed by his unwarranted reaction.

So what? I'd had a life before we met. How dare he make me feel cheap for hooking-up with guys.

"You really wanna know?" I replied, getting up to walk toward him.

I was mad. Mad, hurt, and offended. He didn't say anything, so I continued.

"You asked, so now I'm going to tell you. I've slept with around twenty, maybe thirty guys. I don't exactly keep an accurate score," I answered candidly.

He closed his eyes like a wounded animal. His chest rose and fell with each ragged exhale as if he was fighting back his emotions.

Rage? Judgment? Jealousy? Who knows?

Instead of heading for the sitting room like I assumed he would, he darted for the back door. His capricious behavior startled me as he pushed past me and flung the door open. I flinched, hearing it crash against the opposite wall and slam shut behind him.

I couldn't bring myself to stay in the kitchen, so I walked back through the cabin with listless steps. Austin's outburst left me dazed, and I found myself in the sitting room, perturbed by what just happened. The battered loveseat caught me as I dropped down into it with a heavy sigh. I had a flippant attitude when it came to sex. It was fun. Not so much the intimacy, but the act itself.

Intimacy never appealed to me. I enjoyed the thrill of bedding a brand-new conquest, taking what we wanted from each other. It always gave me butterflies in my stomach. Feeling desired, sexy, and beautiful. Even if those feelings quickly faded. That's all that I craved. Just a fleeting moment because permanence scared the shit out of me. I did not want to end up like my parents. One minute they were madly in love and now they couldn't stand to breathe the same airspace. I don't do relationships.

The injured look on Austin's face made me feel cheap and sleazy. I'd screwed around, and I never cared about the consequences. Until now, sex was just sex. It didn't mean anything to me. I'd slept with guys — just because. There had been endless one-night stands, playboys, older guys, movie stars.

None of them meant anything to me, so why should they mean anything to him?

That was the kind of social circle I derived from. I was a spoiled little rich girl, what did he expect? Too bad if my experience bothered him. I couldn't believe he was acting this way unless he was a . . . could he be? Nah . . . surely not?

Was Austin Rayne still a virgin?

I chewed my bottom lip as the thought crossed

my mind. The more I thought about it, the more it all began to make sense.

He was still a virgin, and I was his first kiss. Oh God, he'd waited for "the one". Then along came me, Little Miss Slutty. What a disappointment I must be to him. He wanted me to be his first and last and hoped he would've been mine. Now I got it. Now I understood why he was hurt.

I debated whether or not I should leave him alone to cool off, but the restless side of me needed to try and fix this. The remorse was unreal. I wanted to take back everything that I had ever done and reverse time, do my life over again and fix all my promiscuous ways.

Thump . . . thump . . . thump.

I went outside to find Austin swinging his ax high over his head, then he brought it down with one almighty swoop, cutting log after log in half. I leaned against the doorframe, watching him vent all his pent-up anger with each forceful swoop of his ax. The sinewy muscles in his shoulders and chest flexed and rolled with each fluid motion. My eyes drank in his magnificence, in full appreciation of his Herculean form.

"Austin," I called out, only to be completely ignored.

I rolled my eyes in annoyance.

Great! The silent treatment. This either ends now, or it'll be one long-ass month.

I twisted my lips, narrowing my eyes into cunning slits, recalling how feminine pre-eminence ensues dominance over the male genitalia.

What to do to get a guy's attention? Gee, let me think.

A malevolent thought popped straight into my head, and my blood thrummed with anticipation. I stripped off my nightdress, screwed it into a ball, and threw it at the back of his head. It was enough to make him stop what he was doing and turn around slowly.

I saw the whites of his eyes as he saw me standing there as bold as brass, buck naked.

I didn't even attempt to hide my body. It was all shamelessly out on view for him to behold. I had always been confident with my physique having done a couple of naked photoshoots for Playboy just to piss off my parents.

"What're you doing?" His cheeks turned crimson.

The deep, reddened blush reached the tips of his ears, and his eyes glanced every other way but at me.

Aww, he was embarrassed. It wasn't the reaction

I was hoping for, but at least we were talking again. I was bored, and he was my source of entertainment. He could take it or leave it.

"Do you like it?" I asked, suggestively, stroking my fingers over my naked breasts to capture his attention.

"Riley, put your clothes back on," he mimicked my earlier tone, poking fun at my overreaction.

My plan worked though. His gaze flicked to my chest, then downtown, back up to my face again, not quite able to maintain eye contact.

"You haven't had sex before," I spoke, giving him an insight into my observations.

It wasn't a question, more a statement of fact. His silence was telling me I was accurate. I walked closer. He threw the ax so that it stuck into the stump beside him, still not giving me a definitive answer and looking like a startled deer trapped in headlights.

"Why are you walking towards me like that with that mean look in your eyes," he stammered nervously.

"Relax. I'm not going to jump your bones," I was quick to reply, stopping within an arm's stretch away from him. "Look, I'm a spoiled bitch. You've figured that much out for yourself. And so what, I've screwed other guys. They meant jack shit to me." I shrugged, speaking the truth.

The truth was a cold, hard, ugly fact. It wasn't pretty, but at least I was honest. I could've lied, spun him a line that I'd only ever slept with one guy my whole life. That he was my high school sweetheart, and I was young, dumb, and nauseatingly infatuated. Most women were dishonest about stuff like that. Especially with how fragile the male ego could be. We don't tend to divulge those secrets, just as men lie about the number of women they've slept with. Most men did, but not Austin. He seemed like one of the good ones, which only made me feel worse.

I continued, "So, can we start again?"

He reluctantly caved, picking up my nightdress, tossing back to me and shaking his head as if I was crazy.

"Aren't you going to say anything to me?" I asked as I dressed.

"Like what?" he answered, struggling to keep his eyes up north.

"You think I'm cheap," I answered him. "It's okay. I can see why you would."

"No, no, it's not that," he huffed, frustrated. "I would never think badly of you."

"Why are you acting like this then?" I asked, shaking my head with confusion. "Those guys are ancient history. And out in the big wide world, people hook-up nowadays. It's what all the kids are doing. Maybe you should get out more."

Austin frowned. "It's just that it makes me sick just thinking about you with other guys that aren't me, that's all," he admitted, looking completely crestfallen.

I threw my head back with a genuine laugh.

"We've only just met and you're already whipped." I chuckled at his cute comment.

Usually, that would be enough to make me want to run for the hills. It was weird how my feet remained rooted to the spot.

"If it makes you feel any better, they couldn't please me," I admitted. "I've always had to finish myself."

He folded his arms, giving a grunt in response.

"You're jealous," I accused, pointing a finger at him.

"Maybe I am," he snapped back, flinging his arms up in irritation. "Regardless of whether they pleased you, it still sucks they got you in the sack so fast. If they were so irrelevant, then why waste your time on them?"

"Boredom. Looking for something I'll never find. And hoping my pussy isn't broken. Pick one. They're all correct," I answered honestly.

Austin scoffed at the last comment. "It isn't broken. You just weren't with the right guy."

I was as sly as a fox when I wanted to be; just as cunning, manipulative, and precocious. A devious smirk swept across my lips, deciding to throw in a curveball. More than anything, I wanted to see how far I could push Austin Rayne.

"So, what are you waiting for? Take me to bed and give me an orgasm I'll never forget. Do to me what they never could," I challenged.

CHAPTER SEVEN

Riley

"Why are you just standing there with your mouth open?" I giggled.

The poor guy's confidence was draining faster than the color of his face. Sex terrified him, which is why he wanted a month to build up to it. Fair enough; I was too direct. So used to getting exactly what I wanted. And this guy was no exception. I usually slept with a guy on the first or second date depending on how drunk I was. There was no way I was prepared to have a month's abstinence.

Sorry bear-boy, that's just not an option.

Even Goldilocks tried out every bed in the house. Well, maybe not like that, but that depended on which version you read.

He licked his lips, running a hand through his already messed up hair.

"What, like now? As in, right now?" Austin stammered, his eyes growing huge.

It was so cute. I had to chew on the insides of my cheeks to stifle my laughter. I could tell he wanted to take the bait. He so wanted to. It was obvious, the cogs were turning around in that country boy brain of his. It made me feel more powerful, superior, in charge. Just how I liked it.

Here, standing before me like a stuttering mess, was a blond-haired, blue-eyed sex god. All I had to do was mold him into whatever I wanted him to be. He was a blank canvas, just waiting to be corrupted.

If only he kept his trap shut, he'd be my ideal man.

"I'm going to take a shower. You wanna join me?" I threw in the casual offer as I breezed past.

I even fake stretched with an exaggerated yawn, making sure he got a good look at my behind as I walked back through the door. The shirt rode up just enough to give him a sneaky view of my ass. I couldn't have been more obvious. But something told me that underneath all that earlier bravado stood an honest, decent, respectful guy who just so happened to believe I was his fated mate.

So, what if he was a bear shifter? His level of hotness blew all human men out of the water. I'd never been with a shifter before – didn't even knew they fucking existed until now.

If Austin didn't follow me, it wouldn't be the end of the world. I'd said shower, not bed. So, if he decided to pass, I wouldn't lose face.

The jerks I dated in the past were all pretentious assholes. Spoiled, chauvinist, trust-fund, mama's boys. This guy was down-to-earth, and his humble family photos were further evidence to back up that theory.

"Um, well, yeah, all right," I heard him deliberate behind me.

We came to a sudden stop at the top of the stairs. I couldn't remember the way to the bathroom. There was an awkward exchange of glances before Austin nervously led the way.

It was a typical cabin-style bathroom, clean and orderly, nothing extravagant. The toilet was in one corner, the sink was underneath the window, there was a towel rail attached to the wall, and a medicine cabinet that doubled as a mirror. It was what I would expect from a cabin in the woods, including a few cobwebs. A free-standing bathtub with a traditional long-necked showerhead took up one wall. It was clean – and that was the main thing.

Austin turned on the shower, then dropped his gaze to the varnished floor as he sidestepped past me.

"Just let me grab a few clean towels, and I'll be right back," he mumbled, his cheeks flushed pink.

I stripped off my nightdress and stepped into the bathtub, only to let out a gut-wrenching scream.

"Argh! It's freezing cold!" I shrieked, bolting back out again.

Austin hurried back, carrying the towels.

"Whoops, thought I turned the dial towards warm. My bad." He cringed apologetically. "I usually take cold showers. It's set to how I have it," he explained.

"It's a wonder you haven't frozen off your appendage," I snapped. "Ugh, never mind, get in." I huffed with frustration.

I stepped in first as Austin stripped off, yanking the shower curtain into place. It was a transparent one with printed images of cartoon frogs all over it in different poses. It soon steamed up as the warm water sluiced down my body. Austin only had manly products, meaning, I had to make do with forest pine soap and shampoo. My breath hitched in my throat as Austin slid in beside me and closed the shower curtain. I honestly expected him to chicken out.

"You're hoggin' all the water. You wanna move over a bit?" he complained.

I rolled my eyes as I turned to face him. "You think we're actually in here to take a shower?" I asked with an amused smirk.

He wore a priceless look of confusion on his face. He did think we came in here to shower. What was he expecting? That we'd wash each other's backs? I sighed exasperatedly as I sank to my knees in front of him.

"A-aren't we?" he stammered.

"What do you think?" I teased.

He was half turned on when I wrapped my hands around his cock, bending it away from his body. I met his shocked gaze before taking him in my mouth, sucking him in, and humming purposely to send vibrations down his shaft. He snatched in a sharp intake, his eyes huge as he watched me, bracing himself against the wall. This little exercise was purely for educational purposes. I was going to make him come back for seconds. This was how I liked to fish. I hooked my prey in and reeled them in my way – the Riley way. Men couldn't resist a woman who took charge.

"Fuck, Riley, that feels good," Austin groaned, panting and rocking his hips in shallow jolts.

I looked up at him through my lashes, enjoying the play of his muscles beneath his firm skin, feeling his ass tighten and relax with every dip and suck. His cock pulsed, balls heavy, thighs thick and powerful, arms long and hard and bulging with muscle, one palm flat against the tiles.

The water was getting just this side of too hot, the stream from above beating down with incredible force, the jets bouncing off his body and spraying me in the face. He moved the faucet so that the wall took the full force of the blast, cascading down the tiles like a warm waterfall.

"Jesus Christ, Riley." His voice was a ragged whisper.

He took my hair in two handfuls and gripped hard, sucking in a rasping breath and groaning it back out. My scalp burned as he threaded his fingers through my now dampened hair, winding it around his hand.

His eyes squeezed shut, his lips slightly parted.

My God, did Austin Rayne look as sexy as hell when pleasure consumed him.

I moaned, more for his benefit than mine; the vibrations made him growl and thrust again, jerking his hips as he fucked my mouth.

Sensing he was close, I kept my lips sealed around the groove beneath the head, sucking and massaging his balls as they tightened and clung close to his body.

I allowed my tongue to swipe over the head, earning some raw guttural groans from him. His hips jerked, and his back arched. He tilted his head back open-mouthed, his face scrunched in a pleasurable grimace. I could feel his legs begin to shudder as he got closer and closer to his release.

I let him move as hard as he wanted, pulling away from his thrusts until he groaned in protest. I had to make this memorable. It was his first sexual encounter after all.

Then I downed him, pulling him away from his torso and taking him into my throat until his balls touched my chin — the deep throat — and he didn't disappoint. My throat muscles contracted around the soft, spongy head of his cock as I massaged the shaft with my tongue.

I felt a moment of triumph that I'd taken that

much of him. The guy was hung like a fucking stallion.

He tugged on my hair twice. "I'm coming, Riley! Oh, shit, fuck, Jesus."

His sack pulled tighter, and his cock throbbed, jerking in my throat. He came with a burst of hot, salty, musky cum on my tongue. I sucked and swallowed, sliding my fingers down his length, massaging his sack to milk the hot streams from his cock. I kept bobbing on him, holding his ass as he growled with enjoyment. He rocked his hips, thrusting his cock into my mouth, and I felt another spurt of cum jerk from him, then again, less this time until he arched his spine, fluttering his hips in small, quick thrusts.

"You are sooo good at this. Ahh, fuck," he groaned.

He was so coming back for more of this; I was sure of it. I sucked at each little spasm of his cock, holding him still against me with one hand squeezing his butt cheek, flicking his pulsing head with my tongue, milking him with my mouth until I knew he was done. I was a relentless bitch, continuing the torture, bobbing my head, and creating as much suction as I could. He gave out strained groans, obviously feeling incredibly sensitive at this point.

Finally, he stumbled backward, wrenching himself from my grip. I let him go and stood, watching him with a casual smirk as he sagged back against the wall of the shower.

His weakness injected a huge boost of power to my overly inflated ego, and I could've burst with pride. This was a man who seemed as if he preferred to be in control; strong, and equally as proud. Cocky and occasionally arrogant. Sarcastic and undeniably cynical, and I had just reduced him to a panting, boneless mess.

CHAPTER EIGHT

Austin Rayne

I couldn't peel my eyes away from Riley's naked body. The first time was awkward. The second time, I was more prepared.

From behind, I took the chance to fully appreciate her. It wasn't like I'd never seen a naked female before. Nudity was a common occurrence with shifters. We don't usually suffer from embarrassment, but this time it was different. She was different. This was the body, the one that would take away my V-card.

She really was something, tempting me to sin like a siren, luring me into uncharted waters, where she would pull me overboard and drag me to the depths. I'd go along with her willingly, completely and utterly enchanted by her. I would either drown, blissfully happy in her love, or she would be the ruin of me.

Her hair was a majestic red, the same color the leaves from the Cherokee Brave turned in autumn. She dipped her shoulders under the flow of water, allowing it to cascade along her creamy skin, caressing the soft curves of her hips and down her slender legs. Those seemed to go on for miles and miles. I was hooked. Blind drunk on Riley . . . whatever the hell her surname was. I'd forgotten.

It didn't matter what her last name was. All that mattered was what her last name was going to be.

For a whole five seconds, I forgot how to breathe. Physically, she was the epitome of perfection. Morally, she was flawed. She was the quintessential high-class snob. She was entitled, spoiled, and conceited. The complete opposite of me, mixing as well as oil and water.

Was it fair to hold such high expectations of her? No, it wasn't. Now that I had a chance to calm down and really think about it, I faced the facts: I wasn't exactly perfect either. Nobody was. I hadn't been with another woman, but I'd made my fair share of mistakes. I'd said and done things I wasn't entirely proud of.

Her scent smelled strange, and I couldn't figure out why. My mate wasn't like me, but she didn't smell like a typical human either. It gnawed away at my curiosity. Her ways were human ways. She appeared to know nothing about my kind. After giving it some thought, I decided I had been way too hard on her. The fact that she hadn't slapped my face and bolted through the door meant something. She was here because she wanted to be. She was staying of her own accord, which was comforting. It meant she was feeling the connection we shared. My mom was right when she told me I'd know when I met "the one", because for the first time in my life . . . I felt whole.

Riley turned around to face me. Water droplets clung to the tips of her lashes, and she had the faintest smile lingering on her lips. This magnificent creation was mine. A ball of fire blazed in my chest and permeated within me; it gave me that warm, fuzzy feeling inside. My eyes followed the journey Riley's fingers made over her saturated body, compelling me to join the hypnotic odyssey as they skimmed her full, round breasts, then traced the groove of her womanly hips, drawing my gaze to the valley between her thighs. Something primitive awakened in me, stirring deep from within my loins, a voracious appetite I couldn't avoid nor control. I glanced south, just as she opened her eyes, following my trail of sight. It was too late to hide the effect she had on me. Her blue eyes flaring wide with recognition.

"You're hoggin' all the water. You wanna move over a bit?" I muttered in an attempt to hide my embarrassment.

My traitorous dick just wouldn't relent, hellbent on becoming acquainted with our mate. The bear inside me roared its approval, sending a reinforced rush of blood straight down to my strained organ.

She rolled her eyes as I spoke, placing her hand on her cocked-out hip.

"You think we're actually in here to take a shower?" She gave a critical smirk, putting me right on the spot.

My eyes darted back and forth between hers, not knowing how the fuck I was supposed to respond to that. I muttered something. At least, I think I did. My brain stopped working the second I saw her tits. But when she got to her knees, eye level with my groin, I swear to God, my heart stopped dead in my chest. Riley's mouth drew toward me, her lips parting, allowing her tongue to sweep away the bead of pre-cum that she'd coaxed from the tip of my cock. Tingles shot straight to my balls, causing my heart to detonate like a grenade. Through hooded eyes, I watched the scene below as if time had slowed right down. I mean, I'm male. I'm not complaining — but shit! I was not expecting that. When she asked to take a shower with me, I assumed she wanted to conserve water. Not devour me for lunch.

She bent my meaty shaft toward her, angling it away from my body. My ball sac pulled tighter as the slightest breath blew against the crown. My breath stuttered with a maelstrom of sensations: heat from the steamy water, the sudden shock from the cold wall tiles, and then the — Jesus Christ! Her soft, moist lips sheathing themselves around my cock. I stumbled backward, bracing myself against the cold wall.

My splayed hand pressed flat against the tiles as Riley began sucking me, bobbing her head, dragging her lips all the way up, then back down again, flicking her skilled tongue over the tip, causing my eyes to roll back on themselves.

She blew my mind; withdrawing her lips to the base of the crown, then began to hum delicious *mmm* sounds, sending deep, sturdy vibrations straight down to the base of my shaft.

She held me right there on a cliff's edge, delivering a ruthless cocktail of torturous pleasure and denying me the release I so desperately craved.

"Fuck, Riley, that feels good," I groaned.

I wrapped her hair around my hand, fluttering my hips, feeling my climax brewing like a volcano ready to erupt.

"Jesus Christ, Riley."

I held a handful of her hair in my fist, losing myself in the cyclone of sensations.

Seconds, minutes passed, I lost all sense of time and space, my brain was shutting down and letting autopilot take over. Just when I didn't think I could take much more, she swallowed me right down to the hilt, her throat greeting me with the most intense massage.

"You're so good at this. Ahh, fuck," I groaned, scrunching my face in a pleasurable grimace.

All I could do was groan, feeling everything her perfect mouth was giving me. Warmth, pressure, suction, caressing the perineum behind my sac with her dainty fingers. Sequence after sequence, her technique ever-changing, sending toe-curling sensations straight to my balls.

My brain had turned to scrambled shit. My dick was now in the driver's seat, thrusting a million miles per second. Each fluttering jolt into those heavenly lips only added to the build-up of pressure. I tried tugging her hair to warn her, but it was too late.

"I'm coming, Riley! Oh, shit, fuck, Jesus!"

Lights flashed behind my flickering eyelids, and I was done, breathing like I'd forgotten how, swept out to sea, carried away by a tsunami of euphoria.

Fireworks in my nuts—that's what it felt like. The orgasmic roar I gave when I blew my load into Riley's willing mouth bounced off every tile in the room.

Oxygen flooded back into my lungs with abundance, my legs quaking like blades of grass in the wind. I fell backward, pulling my highly sensitive organ from her lips. The fog that clouded my brain lifted, leaving me basking in the glow of the aftermath.

That was the most incredible experience of my life.

Riley giggled, getting back up to her feet with a smug look of triumph plastered across her face.

"Wow," I breathed.

CHAPTER NINE

Riley

Austin reached for the body wash and started to lather himself up. He finished off by scrubbing it into his hair and standing under the showerhead.

I openly admit I was gawking. I mean the guy looked like he'd just stepped out of a shampoo commercial. The water cascaded over his head and down his body as if he was standing under a waterfall. I watched the soap trail around and down every dip and groove of his muscles, all the way down to his V-line.

When my eyes snapped back up again, I was met with Austin's oceanic blue ones watching me. A self-assured smile played dangerously on his face.

"Turn around," he spoke in a rough, husky rasp.

He grabbed a bottle from the side of the bath. I heard the sound of the lid crack open and the contents being squeezed into the palm of his hand.

He worked the shampoo into my hair, scrubbing my scalp and lathering my hair thoroughly down to the tips, and then he leaned to the side so the water sluiced the shampoo away.

He backed away again and the water streamed onto my back, allowing Austin to work conditioner into my hair.

While the conditioner soaked into my hair, he applied some shower gel and began scrubbing my back, over my shoulders, and down my arms; everywhere he could reach without moving me.

"Arms up for me." He shifted forward, and I lifted both arms, chuckling as his hands slid round to cup both breasts in his large hands.

Austin washed me all over, getting me clean. His reverent fingertips massaged me gently as if he was afraid of breaking me.

I stared dead ahead at the far wall, feeling a

lump form in my throat. Nobody had ever taken care of me like this before. Nobody had bothered to care. It felt good to be appreciated. My eyes stung as I felt them well up. Tears trembled as they brimmed the edge of my eyelids, suspended right on the edge.

I wouldn't dare face him yet. I took a few quiet breaths, fluttering my lashes in an attempt to soak up the moisture. It didn't work though, not here in the shower. Instead, they spilled onto my cheeks and merged with the splattering of water.

The water was getting cooler now. Austin stilled for a long moment, then let out a long breath and moved past me after he'd shut off the water jets. I wondered what he was thinking about. The towels were stacked on a cupboard next to the sink, and Austin pulled the one off the top and wrapped it around me.

His brows furrowed, his expression remained unreadable, his silent demeanor was a mystery to me. He wrapped a towel around his waist then wiped me dry from head to toe, gently and thoroughly. He then scooped me up in his arms, hesitating as if to bolster his strength, and then carried me into the bedroom.

"I could have walked, you know?" I mumbled,

embarrassed, turning my face so as not to meet his gaze.

I watched him closely, unsure of his emotional state, or his thoughts, or of what he'd felt regarding my little display of control.

Had that been too much? Had I scared him off?

He carried me in silence to the bedroom. With each passing second of silence, I grew more and more apprehensive.

I hoped he didn't think too badly of me.

He placed me down on the bed, standing awkwardly as if he wanted to say something but didn't know how.

"Hey, what's wrong? Didn't you like it?" I asked, feeling mortified in case he said "no"

"No, I mean, yes, of course, I did. It was the best feeling I've ever had in my life, but that's not it. How do I . . . I mean, what do I do?" He fumbled for words.

I reached up and placed a finger over his lips. "Come here and I'll show you."

I kneeled up onto the bed, grabbing his hand and pulling him closer. I loosened the towel, letting it drop to the floor around his feet.

Holy shit, he was fully aroused again.

"That's not normal," I said, pointing to his penis.

His eyes widened looking horrified, "Why? What's wrong with it?"

I made a *tsk* sound. "No, nothing's wrong with it per se. It's huge is what I meant. Regular guys don't get hard straight after cumming, and you're raring and ready to go is what I meant," I explained, pointing out the difference between him and every other male I'd ever encountered before.

I watched as his lips twitched up one side into a smirk. "Oh, so human men aren't made like this?"

"You catch on quick." I shot him a cheeky grin and moved up the bed with a slight bounce, patting beside me.

He kneeled up on the bed. The mattress dipped and creaked in protest under his weight.

He came to rest facing me, propped up on one elbow. His fingers trailed along my face and stopped to cup my chin. He leaned in toward me, claiming my lips with a gentle, controlled kiss. No trembling this time. So much more confident.

I felt my sex pulse between my legs, just from the way he was kissing me. His tongue swept inside my mouth. I clenched my thighs together, feeling a dull, throbbing ache in my center.

"Now you've got me where you want me, you need to heat me up a bit. Start by kissing my neck, keep your hand firm and hold my neck," I breathed the instructions in a soft, sultry tone.

I felt goosebumps trail along his skin. His cock jutted and stood to attention. I could hear the change in his breathing pattern as he got more and more excited.

He placed his hand on the back of my head and began planting kisses down the side of my neck, along the curve, and onto my shoulder.

I felt a little shudder as his tongue escaped his mouth for a second and dipped into the hollow of my collarbone. I could feel he had a natural knack that just needed a bit of guidance, a bit of coaxing out, just a little tweak here and there for him to master his technique. Then I was in for a really good time.

He grew a little more confident as he got a feel for things. He started groping my breasts a little too eager. "Slow down there. If you squeeze so hard, I won't feel anything but pressure. Remember you want me to feel everything, so start slow and build," I advised, schooling him in the art of foreplay.

CHAPTER TEN

Riley

I took his hand in mine and placed it around my breast, moving my hand slowly, guiding his thumb around my nipples, and getting him to gently roll the tip in his fingers. He began to move of his own accord, pinching ever so slightly as he went.

I removed my hand, allowing him to take the wheel; his eyes were clouded with lust, licking his lips as if he wanted a taste. I placed my other hand along the back of his neck and eased him down so that his lips were against my breast. His warm, staggered breath caressed my delicate skin.

"Now, when you kiss my breast, use all of your mouth's tools; breathe against my nipples, flick your tongue over the tip and around the areola, and now and again take it into your mouth and suck."

I pushed his head down onto me so his mouth was against me. He did just as I had said, creating sweet circles with his tongue around my solid bud. It felt good . . . so good.

His innocence of learning for the very first time felt kind of sexy. Usually, I didn't feel any emotional attachment when I was with one of my fuck-boys. All they ever were to me was a quick fuck, end of story.

I was one of those people who could be having sex while thinking of the day ahead. Whether I wanted to go and get my hair done, or if I was gonna go buy those cute new shoes or not. Yeah, usually I would lie back and think of Prada, but with Austin, it was different.

Austin here wasn't half bad. A bit of a novice, but he was certainly warming up and getting used to it. He got a little too keen and started planting wet kisses over my breasts, which snapped me out of fantasy land.

"Stop," I said, "keep it to a minimum, enough with the wet kisses, I've just had a shower. Jeez."

"Sorry," he chuckled, concealing his embarrassment.

"Here try this," I suggested instead.

I opened my legs slightly and took his hand; I brought his middle finger into my mouth and then sucked on it, keeping eye contact with him. I then guided his hand down my body and between my legs, keeping my hand on top of his hand the whole time.

With his moistened finger, I started to run small circles around my clit and long strokes down the length of me. He let out a harsh gasp. It was the first time he'd felt a woman's pussy. I carried on guiding him with my hand, setting the pace, letting him feel how I wanted to be touched.

"See what I'm doing? Now you try on your own," I breathed softly, feeling the pad of his finger circle my moist flesh.

He was doing so well. I liked to be touched exactly like this, and it was turning me on so much I could feel the heat build in my face as my cheeks began to flush.

I could feel myself getting wetter and wetter under his touch. He pushed his finger inside me and back out again to go on stroking my clit. Oh, he was a fast learner. Yes, he was. I couldn't help a rough moan leaving my lips.

He gasped as his finger entered my warm wet pussy. He then added a second and then a third, and began pumping in and out of me while circling my clit with his thumb.

"Oh, God, Austin, right there. Don't stop!" I moaned out loud.

He found my G-spot on my front wall and started stroking, causing a chorus of, "Oh, fuck, yes, God, don't stop," coming from my lips.

My hips started to wander closer to him of their own accord. I was getting hot, very quickly. "Do you have a condom?" I asked a little too desperately.

He looked a little startled but gave a nod. "I picked some up from the men's room at the guest house, just in case." He made a cringe face.

"No, that's good. Good thinking," I replied, relieved.

He stood and frantically fumbled around looking for where he'd slung his jeans, picking them up off the floor and searching the pockets. He pulled out a small square box and ripped it open, pulling out a silver packet.

He fumbled with the packet before ripping it open with his teeth, pulling the condom out, and discarded the foil wrapper. After watching him struggle, I kneeled over and helped to put it on, rolling it down over his long, thick shaft.

I moved back onto the bed, pulling him down on top of me. He knelt between my legs. The missionary position was the perfect way for him to learn the first time around.

Personally, I prefer to be in the driver's seat, but I would keep that one in my back pocket for another time.

I took his cock in my hand and guided him so that the tip was just inside me.

"Now you must start slow and build up to it. I'll let you know if I want it harder or faster."

I could feel my heart beating rapidly; my breathing quickened. I was now struggling to form words.

He leaned over me as he pushed himself inside. Leaning down to kiss me as sheathing himself to the hilt, we both cried out as he stretched my walls. God, I'd never felt so full. He was so wide I thought he'd split me.

I couldn't even clench my walls around his cock he was that big. My sex could only flutter helplessly around it as he began thrusting slowly in and out.

I wrapped my legs around his waist and my arms around his neck so I could hold on for dear life. I cried out as I felt him slam into me deeper.

He leaned forward toward me so his chest was against mine. Skin on skin. His thatch of curls rubbed against my clit.

"Oh yeah, like that. Just like that." My cries of encouragement spurred him on.

He grabbed my ass cheeks with both hands, lifting them slightly from the mattress. I could feel his heavy ball sac slapping against my ass like a paddle.

It felt so, so good. Every part of me was tingling. I was ablaze with a burning desire. Never before had I ever felt so alive, so raw with primal need. I was too into the moment to give out any more sexual orders. I had lost all ability to speak.

I threw my head back, and his lips found my neck, nipping and sucking, his teeth grazing over my sweet spot.

Was he thinking about biting me? It sure felt as if he was for a second, although I may have imagined it.

He kissed me, devouring my mouth in a delicious assault. He grabbed my wrists, pinning them above my head, squeezing my wrists, and anchoring them to the bed as he pounded into me, the headboard thumping against the wall. His cock knocked against my inner barrier, causing a blissful scream to tear through my throat.

"Oh, my God, Austin! I think — I think I'm — oh, God, yes!" I screamed. Lights flashed behind my lids as an incredible wave of euphoria washed over me, tensing my body rigid.

"I can't hold back any longer. Oh, fuck, Riley," he grunted.

He let go of my wrists, planting his palms on the bed. I reached down with my hand and squeezed his ass hard, pressing my nails into him as we both climaxed together.

And now my legs felt like Jell-O.

"How was that?" Austin asked in that cocky tone I recalled only too well.

I groaned with a smile, unable to speak as I melted into the mattress.

CHAPTER ELEVEN

Riley

I woke mid-afternoon with a jolt. I'd forgotten where I was for a few seconds, and the shock almost gave me a cardiac arrest. The slumbering mountain lying next to me turned around and draped a huge, muscular arm across my waist.

"Oof! Austin, wake up. I need to use the bathroom." I heaved the heavy weight of his arm off my bladder.

"Hm, what time is it?" he mumbled sleepily.

The side of his face was smashed into the pillow, and his eyes were closed.

I squinted at the old-style alarm clock on his bedside table. The damn thing looked antique; it was one of those wind-up clocks that had two bells on the top.

"It's ten past one in the afternoon," I replied irritably.

I now had one foot flat on the floor and was attempting to limbo myself underneath his arm.

"C'mon, Austin, lift up! I'm not a damn contortionist," I grumbled as he tightened his grip.

"Go on then. I'll be up in a minute," he huffed and released me from his vice-like grip.

I raced off to the bathroom, desperate to use the toilet. No sooner had my backside touched the seat, the equivalent to Niagara Falls started to flow out of me. I gave a huge sigh of relief and closed my eyes. A slight smile curled my lips as the ache in my bladder ebbed away.

"Riley, are you running a bath?" Austin yelled from the bedroom.

His deep manly laugh rumbled through the wall as he amused himself with his own joke.

I wrapped toilet paper around my hand, breaking off a good handful to clean myself. He was such a sarcastic ass. Although I had to admit, I did find his comment funny and found myself giggling.

I wasn't used to men making me laugh. They usually bored me to death, talking about business or the stock market. Austin was different, I could tell he didn't have much. He wasn't rich. He lived a humble life and came from a working-class background. Not that I minded. He seemed fun to be around. Even if he did tease me a lot, he wasn't exactly unpleasant about it. I knew I'd never get bored quickly.

I washed my hands and dabbed cold water on my face. The mattress creaked as Austin got out of bed, and I heard heavy footsteps walking across the hall.

He tapped lightly on the door. "You want some company?"

I opened the door slightly and peered through the crack. "If I let you in here, we're just showering," I said flatly.

"Just showering?" Austin cocked an eyebrow as if he had other plans in mind.

I left the door ajar as I turned to switch on the shower, then placed my palm under the running water to check that it was warm enough this time.

"I mean it. No sex. I'm starving," I

complained.

My stomach growled as evidence. I stepped in first, followed closely by Austin. At least he was a gentleman and allowed me to wash first. He stood back to admire me while I scrubbed myself from head to foot. I wasn't used to being this appreciated, and to be honest, it felt rather good.

I know this might seem weird, but it felt as if I'd known him for years, like being with him was just as easy as breathing air. I stepped out, allowing him more room to maneuver around as he scrubbed that huge body of his.

"Can I have one of your shirts to wear? I don't have any clothes," I asked, wrapping a bath towel around my naked body.

"Second drawer. Take whatever you want. Put on a pair of my boxers if they'll fit," he offered, splashing water as he rinsed off his shampoo.

I clutched the towel in place with one hand as I ventured back to his room. My wet hair dripped water down my shoulders as I rummaged in his drawer for something to throw on. I let out a snort of laughter as I held up a T-shirt that had Graceland printed on it just as he walked through the door.

"Not that one." He snatched it out of my hand

and folded it back up neatly.

I pulled out a plain, gray marl T-shirt and put that on instead.

"Don't worry. Your Elvis stuff is safe from me." I sniggered as I left him there, now on a mission to find something edible from the kitchen.

I opened the fridge, finding only beers, fish, a tub of butter, and some milk. There wasn't much else to satisfy the palate. There was bread in the cupboard, and a jar of marmalade, so I decided on toast.

While I was waiting for the bread to pop up in the toaster, I switched on a small television that was on top of the kitchen work surface. It was an old-style, analog TV that had a metal coat hanger for an aerial. It didn't have a remote or anything. I had to mess with the dials to pick up a channel.

The toast popped up just as I'd found the CNN news channel. I searched around until I found the cutlery drawer, grabbed a knife out, and began spreading butter and marmalade on my toast. The anchorwoman was busy announcing the daily news. As soon as I heard a clip of my mom's fearful plea, I dropped the knife, causing it to clatter onto the kitchen floor.

"You all right in there, Riley?" Austin called out

after hearing the sound.

"Austin, get in here!" I replied urgently.

He came hurrying in just in time to hear the rest of the news report.

"We have breaking news: Miss Riley Roth . . ."

They then displayed a photograph of me across the screen, and I cringed with shame. It wasn't the best photo ever taken of me. Surely it wasn't necessary to show a picture of me falling out of a limo, drunk, with Paris Hilton, but that's the press for you.

"I fucking hate the paparazzi!" I whined, mortified.

The reporter straightened her papers and continued reading from the script.

"The only daughter of multi-billionaires, Bracken and Sasha Roth, has been reported missing. It's feared that the heiress has been kidnapped with the intention of being held for ransom. Police are appealing for any witnesses to come forward."

They then showed a clip of my car and my room at the guest house. Carl, the guy at the guesthouse, gave a witness statement but had no recollection of seeing me leave. Dad had a GPS chip stashed in my car to pinpoint my location in case of emergency and that's how they knew where to look. As soon as Austin heard how serious things had gotten in a matter of hours, he started to panic.

"Shit, Riley! They've got the fucking FBI out looking for you!" He ran a hand through his hair, cursing at the television screen.

"What did you expect?" I replied, turning the volume up to listen.

The reporter continued, *"There appeared to be no sign of a struggle; all her belongings were left in the room. Forensics are on the scene, dusting for prints. No contact has been made with the kidnappers as of yet."*

They showed a clip of my parents making an emotional appeal for my safe return. I scowled at the screen, shaking my head from side to side in utter disbelief as my parents, who couldn't stand one another at the best of times, hugged each other tearfully, begging and pleading for my safe return. I let out a high-pitched shriek as my dad announced a ten-million-dollar reward.

"Is that all? Ten measly million. Oh c'mon!" I slapped my palm down on my thigh, fucked-off to high heaven. "That's pocket change for them. I'm their daughter! Is that the price they put on me? They can fart ten mil in a day. Fucking cheapskates!" I spat angrily.

CHAPTER TWELVE

Riley

I was livid. Absolutely fuming.

Was that all I was worth to them? They could spend that in the blink of an eye. The pointless shit that they were known for blowing money on was unreal. Then they insult me with this bullshit!

"Riley?" Austin blew out in a breathy voice. "Maybe you should go back." He nervously paced the floor. "We need to fix this quickly before this blows way out of proportion."

"What? You think I should leave?" I immediately snapped out of my thoughts.

I knew what would happen the second I went back. My parents would have Austin's ass thrown in jail for kidnapping. A look of conflict clouded his handsome face. He gripped his hair in both hands, evidently scared about the media storm this had caused.

"Humans can't come snooping around here, Riley. This could put the whole shifter community in danger," he stated in a panic.

"You want me to go?" I asked, sounding a little shocked. His announcement took me by surprise.

I thought he said I was his mate? Didn't it mean that we should be together?

He pinched the bridge of his nose. "Of course, I don't want you to go. Which is why I need to figure a few things out first."

"Look, my parents haven't gotten along like that in like — ever. I think I'm going to let them stew a little while longer. So, if this is an excuse to dump me now that we've had sex, then just drop me off somewhere close to town, and I'll call somebody to come pick me up."

Who the fuck does this guy think he is? Using me for sex!

I'm the user and men are the weak, pathetic play things. This guy is something else.

"Riley, what the fuck are you talking about?" Austin scowled, looking as if what I had said deeply offended him.

"You heard me." I folded my arms across my chest in a defensive pose.

He huffed, giving an exaggerated blink as he shook his head, slowly.

"You're fucking crazy, you know that?" he expressed, placing his hands on his hips. "I need you to understand something." He paused, giving me an agonized look. "Your world and my world are completely fucking different. You and I may belong together, but our worlds can never meet — if that makes sense?"

I didn't answer him, choosing to stare at the linoleum instead. He stormed straight past me, muttering under his breath. That only increased my irritation.

Austin disappeared to the bedroom so that he could put on the rest of his clothes. I sat on the couch in silence as I waited for him to give me a ride. His little outburst hurt more than I thought it would. I'd never felt this kind of connection with anyone before. I refused to let him see me cry though. I had too much pride.

"Our worlds could never meet." What sort of lame excuse was that? It was almost as bad as *"It's not you . . . it's me."*

I glanced around the sitting room of his cabin, looking at all the old-style wooden furniture. The rug was threadbare, the couch was well worn and was torn along one arm, there were two windows in here, but the curtains didn't match. There wasn't even a TV in here, so the portable one in the kitchen was the only one he had.

I was used to luxury, living between my mother's mansion and my father's penthouse, being showered with expensive gifts, and eating at fancy restaurants. I was known for dating film stars as well as partying with socialites. But where I really wanted to be more than anywhere else was right here with Austin Rayne. Everything else was just stuff.

He strained a smile as he grabbed his keys off the side and held the front door open for me. We walked around to the side of his cabin where he kept his battered red truck. I climbed in feeling the cold leather against the back of my legs.

Austin started the engine, looking genuinely upset. His lips were pressed into a tight, thin line, and his blue eyes glistened as if he was holding back tears.

"We'd never have worked out anyway," I muttered, fighting to form words through the burning lump that had developed in my throat.

He cast me a fleeting look before turning his attention back on the road.

"Why do you have to say shit like that to me?" he replied, unable to keep the sadness from his voice.

I folded my arms, feeling anger rise inside me from God knows where. "Because you're chicken shit, that's why. Calling quits on our arrangement on day one." I scowled at him with an air of disdain. My chest heaved, and my nostrils flared. I had to grit my teeth to stop myself from screaming.

I couldn't hold back anymore. "So what if the whole fucking SWAT team burst through the door? I agreed to stay here with you. Not against my will, but because I thought that maybe you would be worth it. I thought, here's a decent guy. Why not take a chance for once? And not only that, you chose me, in case you'd forgotten." My tears gathered on the edge of my eyelids, clouding my vision until I blinked, causing them to spill down both cheeks.

I wiped them away quickly, looking at my wet hands in shock. Here I was, for the first time in my life, crying over a man. My chest burned as if my heart had only just started to beat for the first time. I sucked in a shaky breath as I tried to rub the ache in my chest away with my palm.

Austin did an emergency stop, causing me to jolt forward. "Chicken shit, huh?" He gripped the wheel so tightly I could hear the leather creak in protest.

I let out a sob and crossed my arms. "That's right, I can practically see the feathers sticking out of your butt. I'm actually waiting for you to lay some eggs because I'm still fucking starving." My voice sounded strained as I responded with sarcasm.

The next thing I knew, Austin had slammed the truck into reverse and was driving backward like a maniac up the dirt track. I held onto my seat with one hand while gripping the door handle with the other. The backward motion made me feel as if I had left my stomach behind.

We came to an abrupt stop back at the side of the cabin. I glanced nervously at Austin who was breathing heavily through his nose.

"Did you think that I was taking you back

because I didn't want you?" He threw the question at me.

There was a quizzical edge to his voice that made me crumble internally.

Have I overreacted, reading the situation wrong?

"Why? Wasn't that what you were doing?" I cringed sheepishly.

Austin let out a shocked laugh.

"No. I was going to request some leave and go with you," he replied, making me blush with humiliation.

"Is that why you were pouting and stomping your feet like a petulant child?" He grinned, seeing straight through my stroppy mood swing.

"Maybe . . ." I cringed sheepishly.

"I figured because I caused this mess, it's my job to clean it up." He shrugged.

Ugh, I was wrong. He isn't letting me go. He wants to come with me.

As much as I hated being wrong, I was glad I was this time. Getting an apology from me was as rare as rocking horse shit, but with Austin, I felt the need to grovel.

"Nobody even knows I'm here. I just want to stay with you. Is that so bad?" I winced at the sound of my whiny voice.

Was that me? Did I really just sound so needy?

Austin's gaze burned into the side of my face as if he wanted me to elaborate. Just as I was about to apologize for acting like a bitch, he hit me with a proposal.

"Are you saying that you want to stay here and mate with me?" His bright blue eyes shone with hope as he gazed down upon me.

"Yeah, I guess I am." I didn't even need to think about it.

I knew what I wanted, and that was Austin.

"And to hell with the month trial?" he asked, arching his left eyebrow.

"I guess," I replied, feeling fine about that.

"Once we mate, there's no backing out. You're stuck with me for life." He brushed his large hand up my leg, stopping with a gasp as he realized that I wasn't wearing anything underneath his T-shirt.

I relaxed into the seat, placing my hand on his groin and feeling the bulge that was developing there. He jolted as I ran my fingers along the stiff column beneath the denim.

"Promises, promises," I answered his question.

So that was it. We would mate first, then go back to face the music. Now I just had to convince Austin of the plan.

CHAPTER THIRTEEN

Riley

Back at the cabin, Austin cooked up a plateful of fried fish. It was beautifully seasoned, and it tasted surprisingly delicious. I was impressed with his culinary skills because I couldn't cook for shit.

"This is good." I nodded and pointed to the food with my fork.

I noticed his cheeks blush, and he smiled shyly at my compliment.

"I caught it down at the lake while you were

taking a nap." He tried to sound indifferent as if it was an everyday thing.

Men just didn't hunt for food where I came from. They made a dinner reservation. I wondered if he'd caught it with a fishing rod or whether he'd hunted for it in bear form.

"So, you like to fish?" I asked, making casual conversation.

He looked at me as if I was dumb. "Nooo, I like to pet them and put them back," he muttered sarcastically.

I cast him sly eyes. "All right, no need to be like that."

Just when I thought the conversation was going well, he would always have to say something to ruin the moment. Austin shifted uncomfortably on his chair, stabbing at the last few pieces of fish before letting his fork drop and clatter onto his plate.

"Sorry," he grumbled.

I huffed. "All right, out with it. Something is bugging you. I can tell."

"Not really hungry, that's all," he muttered, scrubbing a hand over his stressed face.

It wasn't hard to see what was going on here. He was concerned about bringing a shitstorm to town. My shoulders slumped as I exhaled a heavy sigh.

We'd been over this. Had I just wasted my breath for the past half hour?

"What did I say, hm? I said I'd take care of it. If we go back now, they'd never let me come back." I knew it was the truth too. My parents would hire bodyguards to watch over me.

I stood, took my plate over to the bin, then began scraping the remaining scraps into it. I then began filling the sink with hot soapy water. A chore I'd never done before.

"Here, pass me your plate." I held out my hand. I hadn't meant to look at him with such a hardened glare, but he was starting to grate on my last nerve.

He kidnapped me, and now he was afraid of the consequences. Boo-hoo! Luckily for him, it was the best thing that had ever happened to me. Nobody would come looking for me here. I was certain of it.

"Huh? You don't have to do that. Here let me." He took three large strides over to the sink and attempted to take over the dishwashing duties.

I stood firm, refusing to budge. "I can manage."

"Yeah, but you probably never even . . .," he started to ramble while we both nudged each other out of the way of the sink, desperately fighting over the soapy scouring pad.

He could have forcefully removed me, but he didn't. I slapped his hands away as he attempted to wash the dirty plate, sending soap suds flying everywhere. I snapped a look in his direction.

"Probably what? There's no probably about it. I've never done a day's housework in my life. I've never cooked or done my own laundry. I've had a golden spoon rammed so far up my ass that when I smile, I could give Goldie a run for his money! So back the fuck up and let me wash the goddamned dishes! You cooked, so it's only fair," I finished my rant, pointing a soap-sud-coated finger at him.

My chest heaved as I gasped to fill my lungs. We had already started bickering and this was only day one. Austin backed away, holding both palms up in front of him. I huffed and wiped a cluster of soap bubbles from my eyebrow with the back of my hand.

Austin grabbed a dishcloth and started to dry the dishes in silence. He gave a frustrated sigh as he snatched the now clean plate from the draining rack.

I hated the awkward feeling that clung to the air. I wasn't keen on angry silences. Just as I was about to be the first one to crumble, Austin broke the ice.

"I have absolutely nothing to offer you." He swallowed thickly. "I'm not rich, I'm nothing like your fancy Wall Street boys." He shrugged as if he thought it was hopeless. "This is just about everything I own right here." He gestured around at the small cabin. "You sure this is what you want?"

I huffed in annoyance and turned to face him full on. "I was born rich. I've wanted for nothing — ever. But you know what I've come to realize? Money isn't everything, and those assholes can't hold a candle to you."

And I meant that right from the bottom of my swinging pendulum — I meant, heart. Austin threw the cloth down on the kitchen counter and stood with his arms crossed, giving me a confused scowl.

"Cut the crap. I saw your car, which was a red Bugatti Chiron, in case you didn't know. You probably got it because it matched your nail polish. I bet you said, 'Ooo! I'll take the red one,' didn't you? I bet you didn't even know what make or model the car actually fucking was." His voice was laced with his signature sarcastic tone.

I was dying to laugh. I had to have a moment to look away before I scrunch my nose and made a cute little grunt noise as if to say, "meh, so what?" It was true. I didn't know what it was until my father mentioned it when he uncovered my eyes and revealed the surprise.

"Who cares? I have another one in blue." I gave an indifferent shrug. "Dad didn't know which color I'd like best so he bought both."

Austin stared at me in stunned silence, unsure how to respond to that.

I rolled my eyes. "Look, what I'm saying is, I'd give up all that crap just to stay with you." I poked his chest with my finger.

Even after one day, so that should speak for itself.

"You're spoiled beyond salvation," Austin muttered, shaking his head.

Austin was right. I did pick the car out of a brochure. I'd pointed at it when my dad asked me what I wanted for my birthday, and I said, "One of those, please." He mentioned that they also came in blue, to which I replied, "Oh, cool." On the day of my birthday, I woke up to two cars. One red, and one blue.

Thank you very much, Pop!

"Thanks," I said, keeping my voice sugar-sweet, despite his snarky comment. I wasn't going to rise to it.

"You've shown me more affection in the past twenty-four hours than I've ever felt in twenty-two years. I like you. Everything else is just stuff. My parents throw money at their problems, thinking it solves everything, but it's the little things that count." I felt my face flush with heat as he pulled me by my waist.

"You like me, huh? And you want to mate with me?" he asked as if he still couldn't quite believe it. I could smell his warm, masculine cologne, which left me feeling light-headed and intoxicated.

I slid my palms across his rock-hard chest and looked deep into his eyes. "For the love of Prada, it's a definite yes."

"And you want to stay here with me, in my humble abode?" he questioned again.

I growled in frustration. "Does a bear shit in the woods?" I realized what I just said, then tried to recover. "For the last time, yes!"

I thought he was going to come back with a sarcastic retort, but he didn't. Not this time — thank God!

He blew out a breath of relief. "Do you want to meet my family and join the crazy bunch? I've got to warn you, they're pretty rowdy."

I cocked an eyebrow. "You want me to meet your mom?" I couldn't keep myself from smiling.

Here was the perfect example of boyfriend material standing right in front of me. He, who wanted to form some kind of marriage bond, and who looked as if he was hand-sculpted by the Gods themselves, was asking me — yes, me — whether I was feeling okay about it. From where I was standing, it was pretty much a no-brainer.

"Sure, I'll meet your folks. That's fair." I sucked in a breath through my bared teeth in an apologetic grimace.

"You will, unfortunately, have the displeasure of meeting mine." My honest comment made him laugh.

"Looking forward to it." He widened his eyes with sarcasm.

We rummaged through piles of clothes in his closet for something remotely half decent that would fit me. He handed me a pair of jeans that were his when he was fifteen and a couple of shirts I could use to tie at the bottom.

I took a pair of scissors to the jeans and turned them into shorts instead. Then I tried on the make-shift outfit, along with an old pair of Austin's boots from his younger years. Teamed together, it didn't look half bad.

Austin wolf-whistled playfully as I came to show him, twirling around for a grand finale.

"Look at you, looking all country chic." He leaned down for a quick kiss.

I wrapped my arms around his neck so he couldn't get away, turning it into a full-on make-out session as I went straight for the goods. He ended up naked and pinned to the sitting room floor while I remained fully clothed, rocking his world with my oral skills.

I felt accomplished as my handsome mountain man recovered himself from a mind-blowing orgasm. I didn't expect him to return the favor. That was my little display of gratitude right there.

"Am I your girlfriend now?" I nearly held my breath while I waited for him to answer.

What the fuck am I saying? I sound like a needy bitch. Hell would have to freeze before I – Riley Roth – chased a guy and waited with bated breath to hear him call me his girlfriend. But here I was, desperate to hear him say it. Ugh! I hate myself right now.

He answered a little too eagerly "Yeah — yes, absolutely."

I felt my heart flutter as he confirmed what I

wanted to hear. Fireworks exploded inside my chest. I was Austin's girlfriend. My chest swelled with pride at hearing him say it.

"When can we go see your folks?" I asked a little apprehensively.

I wanted them to like me more than anything in this world. Usually, it wouldn't matter whether they liked me or not, but this was different. Being with Austin felt different. It felt real. And this was something I had never experienced before.

Austin was busy doing up his jeans as he spoke, "Ahh, well, you see . . ." He fumbled around for the right words.

I leaned against the doorframe as he straightened out his clothing.

"Are you all right?" I inquired, noticing how awkward he'd become.

"Yeah, um, Riley, my folks are what you call old school." He rubbed the back of his neck sheepishly.

"Old school?" I repeated his words, not quite getting what he meant. "In what way?" I titled my head, narrowing my eyes questioningly.

"They don't believe in cohabitation before mating," he said, cringing.

That kind of old school.

My eyes widened with realization.

"Well, why don't we just mate then?" I looked at him as if to say "duh".

"We could if you're ready?" he replied, his tone light with surprise.

Hallelujah. Finally, this hunk of a bear shifter had found his sexual confidence and was about to grant me my wishes.

"Let's get straight to it then." I went to remove my clothing.

I knew he could be ready and raring to go in a matter of seconds. That was his super skill. A gift from the Gods. My eyes looked toward the ceiling as I inwardly thought *thank you!*

Austin waved a hand in front of him. "Riley, stop, I need to do it out in the open. There's not enough room here."

I scrunched my nose. "What?" I looked around the sparsely furnished sitting room. He wasn't making sense. At all. "There's plenty of room," I scoffed. "Don't be so ridiculous, what do you want to do, swing from the light fitting? Which I'm totally game for, just so you know."

The color drained out of Austin's face. It looked as if this was the part of the conversation he'd been dreading to have with me.

"I need to partially shift when I bite you." He winced at my reaction.

"Bite me? What the hell do you mean, bite me?" I shrieked, completely horrified.

He moved toward me in a desperate attempt to calm me down. "Wait, wait, it's natural for us shifters. It's a mating mark, which means it'll show other shifters that you belong to me."

"Will it hurt?" I shuddered at the mere thought of it. I hated the sight of blood. I was so squeamish I couldn't even watch Grey's Anatomy without hiding behind a cushion.

Austin dragged a hand down his face, seeming unsure how to continue our conversation. "Yeah, it'll hurt a bit, but I'll be as gentle as I can."

"And you say you'll need to shift to do this? So, what, you're going to fuck me as a bear? Are you kidding me?" My voice sounded shrill as I had a miniature panic attack.

He groaned and gripped his forehead. "You're not listening. I need to partially shift. Don't worry, it's not the same as bestiality."

I tried to swallow, but my mouth had run dry. "It better fucking not be," I warned, my voice tainted with revulsion. "How come we can't just do it here? I'm confused."

Austin spoke soothingly, pulling me into his chest as he rubbed the center of my back in small circles. "To complete the mating ritual, we need to be out in the open."

I blanched.

"Out in the open? You mean outside?" My voice sounded strained as I realized just what he meant.

It was one of my biggest phobias coming true. I could feel my pulse pounding in my ears.

Austin paused before he spoke. "Riley, I'm gonna need to take you in the woods."

CHAPTER FOURTEEN

Austin

I saw the color drain from Riley's face. She looked terrified. I guess her childhood phobia was more serious than I thought. Her breathing was all over the place as she paced the floor, and if I had to hazard a guess, I'd say she was having a panic attack.

Instinctively, I reached over and pulled her against me. She was so much smaller than me she barely reached my shoulders. I buried my face into her soft red hair, stroking her back while she sobbed.

She mumbled against my chest. "I'm sorry. I feel so fucking stupid. I don't usually cry like this."

Why apologize for crying? Didn't she know that it's all right to be scared?

"Shh, it's all right. We don't have to go. I'm not going to force you to," I reassured.

Riley pulled back and looked up at me. Her tear-soaked face made her skin look paler than before, almost translucent.

"No." She flattened her palms out on my chest. "I have to. I don't want to." She widened her eyes and gave a small, pained laugh. "I've got to. Besides, having you with me means that it won't be as bad."

Is she saying that she feels safer with me around?

I held the sides of her face in my large hands. She looked like a fragile porcelain doll, a cute one, not like one of those creepy-ass ones my sister used to collect. Those things followed me with their eyes whenever I went snooping in her room.

I brushed her tears away with my thumbs and instinctively bent down to kiss her. She wrapped her arms around my neck. It wasn't comfortable for me to hunch over like that, so I picked her up and walked her into the kitchen, placing her onto the counter, not once breaking the kiss.

"Austin?" Riley snatched herself away from me. "I don't want to wait. I think we should just go get it over with." Her blue eyes darted between mine.

"Thanks a lot." I rolled my eyes with a chortle.

She huffed softly. "You know what I mean."

I narrowed my eyes, pretending to be offended, but I knew exactly what she meant. That was what I liked most about her; there was no bullshit, no games, no fooling around. I didn't need to be psychic to know what she was thinking because Riley got straight to the point with what she wanted. She was my ideal woman. A little high maintenance, but nobody's perfect. I watched how her shoulders slumped and her brows knitted together, all concerned that she'd said the wrong thing and upset me. She was so easy to tease. Spending years all alone out here didn't exactly improve my social skills. I knew I needed to work on them. All this time alone had made me crabby.

"I'm kidding." I caved in at the sight of her big blue, teary eyes.

Riley gave me a look to suggest she was pissed off with me goofing around all the time. I could hear her pulse pounding as her blood raced around her body. Her nostrils flared with each forceful huff. Her arms folded tightly in front of her chest and she pouted like a spoiled brat.

"Do you have any idea how fucking sexy you are, right now? Looking all indignant and mad at me. God, the hormones you're throwing off are going to be the death of me." I leaned against the opposite kitchen counter, mirroring her stance. My eyes narrowed with amusement, tilting my head to the side with my signature smirk playing on my face.

Her expression softened.

"You're safe with me, Riley. I swear on my life," I told her.

I could see the trust settling in her eyes, then she nodded.

"Okay." She held out her hand. "Let's go before I change my mind."

Riley

I clung to Austin as we walked through the woods. He was taking me to some sort of mating ground where all bear shifters took their mates to form the bond. Thankfully, it was broad daylight as we ventured through the trees. Austin brought along some camping equipment. He said he had plans to make this like a special romantic getaway, and that we could look back on it with nothing but fond memories.

We walked for around for an hour with me pressed against Austin's side the entire time. Both of us were talking about our families, sharing stories. He succeeded in taking my mind off the fact that I was doing something that would normally scare me shitless.

"Then she said. 'Austin, if you fall out of that tree and break both your legs, don't come running to me!'" He chuckled as he finished telling me a story from his childhood.

I erupted into a fit of giggles. "Your mom sounds awesome. If that was my mom — no wait, that wouldn't have been my mom because I was raised by the nanny."

"You must have some fond memories of when you were growing up?" Austin scrunched his brows.

I thought for a minute. "I do. I remember one Christmas Eve; I thought I heard sleigh bells on the roof. So, I ran into my parents' room, and they weren't there. The alarm clock seemed to be stuck twelve minutes past midnight. I crept downstairs and found my parents putting all my gifts under the tree. Dad knocked back the brandy that I'd left in the glass, and Mom took a bite from the mince pie, even though she hated them."

I looked up and saw him smiling slightly. "It was at that moment when I realized that Santa wasn't real. But also, it made me realize that my parents did all that just to make me believe that he was. Those were the good ole' days when they actually worked as a team. I miss that." I wiped a stray tear from my eye.

Austin kissed the top of my head as we walked. "That'll be us one day. Playing Santa and the Tooth Fairy. I can't wait."

We chatted about everything. From what our favorite TV show was, right down to what got on our nerves the most. Before we knew it, we'd arrived. He had brought me to a lake with a waterfall.

"Here we are." Austin dropped the rucksack he was carrying onto the ground. The sun had well and truly set by now, and the only light source came from the glowing full moon.

"You stay right here. I'm going to catch us supper." Austin shucked his jeans and pulled his T-shirt over his head. By the time he'd got down on all fours, he'd transformed into a bear.

The moon shone down, illuminating everything around us in blue. The lake was as still as glass, mirroring the image of the moon and the outline of Austin's bear form as he stood proud, fishing from a rock. A gentle breeze lifted my hair off my shoulders, and I took the first slow steps toward my bear.

He was mine. All for me.

CHAPTER FIFTEEN

Riley

I watched his magnificent movements with fierce pride. How his huge paws swatted the water, catching fish after fish, picking them up in his powerful jaws and tossing them down onto the embankment. They flipped and flopped around, gasping for water until they stilled.

I pulled off my boots, peeled off the shirt he'd given me, and cast it aside. I stepped out of my cut-off shorts and kicked them over to where my shirt and boots were. I stood at the edge of the water in my full naked glory with my toes sinking into the sand.

I looked over to the left of me. Austin stopped fishing and turned to watch me. His ears pricked to full alert, then he turned and pawed at the lake again. The lake rippled with each disturbance in the water.

Austin shook his fur, ridding himself of the water and growled. I turned my attention toward the far side of the lake, admiring the waterfall with awe. It was beautiful, all illuminated in the moonlight, looking a bluish-silver color as it crashed down along the rocks, then turned white as it churned at the bottom.

I saw my reflection in the soft rippling waters, seeing myself as Austin saw me.

My skin gleamed white, contrasting with my red hair that cascaded down my back, blowing slightly in the breeze. My breasts rose and fell with each intake of breath. My nipples pebbled, forming stiffened peaks. The cool, gentle breeze covered my skin with gooseflesh.

I dipped a toe into the water, causing me to shudder at the cool temperature. The lake was shallow enough to wade through from where I stood, and I bet I could walk with ease all the way over to the opposite side. I could see the darkened areas farther along where it deepened. The water was cool but not cold. Not unbearable. I felt confident enough that I could swim comfortably without running the risk of getting hypothermia.

I wrapped my hair behind my head in a makeshift knot and walked in until the water level reached my knees. Austin growled. I could see his shimmering reflection before me. I took a breath and made a shallow dive into the water. The startling coolness on my skin caused me to gasp and my body to tense. I managed to swim to the rocks where Austin stood and treaded water in front of him.

He sat back on the rock and watched me. I felt like a water nymph as I floated naked before him. He watched with predatory eyes as I kicked backward and floated on my back, my hair coming loose and drifting around me.

Austin clawed at the rocks again, scratching grooves into the stone and reared back on his hind legs. Unable to sit back and watch any longer. His fur rippled and receded. There was the snapping sound of bones contorting, then he stood before me again but this time as a man.

My naked and glorious man. Beads of sweat

coated his skin, and it glistened in the moonlight. His engorged appendage stood bolt upright with a short thatch of blond curls around it.

The muscles of his thighs rippled as he took a step back, then launched himself forward into a dive, straight in at the deep end. He disappeared under the water for longer than I thought was normal. Panic took over me, turning around in a frantic search and scanning the waterline.

"Austin! Austin! Where are you?" I called out.

I squealed as I felt a hand grip my ankle and flung myself backward with a splash. Austin emerged alongside me with a whoosh of water, grinning wildly and clearing his vision. He shook the water from his hair and swam in front of me, his blond hair dripping over his forehead. My heart fluttered as his blue eyes met with mine.

"Riley, we can't use protection during the mating ritual. Are you all right with that?"

I nodded. "It's all right. Will I get pregnant though?" I asked cautiously.

I wasn't sure I was ready to take that giant step.

"We can usually scent when our mates are at their most fertile. You're not yet, so the chances of getting pregnant are highly unlikely," Austin explained.

He wrapped his arms around me and drew me to him tightly. He crashed his lips against mine and kissed me with what words could only describe as raw, primal, and fervent. He lifted me, wrapping my legs around his waist, and brought me down, sheathing himself to the root inside me with one nimble movement that made me gasp with the sheer thrill of it.

Austin kept his arms around my waist as he kicked back through the water. I wrapped my legs around him, clenching my pussy tight to keep myself well seated. He was huge, hard, and filled me completely. My body shivered with the twin sensations of Austin's throbbing hot cock inside me and the swirling cool water surrounding us.

Before I knew it, he had us back onto the shore. He walked us out of the water, and I managed to keep my legs wrapped around him tightly as he laid me down onto the wet sand.

"Make love to me," I whispered, my teeth chattering with the cool night air on my wet skin.

Austin's eyes blazed. His white teeth nearly glowed in the moonlight as he began to pump and thrust into me, slow and steady. He spread my legs wide with his huge muscular hips. He was hard and hot, my pussy clenched and shuddered as he set the rhythm he needed.

"I love you, Riley," Austin whispered as he trailed his lips along the curve of my neck.

Those words shook me to my core. I'd never been in love before, but I knew one thing—when I was with Austin, I felt more alive than I'd ever felt in all my life. I needed him like I needed air to breathe. There would be nothing I wouldn't give up for him. Fuck the money. Fuck the family business. My inheritance. All of it. There was only one thing I cared about most in this world, and that was Austin Rayne.

My eyes stung with unshed tears; my throat and my chest burned. But not because I felt sad. No. This was the happiest moment of my life. Gazing down at me with his gorgeous blue eyes was a man who loved me—as in really loved me. And that feeling I got as soon as he told me made my heart swell. That feeling alone, you couldn't put a price on.

"And I'm falling in love with you," I replied.

I gasped as he raised my wrists in one hand, placing them over my head, pinning me against the ground. I lay spread open before him as he rocked into me with powerful thrusts. Our breaths ragged, grunting, moaning, and crying out with pleasure.

"What have you done to me, Riley?" he said through each punishing thrust. "I can't get enough of you. Do you know that? I can't eat, I can't sleep, I can't breathe unless you're with me like this. I need you, Riley, always and forever. I want you to have my cubs."

"I want that," I gasped, wrapping my legs around him. "Don't stop. Oh God, Austin, don't stop." I could feel my pulse pounding in my wrists as he pinned me. His body heated mine. With each thrust of his cock, I felt myself open even wider. I bit my lip to contain the sensation.

"Babe, scream as loud as you want," Austin said breathlessly. "There's no one around."

"Yes! Don't stop!" I cried as his pace quickened. Austin let go of my wrists and planted his hands either side of me on the wet sand. I clawed at his broad, muscular back to brace myself as he kept up his driving rhythm.

His blue eyes changed color to onyx black, and I knew he struggled to keep his bear contained. A part of me wanted him to let it go and give it to me. I wanted the bear just as much as I wanted the man.

"Mark me," I panted. "I want it, Austin. All of it. All of you. I want to be with you." And it was true. This was my life now, Austin and me.

The harder we fucked, the more I wanted. I clawed at Austin's back and thrust my hips upward as he pressed his hands against the ground. Austin leaned down and took my nipple between his teeth. He pulled back as he sucked, letting it go with a pop.

"Yes. Austin. Oh, God. Just like that!" I screamed. I wanted it rough. I wanted him to fuck me, dominate me, and make me all his.

He pulled himself out, leaving me with the feeling of being empty. He grabbed my ankles and flipped me over, jerking me up on to my knees, then forcing me down to all fours. My pussy was on fire and dripping for him. Oh my God! Austin had turned into a ravenous sexual beast! Oozing confidence and owning it.

My legs quivered in anticipation as he lined himself up to enter me again. He put a hand between my shoulder blades and pushed me down, right down so that my chin was a mere inch away from the ground, angling my ass high for him. He got one knee between my legs and forced me to spread them even wider. The sand moved along with my knees.

"Please!" I gasped again. "Give it to me. Fuck me! Please!" Austin gripped my hips, holding me into position.

My pussy pulsed, waiting to be filled again. He got a scream out of me as he rooted his cock deep inside my high-angled pussy, placing a hand on my shoulder and another holding my waist. I craned my head round to see him. He still looked like Austin but much more primal. His skin rippled, and his cock seemed to grow larger inside me, applying further pressure to my already soaked and stretched walls.

Austin picked up his pace as he rooted himself deep with each thrust. He let go of my hip and reached around, sliding his fingers over my throbbing clit. I cried out from the pleasure of it. Austin growled with satisfaction. A deep rumbling growl that made the hairs on the back of my neck stand on end.

I screamed, giving in to it. I was having the most powerful orgasm ever. I was shameless, wanton, greedy, and begging for it. My back arched, my breasts swung wildly, and my teeth rattled in my head. Yet I still begged Austin to go even faster. I belonged to Austin. He filled my body as well as my mind.

"Yes!" I cried out.

I couldn't control myself for another second. I came hard and fast, my orgasm tearing through me. I screamed through it, rearing backward. Austin showed me no mercy. Instinct took over, and I offered him my exposed neck, moving my hair to one side.

Austin let out an almighty roar and pulled my back against his chest. Pleasure and pain engulfed me as his teeth pierced through my skin. Right in the hollow of my neck. Austin's cock jerked five or six times as he filled me with hot pulsating jets of semen. He gave one last deep thrust, and I felt his seed shoot straight up into me as my orgasm crested down.

When he was through, Austin helped me stand and turned me to face him. He whispered my name as he lifted me in his arms and carried me back to the lake where he washed us both. He lapped and kissed the wound on my neck. The pain I felt initially ebbed away. Now when he pressed his lips there, heat enveloped me and warmed me from the inside out.

The fur that coated Austin's body began to

recede, leaving behind glistening skin. "Have you ever eaten food that's been cooked on an open fire?"

I shook my head. "I've never been camping before, so no," I replied in all honesty.

Austin mumbled something along the lines of "Humph! You've never lived!"

He managed to get a campfire going within minutes. We had to get off the beach and find a clearing where we could pitch the tent. I couldn't see past the end of my own nose. Luckily, Austin could.

He cooked us the fish he'd caught. Expertly removing the bones with a single sweep of a hunting knife.

"It tastes so good," I said with my mouth full.

Austin raised his brows as he spoke pleasantly. "See, it's not so bad being out in the woods, is it?"

"Only because you're with me. I feel safe with you," I confessed.

His chuckle was sexy, husky and with a hint of amusement. "Don't worry, baby, I'll save you from the Blair Witch."

I swatted his arm. "Jackass!" I grinned.

"You said you were falling for me." His eyes

blazed with pride, captivating me as I gazed back into them.

He squeezed my knee with his large hand, as I gazed at him like a loved-up teenager.

"I am," I admitted.

I had surpassed the falling stage, having fallen hook, line, and sinker for him.

"Well, we should get some sleep because tomorrow I'm going to take you somewhere." His voice was as smooth as velvet as he gazed at me lovingly in the crackling firelight.

I tilted my head with curiosity. "Where to?"

Austin stood and unzipped the tent, holding the panel to one side for me to crawl in. "To meet my parents," he replied.

CHAPTER SIXTEEN

Riley Rayne

The morning after the mating...

I woke at the first sign of daylight. It had been freezing down by the falls last night. I had a stiff neck and a sore back from lying on top of a wafer-thin camping mat. Austin and I had snuggled inside a doubled up sleeping bag. Austin's chest was great as a heat source to cuddle up to, like a life-size hot water bottle—but jeez, it meant I'd slept awkwardly. I'd never spent the night in a tent before, and given the choice, I wouldn't repeat the experience.

I'd been converted to hot sex in the woods, but after that it'd be straight back home to a nice warm cabin, followed by a hot shower.

Although I must admit, last night was incredible. Austin and I became one. It really felt as if it completed me, and there was no way I could ever contemplate spending a single day apart from him after this.

We both woke together as soon as the sun came up, cuddled together with my fingers entwined with his. He was stroking the back of my hand softly with his thumb. My heart melted feeling his lips press against my forehead as soon as I woke. It didn't matter that I'd only known him a short time. I had fallen madly in love with him, and I was deliriously happy.

I caught him watching me like a creep.

"Morning," he asked, his voice sleep roughened.

"Good morning," I replied.

Austin's blue eyes were already fixed upon me with an intense look of someone who was head over heels in love. It made me paranoid as to how long he had been watching me.

"How are you feeling, Mrs. Rayne?" he asked as if testing how it sounded out loud.

Mrs. Rayne!!! I squealed internally.

My heart fluttered hearing him call me that.

"Great, thank you for asking."

I chuckled softly as he played with my hand. He rolled each one of my fingers between his forefinger and thumb until he reached my wedding finger.

"Do you want a wedding ring?" he asked, wiggling my finger.

I knew Austin wasn't a wealthy man, and that didn't bother me. I didn't need a piece of jewelry as a symbol of our union. The mark on my neck was proof enough. That meant more to me than gold or silver ever would.

"I don't need a ring," I told him honestly.

I also didn't want him wasting his money on one. I knew he couldn't afford to, but there was no way I'd ever tell him that. He'd get offended for sure, not to mention it would be incredibly insensitive.

"I already know what you're thinking. How's a broke guy like me gonna find the cash to buy you a wedding ring?" His response was so blunt it caught me off-guard. It left me paranoid that perhaps he could read my mind.

I opened my mouth to reassure him that it didn't matter, but he cut across me before I had a chance to speak.

"The answer to your question is, I robbed a jewelry store," he replied, straight-faced.

"What?" My eyes bulged with shock.

Austin burst out laughing. "I'm kidding!" He hid his face with his hand as his stomach spasmed between gasps of snatched breath.

He got me good. For a second, I'd fallen for his prank. I'd have to remember to take whatever he said with a pinch of salt just in case it was a wind-up.

"I'm sorry." He grinned. "You should have seen your face."

"And now I'm stuck with a giant clown for the rest of my life, aren't I?" I retorted.

"Yep." He pulled me into him for a cuddle. "Just wait until you meet the crazy bunch. Help me pack away the tent, and I'll take you to the madhouse."

Every time Austin referred to his family as crazy, it made me nervous to meet them. I'd developed these wild assumptions in my head about what they were going to be like. I bet they were nothing like he said. I was sure that if they could raise a guy as great as Austin, then they were bound to be nice people.

Once we'd packed away the tent, we went back

to the cabin to grab a shower and freshen up. After a few mugs of much needed strong coffee, we jumped in his battered red truck and set off toward the main town of Forest Hills. Austin was taking me to meet his parents for the first time, and I was nervous as hell.

Austin pulled up outside a small cluster of dwellings that were tucked away out of sight along a side road. They all looked similar in style: cute little log cabins with a window on either side of the front door and three windows along the upper floor, all with pretty, matching, red gingham curtains.

Austin put his hand up to one of the neighbors who had waved at him from across the way. I noticed a few people peeking out from behind the curtains to get a sneaky look at us when we got out of the car. It seemed like a nosey, but nonetheless, tight-knit community.

It looked as if they all sat outside along the front of their properties to gather socially. What gave that away was the ocean of deck chairs along each porch and the fact that they all had barbecues along the edge of each lawn. Austin's family home had a weather-worn double swing seat on the porch; the blue-and-white striped chair cushions looked as if they'd faded over time.

The small lawn at the front of the cabin had the odd scattering of bald patches in the grass. As if children played on it often. Scattered along the edge of the porch were potted floral arrangements and garden ornaments of little woodland creatures.

Across the floor decking, there was the odd scribbled picture where a child had been coloring in between the grooves of the wood with colored chalk. It looked as if someone had been coloring on the front of the house with chalk too. I guessed Austin's parents were also grandparents. I didn't recall him ever mentioning having any younger siblings, which meant he could possibly be the youngest.

Directly at the foot of the front door, there was a mat to wipe your feet on. It had a slogan that read: "Oh no, not you . . . again!"

There was a sign next to the door that read: "An old bear lives here with his honey."

Austin put his arm around my waist as he opened the door and walked straight into the house. "Mom, it's only me," he called out.

A female replied in a sing-song voice, "We're through here in the kitchen."

I smiled as I read the family rules sign in the small entrance hall. It was a long rectangle canvas that had the words Mom's Shit List printed on it, along with: don't break shit, don't fight over shit, clean up all your shit, don't act like a shit, but mostly, don't make me lose my shit. An amused grin spread across my face.

Austin caught me reading it, pressing his lips together in a shy, tight smile. Was Austin embarrassed to introduce me to his family? The thought struck me by his sudden change in demeanor. It seemed like we were both worrying about the same thing—what we would think of each other's families.

"Go through to the den, Riley, I'll be right back," he said.

CHAPTER SEVENTEEN

Riley

He ushered me into a cozy sitting room, filled with bespoke wooden furniture, a plump and inviting couch, and a matching armchair beside the fireplace. So much stuff had been crammed inside such a small space, there was hardly enough room to move around without bumping into something.

It wasn't untidy, shabby, or anything like that. It was dust-free and clean. It had a cottage-like feel to it, and the scent of potpourri clung to the air. Fresh wooden logs had been stacked ready to be lit in the fireplace, and the handcrafted oak cabinets had an array of framed photographs on display. They were arranged amongst ornaments along the shelves, all ranging from a selection of baby pictures up to adulthood. The most recent group photo was of Austin standing next to three pretty women, similar in looks, who were holding babies of their own. It was easy to spot Austin as a child amongst all his family photos. His eyes were one of his best features that hadn't altered much over time.

There was a photo of him with an old woman with white hair. I'm pretty sure it was his grandmother. He was sitting beside her with a genuine, happy smile. They both were wearing knitted Christmas sweaters and paper hats that you got from inside a Christmas cracker. There was a decorated Christmas tree in the background with handmade ornaments. Austin looked younger, possibly around sixteen. This looked like a tender moment that had been immortalized in a photo. The way she looked at him adoringly as if he were the apple of her eye was one of the sweetest things I'd ever seen. It was a beautiful photo, and they both looked blissfully happy.

I let my fingers brush along the intricate silver frame. Every one of the photos radiated happiness and love. I couldn't help the feeling of envy as I admired each one. We had nothing as natural as this in either of my family homes. Not at my dad's nor my mom's. Our photos were organized professionally, and although they looked beautiful and flawless, there was something superficial about them, a coldness like each smile wasn't genuine.

"Riley, come through." Austin popped his head around the door while holding onto the handle.

His eyes darted to the picture I was touching. "She was my grandma; she died a couple of months after that was taken."

My heart sank, and I removed my hand from it quickly. "Oh, I'm so sorry, Austin," I apologized. I hoped I hadn't upset him by looking at it.

He managed a slight smile despite the brief look of sadness on his face. "Don't be. She led a full and happy life. She passed away peacefully while sleeping."

I hated seeing the grief in his eyes. I immediately tried to comfort him. "I can tell by the photo that she loved you a lot."

"She was the nicest person I'd ever had the pleasure of meeting. I only wish she'd have lived long enough to meet you," he replied sadly. "Are you ready to meet my family?" Austin changed the subject, blinking away the excess water that had pooled in his eyes. I nodded quickly, despite not feeling very brave.

Ahh! This was it.

I blew out a forced breath as my heart just did an impression of a brass band in my chest. The first meeting with my in-laws.

God, please like me. Oh, I hoped they liked me.

I crossed my fingers behind my back.

Austin must have sensed my nerves, stopping to kiss me in the hall and whispering, "Don't worry," in my ear.

Nothing had ever mattered to me this much before. Hell, I didn't even care if my real parents liked me, but it was really important to me that Austin's parents did.

I walked behind him as he led me into the kitchen. I felt as if I was being put on show as all eyes landed on me, and I swear for a few seconds, I forgot how to breathe. His mom, a cheerful-looking woman whose age I couldn't determine, was sitting at a long, rustic wooden table. Her blonde, curly hair fell past her broad shoulders. She had bright blue eyes just like Austin, but despite her kind smile, she was sitting at that table watching me like a hawk.

Austin was not only her only son, but he was also the youngest out of all her children. It suddenly dawned on me that I was a little fish swimming in uncharted waters amongst sharks, and I knew for a fact that I was the first female he'd ever brought home before. I could tell this was a pretty big deal.

His dad, a well-built guy with graying hair and blue eyes, looked up from reading the sports page of the paper and shot Austin a wink. It looked like some sort of guy-code the way I saw Austin's face flush red. His blush spread across his face and reached his ears. He tucked his fingers in his pockets and hunched his shoulders. I could imagine the wink put into words: "Congratulations, son, on losing your virginity."

It was hard to miss the three similar-looking women sitting around the table eyeing me like vultures waiting to strip meat from a carcass. They all had the same blonde hair but cut into different styles. All three had the same vivid blue eyes. From what I could make out from the family photos, they were Austin's older sisters. I don't know why, but the way each set of female eyes pierced into me made me feel intimidated and pinned to the spot.

I could tell he was the baby all right.

Austin shifted his weight from one foot to the

other nervously. "Everybody, this is my mate, Riley." He glared at his sisters, sending them a silent warning with his eyes. "She's very important to me, so I want you to be nice to her."

I sensed the "or else" tone in his voice.

Austin glanced at me and flashed a sweet smile. He removed his hands from his pockets and pulled me into his side, wrapping an arm around me tightly.

"Riley, this is my mom, Eliza, and she's a doctor. This is my dad, Brian, and he's our local sheriff, both here in Forest Hills and Lakewell." He nodded over toward the three women who hadn't taken their eyes off me once. "These are my sisters, Melissa, Jackie, and Stacey."

I smiled my best forced smile, to the point where my cheeks were aching. There was an awkward moment as we all mumbled, "hello". I watched Austin's mom's eyes searching my neck for his mating mark. As soon as her eyes landed on it, I saw them widen.

Shit! His mom now knows we've had sex.

CHAPTER EIGHTEEN

Riley

"She's really pretty, isn't she, Brian? You two will need to sign the new mates register." She nudged her husband. "Won't they, Brian?

But Brian hadn't been paying attention.

"Brian!" she yelled.

His dad jumped while reading the paper. "Huh? What?" he muttered, having assumed the introductions were over.

They both started squabbling over him being rude, reading the paper while they had a guest and how he wasn't paying attention. He folded up his paper like a scolded dog and apologized.

"Sorry, I only wanted to read about Beast's retirement from cage fighting." He glanced up at Austin, but Austin rolled his eyes. Stacey almost choked on the mug she'd taken a swig from. Her cheeks burned an angry shade of red and Austin shot her a death glare.

Brian's face filled with awe as he spoke about his sports hero. "Did you know he's never been defeated, not once?" He shook his head in amazement. "What a record, and a local guy too."

Austin huffed as if he was unimpressed. "Dad, I've met him, remember? We fought alongside each other in Whitevale. He saved my ass, I saved his, big deal." He gave an indifferent shrug.

I hadn't a clue what they were talking about. They all started talking about some fight over land and a girl called Leah. That the whole of Whitehaven's water supply had been poisoned and only recently became safe enough to drink from again. It all sounded rather scary, and to be honest, I'm glad to hear that it was all over. Brian told him each community was busy repairing the damage that was caused. Austin told his mom he'd been sent to check there were no hunters left lurking around the edge of Lakewell, and that was when I'd almost run him over on the road.

His sisters erupted with laughter at how we met.

"He sabotaged my car and carried me off to his cabin while I was sleeping. I woke up to find him spooning with me, completely naked," I told them.

They all responded with a wide-eyed, "No way!" To which Austin fidgeted uncomfortably on the spot.

Austin and I took a seat around the table while they all chatted, laughing and joking and throwing the occasional sarcastic remark at each other. I could see that he got his sarcastic streak from his mom. They all gave as good as they got, and when they laughed, they were loud and proud. My nervousness ebbed away, and I found myself joining in on the conversation. I hadn't laughed so hard in years, and it felt really good to be included.

His mom laughed with tears streaming down her face. "Honey, him running around buck naked is nothing new. He's always been one for stripping off. My little naturist." She pinched his cheek. "He used to strip off all the time and run off down the street with it all hanging out, just flapping in the wind there." She accentuated her words with hand gestures.

Austin groaned and dragged a hand down his face. "Mom, I was three!"

Eliza leaned forward as she carried on telling me stories. "It's a wonder it works at all after he got it stuck in the vacuum cleaner after his fourteenth birthday. One minute I'm telling him to clean his room, the next he's screaming like a little baby girl. Yep, cock and balls, all the way in the tube. We tried switching to blow-out but that just caused you more problems, didn't it, honey? I had to take him to the emergency room in Lakewell. He begged me not to take him to the surgery here. No. Didn't want to risk his school pals seeing him with half the vacuum hose attached to him. That's why we nicknamed him Tripod." There were howls of laughter around the table.

Austin pinched the bridge of his nose with another groan. At that point, I was in such a state that I'd almost peed my pants, unable to stop myself from laughing so I could breathe again. Even Austin found it funny. Each time our eyes locked we'd burst out laughing.

As he was busy getting roasted, my eyes wandered around the well-used yet clean kitchen. It was a room I imagined them all congregating in rather than using the sitting room like this was the heart of the house. Along the walls, there were quite a few canvas prints with witty slogans printed on them. It gave me an insight into Eliza's down-to-earth personality. They read, "Tonight's menu consists of two options, take it or leave it," and the other said, "One tequila, two tequila, three tequila, floor". There was another one above the stove that read, "Open the oven, take a look, the first to complain is tomorrow's cook". My eyes kept darting around the room as each quirky canvas caught my eye. The control it took for me not to laugh was taking up all my concentration. There was one that almost had me in stitches. It read: "It's all shits & giggles until someone giggles & shits." Even the coffee mugs his parents were drinking from had funny quotes printed on them. His dad's mug had one that said, "I'm not lazy, I'm just in energy-saving mode." While his mom's mug was the best. Hers read, "I don't have a bucket list, but my fuck-it list is a mile long."

I honestly don't know why Austin was so worried. All parents like to embarrass their offspring, but his family was amazing, and I really loved his mom.

Eliza loaded the table with food. Homemade beef casserole with mashed potatoes and crusty bread rolls. I copied them all as they ate, dipping their buttered bread in the gravy and devouring it. I licked my fingers, enjoying the freedom to eat however I pleased without having to put on airs and graces. It was good, wholesome food that filled my stomach. Nothing like the à la carte rations my chef usually served.

Eliza got up from the table and came back with a bottle of champagne and seven mismatched glasses. "Here, we were saving this for a special occasion, which is what this is. It's nothing fancy. I won it at the hospital raffle last year."

She popped the cork and filled each glass with the sweet-smelling, pink effervescent liquid. I picked up my glass at the same time as everyone else. Eliza made a teary-eyed toast. "To Austin and Riley. May your lives be filled with as much happiness as mine and Brian's has been, and may my son's loins be fertile enough to spawn me plenty of grandcubs."

Austin spat his mouthful out with shock. "Mom!"

He shot me an apologetic look. "She gets like this. Don't take any notice," he groaned with embarrassment, and I placed my hand on his knee and squeezed it.

"It's fine." I rolled my eyes as if he was being ridiculous. "Relax, will you?"

He mumbled something about first impressions and that it was his turn next to meet my parents. The thought filled my mind with dread. My parents weren't as fun, easy-going, or as welcoming as Austin's parents were. I might as well throw him into a pit full of hungry lions and watch them tear him limb from limb. It'd be less painful.

When and if that time came, I'd hope my parents were as warm and welcoming as Eliza and Brian because if they weren't, I'd already decided that they'd never hear from me again. They could shove their inheritance up their egotistical, overprivileged asses.

We finished up and said our goodbyes. Austin's sisters all started to leave, too, saying they had to get back to their mates and cubs, and that the next time we all got together the following week, I'd get to meet them too.

Apparently, they didn't want to bombard me the first time they met me, which was sweet, but I wouldn't have minded. They also gave me a bag full of clothes and a couple of pairs of shoes to wear. It didn't matter that they were too big; I was grateful.

Brian kissed my cheek and Eliza pulled me in for a strong bear hug—excuse the pun.

I noticed a few more curtain twitchers peeking through the windows as we climbed back into Austin's truck. His mom asked him to hang back for a minute while she talked to him. I saw her stuff something into the palm of his hand and closed his fingers around it. I glanced away out of respect for their privacy as they hugged each other, tearfully. It was none of my business to ask, but I wondered what they were talking about. I didn't mention anything as he got into the truck with reddened eyes.

"Where are we going now?" I asked as he started the engine.

Austin cleared his throat. "Townhall," he replied. His voice was thick as if he'd been crying. However, he didn't appear sad.

CHAPTER NINETEEN

Riley

"How come?" I asked, scrunching my brows as curiosity got the better of me.

"We've got to sign the official clan register and get our mating license," he reminded me.

I knew that we had to sign something, but I wasn't aware it was that official.

Mating license?

"Huh? Do you need a license for that?" I asked.

Austin chuckled as he drove. "Yeah, like a license to thrill." He wiggled his brows.

I shook my head in amusement, muttering, "Such a dork."

Austin started to explain, "It's the equivalent to a human marriage license. It means the Council of Elders have more of an idea about the number of residents we have in town. You have to register births the same way as humans do too. We are the only shifter community who does that. The cats don't bother because their numbers are too few, and the wolves can form a pack link, so they don't have any need for a register."

"Oh okay, that makes perfect sense," I replied, having thought about it.

"If I just pull up out front, we can run in and sign the register before they close," he mumbled, determined to park up along the busy road.

We stopped outside an old black and white painted building in the center of town. It did look as if they were getting ready to close for the day, so we hurried out of the truck.

"Quick." Austin grabbed my hand as we half ran along the pathway and up to the black double doors.

It all looked official inside, like a courthouse. It reminded me of an old library and smelled of musty old books.

The craftsmanship that had gone into the construction of the building was extraordinary. I mean the architecture was like nothing I'd ever seen before. The way the wooden beams along the walls and ceilings were carved and sculpted into patterns looked like it would've taken years to craft.

The furniture was made from honey oak. Each piece had been carved and crafted by hand. Whoever made it must have been a highly skilled carpenter. One thing I knew for sure was these bears had a keen eye for style. I could name a few billionaires who would pay a fortune for these pieces.

I could make out the long table at the far end of the room where I guessed all the elders must sit. It made me realize that I knew nothing much about Austin's world. Presuming that I'd be living here for the rest of my life, I made a mental note to ask him to fill me in with his customs.

We approached a wooden desk that was littered with paperwork. A flustered woman was sifting through it all, muttering about nobody knowing how to file properly. I'd hazard a guess she was around thirty. She was dressed respectably in a stylish black and gray pinstripe trouser suit, and her brown hair was pulled back into a tight French plait.

"Excuse me," Austin announced our presence. She glanced up and smiled professionally. "Hi, are you both here to register?"

"Yes, please," Austin replied.

He cast me a subtle side glance as he bounced on the balls of his feet while she went off to fetch something.

She cleared away a stack of paperwork to make room on the desk, then dropped a huge, heavy, leather-clad book onto it. The thing was enormous, and she struggled to carry it.

"Here, let me just find the right page," she mumbled while flicking through the musty parchment.

"Here we go." She handed Austin a quill.

A fucking quill. A bird's tail feather that had been dipped in a pot of black ink.

"Sign here, sir." She tapped her fingernail on the area where he had to sign his name on the page.

The form looked just as official as any legal document. Austin signed and printed his name along the line, neatly. Her gaze flashed to me.

"And could you please print your full name here

and then in that section there, print your mated name." She tapped both places where I had to sign.

Austin handed me the ancient writing tool, and I hovered it over the dotted line.

I remembered Austin calling me Mrs. Rayne this morning, so that meant that I would be known by his surname. "Okay, my signature won't look very good, I'm afraid, I've spent years perfecting my old one," I joked. It was hard to change your signature at the drop of a hat. I let the pen glide across the thick paper as I signed my new name as neatly as I could.

Austin's chest swelled as he spoke with pride, "I think Riley Rayne sounds pretty awesome to me."

As I signed my new surname, I got a weird feeling inside. Not a bad one, the complete opposite. It felt like the start of something new, like a clean slate. I wasn't Riley Roth anymore. I was leaving all that behind me. I always envisioned myself keeping my maiden name and opting to have a double-barrel surname.

Yet here I was, standing here in an old pair of cut-off jean shorts, old boots, and a man's oversized shirt. Nothing like the designer clothes I was used to wearing.

I didn't have a scrap of makeup on, and my hair was scraped back off my face in a loose knot. I didn't have my money, or my car, or any of my luxuries with me, but I'd never felt as happy as I did right now, signing my new name as the start of my new life.

Would it really be so bad if I never returned home again? Couldn't I just disappear and live a normal, happy life with Austin? Have kids and raise them all in Forest Hills?

The registrar handed us a copy of the license, and Austin took it, placing it inside his jacket pocket for safekeeping. "Can we go home now?" I asked, pleading with my eyes.

"You don't know how good it is to hear you say that." Austin put his arm around me while we walked side by side back to the truck. "I'm so happy that you decided to stay with me. So much for me only getting a month, huh?"

"I love you, and I love where we live, despite it being in the woods," I told him honestly.

He swung me around, causing me to squeal with shock, lifting me off my feet as his lips met mine and devouring my mouth mercilessly. He poured all his feelings into it, and so did I. We gasped breathlessly as we broke apart. Our lips were still swollen from the kiss.

I rather enjoyed the peaceful drive back to the cabin. Neither of us spoke much, but it wasn't awkward. We didn't need to maintain a constant conversation to feel comfortable. This was nice. It was effortless. Just like breathing air.

"Home sweet home," Austin announced as we pulled up outside the cabin.

"I'm gonna need a massage after sleeping rough in that tent." I gave a subtle hint as I got out of the truck, faking a backache, and praying he took the bait.

Austin, whose sexual confidence was growing by the day, came back at me with a typical male response. "If you want a back rub, I want a front rub. Fair's fair, babe," he finished, with a suggestive wink.

"Okay, Tripod, lead the way." I gestured for him to go first.

The moment I called him by his nickname he sucked in air through puckered lips, narrowing his eyes at me as if I was asking for trouble.

"Just wait until I meet your mom, I bet I'll learn a thing or two about you." He sauntered off into the kitchen, mumbling something about revenge being sweet.

I went around the cabin closing all the curtains while Austin boiled some water to make us a hot drink. He came back to the sitting room with an armful of chopped wood to build a fire in the fireplace. I left him to it, hurrying up the stairs so that I could get changed into one of Austin's oversized T-shirts. I then put away all the hand-me-down clothes I'd been given.

I felt fully content, humming a tune as I hung the garments in the wardrobe. I heard footsteps coming up the stairs and turned to find Austin rubbing his neck nervously in the doorway.

I giggled. "What's wrong with you? You're acting all weird. If you're waiting for your front rub, I'll be done in a minute."

Austin waved a hand in front of him "No, you'll see. Close your eyes." There was a determination in his face as if he wanted me to play along. Either he had some sort of surprise planned, or he was about to pull a prank on me. It was one or the other.

There was a smile still lingering on my lips as I waited in anticipation for what he was likely to do next.

Austin took hold of my left hand, and I felt him slide something solid onto my third finger, then brought my hand up to his lips and kissed it.

"You can open them now." His voice slightly trembled with excitement as he held my hand in his.

My eyes fluttered open and landed on the gold diamond-cut wedding band on my finger. I slapped my other hand over my mouth as I gasped with shock, tears of happiness clouding my vision.

"Oh Austin, it's beautiful," I breathed.

The corners of his eyes creased as he smiled back, lovingly. "It was my grandmother's. She left it for me to give to my mate, so now it's yours."

Words failed me as my mouth flopped open and closed. This was more than sentimental. This was given to him by the most influential woman in his life besides his mother. She meant the world to him, and by wearing this, I'd be honoring her memory.

"I love it." I found my voice again before throwing my arms around his neck and drawing him close.

"What's that sound?" Austin's forehead creased with confusion as he strained to listen.

The pulsating sound of blades chopping

through the air got louder and louder, our eyes widening as the sound became more and more distinguishable.

"Uh-oh." My voice trembled. The color drained from Austin's face as we both recognized the sound.

It was a helicopter hovering over the property. It was only when a strong beam of white light shone in through the closed curtains that we realized the severity of the situation.

We crept over to the window, hesitantly moving the curtains aside so we could peep through just enough to see without being spotted. I let out a strangled cry at the sight of the armed police and news vans screeching to a stop outside.

The wind vortex that the helicopter blades were creating caused the treetops to bend and sway. I clung to Austin as we both flinched back from the windows with wide-eyed horror.

My heart was pounding in my chest like a jackhammer.

"Shit!" I ran my tongue over my dry lips to moisten them, running a hand through my hair while I paced the floor trying to think on the spot. "I'll go out and talk to them first, I mean, how bad can it be, right?"

Have you ever heard the phrase, famous last words? Yeah, well. Just as I spoke, we heard one of the police officers speak through a megaphone.

"We know you're in there! Release the hostage and come out with your hands on your head!"

CHAPTER TWENTY

Riley

"Okay … I've got it." I spun on my heel to face Austin after having an epiphany.

He flinched at the sound of the police giving another loud rasping knock on the front door.

"What have you got in mind?" His nerves were getting the better of him as his eyes desperately searched mine.

"Just trust me and go with it," I replied while smoothing my hair and straightening my appearance.

I held out my hand for Austin to take, curling my fingers around his as we walked down the stairs, our boots making a light thud down each step.

"Now remember, let me handle the press. I know how to play them to our advantage. The police will have to back off when the story of our star-crossed love is splashed all over the news," I spoke with an air of confidence.

All right, I may not have had any experience with this kind of scenario, but I was pretty much an expert when it came to manipulating news reporters. You had to be cunning in my world. As sly as a fox, some might say. Those guys were vultures if you weren't careful. They could ruin your life in seconds.

Austin scrunched his face confused. "Star-crossed, huh?" he asked as if to say, "What the actual fuck?"

I cleared my throat, and then opened the front door. The sound of weapons being locked and loaded, the blinding flashes that came from the cameras, made the scenario very real indeed.

Shit, here goes absolutely nothing.

An officer, who looked more like a Swedish porn star with a handlebar mustache, called out. I didn't know whether to laugh or take pity.

"Release the hostage," he yelled, then beckoned me to walk toward him slowly.

The police had their weapons raised and pointed them directly at Austin. It looked like they would open fire the second I stepped away, so I nestled closer at his side.

I held my left palm out in front of me, my right hand clenched tightly onto Austin's forearm.

"Wait! This is my husband," I announced, to which there was a series of shocked gasps all around us.

The commanding officer narrowed his eyes as I turned my hand around to show off my ring.

"See? We're married." I shot Austin a reassuring smile, then winked in an attempt to signal to him that I was activating the second part of my plan.

Turning toward the horde of reporters who were all standing there open-mouthed, I called out, "And all this stress isn't good for the baby." I placed my hand over my abdomen protectively. "So, if you don't mind. I need you to leave."

We were then engulfed in a series of blinding, flashing lights from the cameras as well as bombarded with question upon question, which meant one thing — it was working.

"Wait, Miss Roth! Miss Roth! Is this true? Are you married to this man?"

"Did you marry because of the pregnancy? Was it unplanned?"

"Who is this mystery guy? He's not the type you usually go for, but I'll admit, he's hot!"

"Does this mean that Kain Cox is definitely off the scene now?"

"Why all the secrecy, Miss Roth?"

I waved my hand as a sign that I wanted to speak.

"First of all, Kain and I were never a thing. We're just friends. And I'm happy to answer any questions you have, but please, we just want some privacy. This is our honeymoon, after all. And my name is Riley Rayne now. Get used to it because it's the only name I'll answer to."

I felt Austin's posture stiffen beside me.

"Kain? The galactic space orc from Mars, Kain Cox? You gotta be fucking kidding?!" he whispered abrasively.

My eyes blazed as we argued about that in frantic whispers. But I had to admit, I was surprised Austin had seen that movie. It had been such a huge box office flop.

"Fuck no, those were just rumors. I passed out

drunk on his yacht . . . that's all! I did not - I repeat, did not fuck Kain Cox. I heard he only had a small . . ." I wiggled my little finger to indicate he had a tiny penis and was hardly worth taking my panties off for, which is why I didn't go near it. "And as you know, I only play with big boys toys."

Austin huffed. "Not a boy, darlin', in case you need reminding."

We didn't have time for this now. Not with the press hungering for our blood. I composed myself and addressed the reporters with a practiced smile.

"How come you didn't tell your parents?" a reporter asked. "Why elope to the middle of nowhere? Don't they approve of your relationship?"

"Since when have my parents ever shown an interest in the guys I've dated?" I met Austin's questioning gaze with an apologetic smile. "So we did something spontaneous and romantic. The last time I checked, it wasn't a crime. And yeah, the baby wasn't planned . . . it's the product of our love."

He leaned close, his lips barely moving as he muttered. "They're not seriously going to swallow all this baby crap."

I nudged him with my elbow and hissed, "They will . . . just go with it."

Austin laughed nervously. "Um, yeah, we're really happy. Riley knocked me off my feet. She's a wild one." Austin put his arm around me and pulled me closer to his side.

The police officers began lowering their weapons, some rolling their eyes as if this was a waste of their valuable time. The rich and famous were renowned for doing wild, spontaneous shit like this.

"Almost ran me over with her sports car; that's how we met. Then—Bam! Love at first sight," he continued with a slight exaggeration.

"All right, that's enough," I whispered, giving him a dominant glare. "Let *me* do the talking."

The reporters were loving it. They were lapping up every word. Even the police were backing away. All was going so well, then Austin reached inside his jacket pocket to retrieve the mating license to offer as proof and found himself unexpectedly tased to the floor. There was nothing on the documentation to suggest he was a shifter. To the outside world, it was nothing more than a certificate of marriage and that was that. One officer fired, then another, wires crossed over Austin's convulsing body to the point where he was foaming at the mouth.

I screamed in shock. I initially thought they'd

shot him, but they hadn't. They could have — easily, but they'd only tased him. They thought he was reaching inside his jacket for a weapon. Not a piece of paper. A pair of strong hands grabbed me from behind, just as I managed to pick up the mating license from where it landed on the ground.

"It's all right, miss, you're safe now," a familiar voice said, but I was too preoccupied with what happened to Austin to notice who it was.

"No, look I have proof." I waved the certificate around. "We're married. He's telling the truth," I cried out desperately.

If only they'd just read the fucking document, they'd see it for themselves.

I wrestled against a strong pair of arms in a desperate attempt to free myself from being restrained.

"Get off me. You're making a huge mistake!"

Cameras flashed. The press were roaring cries of protests toward the police for being unreasonable. They had thankfully bought my story and were showing concerns for the "baby."

I watched in horror as they placed an unconscious Austin in handcuffs and bundled him into a police van.

"Where are they taking him?" I demanded.

"Austin! Austin!" I screamed while being dragged away.

"That's not your concern, Miss Roth." The officer struggled to form words while restraining me.

"Yes, it is. I'm his *wife*! Get me my lawyer!" I screamed, outraged.

"Miss Roth, uh, I mean, Mrs. Rayne," a female reporter called out, thrusting a microphone in my face. "Can you tell me why a resident of Forest Hills tipped off the police with information about your whereabouts?"

What?

My eyes narrowed as I scrunch my face in confusion.

Who would do something like that?

Then it occurred to me that they might for the ten-million-dollar reward. There were plenty of nosey bastards living in the cul-de-sac where Austin's parents lived. I couldn't see his parents doing that to us, and I could think of no one else it could have been.

"Are you familiar with the name Rebecca King?" she asked, rushing her words.

I shook my head, baffled. "No, I've never heard of her."

Who was this mystery woman?

My nostrils flared with anger.

No way was she benefitting from the ten-million-dollar reward, although she may be needing it to pay for plastic surgery as soon as I rearrange her face for what she'd done to Austin.

CHAPTER TWENTY-ONE

Riley

The officer dragged me over toward the helicopter that was waiting to take off.

"I'm just doing my job, Miss Roth," he huffed in irritation at my last attempt to struggle.

I fought as he forced my head inside. I was being dragged home whether I liked it or not. As I turned to scowl at him and recognized him as my mother's personal security guard, Reed.

"Your parents are waiting for you at home,"

Reed said as he slid the door panel shut and backed away from the revolving blades.

My father's head of security, Gabe, short for Gabriel, was sitting in the helicopter, waiting for me. He wasn't a tall guy at five-foot-five inches, but he was stocky. He always wore black sunglasses whether it was day or night. I cast him an icy glare as I strapped myself in. I needed to find out where they'd taken Austin and convince my parents that this wasn't a kidnapping. I felt the folded-up mating license between my fingers and opened it out; my eyes burned with tears as I read the document.

Gabe cleared his throat.

"Congratulations on your mating, Mrs. Rayne."

My head snapped to look in his direction, surprised he called me by my mated name.

"Huh? How do you know? What did you say?" I stuttered, shocked that he'd just said mating and not marriage.

I could barely make out his face due to the darkness that engulfed us. A shadow cast over him, darkening his coppery red hair. The only light source came from the moonlight that spilled in through the windows, illuminating the lower half of his face.

"Your father will be interested to know that you

found your mate at last. He'll be a little shocked that he's a bear. He thought you'd mate with your own species," he added, sounding amused by the recent revelation.

My mouth flopped open and closed as I tried to digest the crap Gabe was spouting at me.

"Species? How fucking dare you!" I replied, feeling fed up to hell and in no mood to be fucked with.

"Don't play the innocent act with me, vixen. You're your father's daughter, and sharp as a whip. You know exactly what I meant by that." The leather creaked as Gabe relaxed into his seat, then yawned lazily. "You stand a better chance of getting your mate back if you approach your father for help. Your mother isn't all that keen on shifters after the shock of finding out about Bracken being one, but saying that, your little disappearing stunt caused them to reconcile." He took off his sunshades, allowing the moonlight to reflect in his sharp blue eyes.

Had I just heard him right? Was there any truth in that or was he just fucking with me? He knew about mates, so if it was true, there was a strong possibility that Gabe was one too.

"My dad's a shifter," I said, and then dragged in a shaky breath as Gabe nodded in affirmation.

"That was why he and Sasha divorced," Gabe revealed.

I can vaguely remember my mother screaming at him about having lied to her. That's what it was all about. She accused him of being a lying, conniving, manipulating cheat. Those were her words. Dad did nothing to dispel those rumors. Why didn't he fight harder for her if she was his mate? Unless she wasn't. *Oh, God. What if she wasn't?*

Gabe's lips twitched up into a cocky smirk. "Your dad isn't just any shifter. Bracken Roth is a fox shifter. He's the most powerful man in the world, you know. Ever heard the phrase 'as cunning as a fox?' He may be a sly, cold-hearted bastard, but he never cheated on your mother."

"He didn't?" I asked, hoping to cling onto a tiny shred of hope.

Gabe shook his head as a sign for 'no'. "The only thing he was guilty of was hiding his true identity from her. She just thought that he was into some weird, kinky shit when he marked her. But if I'm gonna be totally honest with you, your mom is a bitch, who could be mistaken for a dragon. If dragon shifters existed. As for your father, the guy's a legend, an inspiration to us all. Our kind have infiltrated governments all across the world, protecting the secret state of Whitehaven and protecting our identities. It's all thanks to the influence of Bracken Roth. Don't underestimate your father's capabilities, Riley. Go to him. Appeal to his better nature."

My father has a better nature. Are we talking about the same guy?

"So, you're a shifter too?" I cast him an evaluating look.

He was loyal to my father, that much I knew. But was he sympathetic toward shifters in general? That remained to be seen.

"Yes, I'm a fox shifter like your father. Just like everyone else who works for him," he revealed.

"What?! That's insane," I gushed, feeling mind-blown. "I can't believe I've been surrounded by shifters my entire life and I never knew it."

My mind was bombarded with thoughts, memories of all the niggling doubts I'd had over the years. Dad had never once gotten sick, never needed a trip to the doctor, dentist, nor did he need to wear glasses, and thinking back, neither did I. Whenever Mom coughed or sneezed, I used to avoid her like a plague victim in the hope that I wouldn't catch it. And all this time, I was immune.

We sat in silence for the rest of the journey, and I remained lost in my thoughts. I wasn't angry with my father. I probably should have been. But I was always so guarded when it came to sharing my feelings. We didn't talk about things. We didn't share. That was never encouraged. If I had a problem, I talked to a therapist. My problems would remain in that room, protected by patient confidentiality - and a non-disclosure order for safe measure. But since meeting Austin, my feelings were all I could think about. My wants, needs, and also Austin's feelings. How my choices impacted him. So, Dad lied. Not telling is kind of the same as lying, whether he did it for selfish reasons or to protect us. He chose not to tell us either way. But he was still my dad, and his DNA ran through my veins. And now I was mated to a bear shifter.

It'll be interesting to see how our kids turn out.

But now I'd come to terms with that, it was time I got to grips with the bigger issue that had been bothering me.

"Do you know anything about this mystery female who ratted us out? Some woman called

Rebecca King." I tried not to sound like a jealous bitch, but I failed miserably.

"Ahh," Gabe smirked. "Miss King. The bitter ex-best friend of Mr. Rayne."

My heart jolted with alarm. "What?" I blinked and shook my head quickly. My girly brain registered "ex" before the rest of the information had the chance to filter through. "Ex-best friend as in 'no longer friends?'" I asked curiously.

Gabe picked up on my little flash of jealousy and decided to torture me by being vague with information. "Oh, Miss King and Mr. Rayne had been friends for quite some time, since they were cubs."

I swallowed the dryness in my throat, not liking the sound of that. The thought of Austin having a jealous female friend left a sour taste in my mouth. For starters, why was she jealous if they had been 'just friends' and had there been something more going on between them?

"Am I right in believing she lives right by Austin's parents?" I asked, even though I was already second-guessing the answer.

Gabe's deep husky chuckle filled the cabin.

"You'd be correct. She called as soon as you left his parents' house, rambling something about you not being right for him, and that he and she should be together instead. She was under the impression that you were just merely a human—not that she came out and said it, but it was implied that way."

"Wait-wait-wait. So, this bitch wants to get between us?" The green-eyed monster in me growled, wanting to scratch her beady eyes out. Whoever the hell she was.

"Is that all you're bothered about?" Gabe laughed out loud, trailing off with an amused expression playing on his face. "You don't want to ask me about whether or not you have the ability to shift? You're just concerned about having competition for your bear's affections?" Gabe sat there, grinning his ass off. Luckily for him, I was strapped into a harness. He wasn't even within slapping distance, and there was nothing around me that I could throw at him.

"Oh, c'mon, Riley. I think it's sort of cute. I've never seen you so concerned about anything before. Except when your mother wanted to donate some of your toys to charity. You threw such a tantrum that you—"

I cut him off bluntly. "Shut up!" I screeched. "Just stop judging me. You don't know the first thing about me." My eyes set into a hardened glare.

Gabe looked taken aback. He'd hurt me by dragging up my childhood, and he knew it too. My parents could sugarcoat it all they wanted, but my childhood was far from a happy one. Kids didn't just want their parents to buy them stuff; they only wanted their time. The one thing that didn't cost a damn thing was the one thing that they could never give me.

"You think you got me all figured out, don't you? That I'm a spoiled little brat who had everything. But you know what? I didn't. My dolls were the only real company I had, and when my mom gave them away, she said, 'we all have to grow up some time'. Do you know what it's like having no one to talk to? I've been lonely for as long as I can remember. No one has ever cared about me like Austin does. I want him back, Gabe."

My voice broke off, and I hid my face in my hands. I'd never broken down and cried my heart out, until now.

It's true what they say—love hurts.

Gabe fell into remorseful silence.

"Will you help me, please?" I looked to him, begging, my eyes full of desperation, not knowing what else to do.

"I'll see what I can do. Your bear is from

Whitehaven. His elders will want him back. And anyway, there's someone else who owes your father a favor," he answered in a softer tone, seeming regretful for how he teased me earlier.

Gabe pulled out his phone, his thumb scrolling through his contacts before he pressed to dial and placed the phone to his ear. His lips curled over his teeth into a grin as soon as the person on the other end answered.

"Hey, Alec, long time no see," Gabe chatted on the phone as I sat listening. "I'm not bad, buddy. Congratulations on getting mated. It's been a long time coming." Gabe listened, adding, "Uh-huh," every once in a while. "Yup, I'm glad we're in agreement. We need to get him out of there before things turn grizzly. I'll tell Bracken to expect you both. See you soon." Gabe ended the call looking kind of smug with himself.

Meanwhile, I was left nervously hanging, holding my breath, and practically clawing at the leather upholstered seat with anxiety.

"Well? What did he say?" I blurted impatiently.

Fucking guys and their vagueness.

Gabe grinned. "You just got yourself a damn good lawyer, that's what."

CHAPTER TWENTY-TWO

Riley

The pilot announced through our headsets that he was preparing to land. I always hated the landing part and braced myself in my seat. It was that feeling of dropping, of going downward. It was the same with roller coasters, too. That tummy flipping motion, messing with my sense of gravity, churning my insides, and giving me the sensation of moths instead of pretty butterflies fluttering around in my abdomen.

In an attempt to lure my mind away from the

descent, I concentrated on the billions of pretty lights that made up the lively city below. Everything looked so serene from way up here. Peaceful, away from the hustle and bustle of the city that never sleeps. I had no concept of the time. Although, I guessed it would be pretty late by now. I missed Austin, and I was worried sick about him.

My mind whirled with bad thoughts that played on a loop in my brain. Where had they taken him? Had they hurt him? And how soon could this damn lawyer of ours get here? I was itching to get off this helicopter, anxious to confront my parents, and deal with that bitch from Forest Hills.

The moment the landing gear touched down, I unclipped my harness and switched back into bitch mode. Gabe was the first to climb out; he then held out his hand to help me. I frowned at it, but then grudgingly accepted a hand to get out. My annoyance wasn't directed at Gabe, the poor bastard. He was on the receiving end of my bad mood.

"Thanks." I flashed a chaste smile.

The rotating blades spun above us causing a strong vortex of wind that made the cool night air seem even colder. The wind swirled around me and blew my already messed up hair all over my face.

Gabe directed me over the far side of the grounds to where a black stretched limousine was waiting for us. I caught a glimpse of my sorry sight in the reflection of the blacked-out windows and attempted to smooth down my unruly hair.

"Miss Roth," My mother's head of security, Reed, referred to me by my maiden name as he held open the door. His tousled blond hair moved around with the wind, and his hazel-green eyes narrowed on Gabe.

"After you, sweet cheeks," Gabe said to goad him.

Reed's jaw clenched and pulsed, clearly not appreciating that comment.

"Don't fucking talk to me, asshole," Reed seethed in retaliation.

A moment of hostility passed between Gabe and Reed. The two of them didn't seem to get along and I was worried I would have to break up a fight.

"Just get in the car," Gabe told him, gritting his teeth.

Reed got in and shuffled across the backseat as if to sit far away from Gabe. I climbed in next and sat close to the driver's hatch. It was closed. Gabe got in last and shut the door. He made sure to leave a massive gap between him and Reed on the backseat. Both men glared through the opposite windows, their tensed jaws hard enough to crack walnuts. They were both emanating enough testosterone to power a rocket ship back to planet Uranus, where I was more than convinced those two assholes came from.

Men . . . Ugh!

It didn't take long for the cold leather interior to warm beneath my bare legs, enabling me to relax and enjoy the ride home.

Home.

It didn't feel right to call it my home anymore. My home was with Austin. Being with him made me rethink my whole life. I had kissed my way through a pond filled with frogs to find my Prince Charming.

The limo driver brought us to my childhood home, a mansion made from tinted glass and structured steel. It felt weird coming back here after my parents went their separate ways all those years ago. This was to be part of my inheritance. But it was just a house without a heart, standing cold and uninviting at the foot of the mile-long gravel driveway.

"Finally," I breathed impatiently the second we came to a stop.

Gabe was first to get out, followed by me, then Reed. My boots crunched over the loose stone as I strode up to the front door, taking the stone steps two at a time.

"Mom!" I yelled as I burst through the door.

Through habit, I took off my boots in the hall. We had a pristine cream carpet that ran throughout the house. Mom had always held a "no shoe" policy. We had to change into a pair of slippers the second we set foot through the door.

"Riley, you're back!" she called through from the sitting room.

I followed the direction of her voice and found her draped across the black leather sofa with a glass of her usual: a Bloody Mary, complete with a stick of celery. The skimpy nightdress revealed plenty of skin, especially what I now recognized to be a fresh mating mark in the crook of her neck. I'd asked her how she got the original, and she said an animal had taken her by surprise and bit her, which I guess was close to the truth.

"Mom, what the fuck are you wearing? We have company," I snapped.

Instead of her usual business attire or designer

clothing, she was wearing a plain black silk negligee and slippers. She stood up and threw on a matching robe the second she saw my horrified expression.

"It's night. I'm having a nightcap before bed," she excused, sounding flustered.

I cast my eyes around the living room, looking to see who else was here. Our living room was modern with all the latest technology. Everything was voice-activated, the TV, the music, the lighting, heating, and the fireplace. Every piece of highly polished dark wooden furniture cost a small fortune. This was supposed to be my house now. I wasn't sure what the hell my mother was doing in it, and so scantily clad, too. My eyes bulged at the sight of my father who emerged through the patio doors in nothing but his boxer shorts. A cloud of cigar smoke lingered in the air behind him.

"Riley," he greeted me, his eyebrows raised with surprise. "Thank goodness. We were worried about you."

"Really?" I folded my arms, doubting that. "So then why does it reek of sex in here?"

Dad gawked at me, shocked, and Mom flushed with embarrassment.

"Never mind what we were doing," Mom rounded on me. "What about you? Eloping to the country with some hillbilly hick you just met. Please tell me you were just doing this to punish me for setting you up with a job. We can fix it. I'll call my lawyer, and we can get this sham of a marriage annulled." My mom's pleading face angered me, and I felt compelled to defend my man.

Austin and I had a rocky start, but I soon fell for the guy. He was mine, and there was no way I was going to stand there and let her trash him or talk me out of moving to Forest Hills.

"What is it, Mom? Isn't he good enough for me? Just because he's not rich, you think he's not good enough? Can't you just be happy I've found someone who loves me for me and not because of my net worth?" My eyes darted back and forth between my shocked parents.

"Are you saying you actually like this guy?" Mom asked, scrunching her face with incredulity.

"I love him," I corrected her. "Whatever you've said to the police, you better fix it. I want my *husband* back tonight." I pulled out the mating license and opened it up, holding it up as evidence. I saw my dad's eyes close as he cursed, whereas my mom could only look on with shock.

"Mr. Roth, if I may speak freely," Gabe spoke up from behind me.

My dad nodded sadly, allowing Gabe to continue. "I tried to contact you earlier, but you were otherwise engaged." Gabe glanced at my mother who had now turned crimson. "We located your daughter in Forest Hills after Miss King reported, what she assumed was a human, in town. She called the helpline number and Reed did the rest."

Dad scrubbed his hand over his stressed face. "What a mess," he mumbled exhaustedly. "You deal with your mate, and I'll deal with mine," he added, earning an agreeable nod from Gabe. "Where is he now?"

"Sulking," Gabe answered smugly.

"Well, how was I to know that Riley wasn't in any real danger?" Mom shrugged defensively. "We both thought she'd been kidnapped by blackmailers."

"But Reed must have told you about the call," Dad replied, his tone tense.

Mom's guilty splutter told him all he needed to know. Reed had told her, and she acted without consulting Dad. He glowered at Mom, a silent message that she ought to have known better. And now I knew what the beef was between Gabe and Reed, they were mates and didn't seem too happy about it, I could agree with Dad - this was a holy fuckery of a mess. Especially if Reed had been kept in the dark about shifters, which I suspect he had or else he would have let Gabe handle things. Austin had been worried about humans coming to Whitehaven and poking their noses around where they weren't wanted. How was Dad going to fix this catastrophe? We were going to need a miracle.

"We can't leave a shifter in human custody without risking the exposure of Whitehaven," Gabe mentioned to Dad.

"Agreed," Dad replied, to my relief.

"I've already taken the liberty of contacting Alpha White as it's now a matter for the United Shifter Council to handle," Gabe informed him.

"Of course." Dad looked defeated, pinching the bridge of his nose as he scrunched his eyes closed. "I understand the protocol, Gabriel. I am on the damn committee."

"United Shifter what?" I asked, feeling really fucking confused. "Will someone please explain to me what the hell that is and how it can help get my husband home?"

CHAPTER TWENTY-THREE

Riley

Gabe opened his mouth to speak but Dad cut in first. "The United Shifter Council. It's a newly established governing body that oversees the whole of Whitehaven. Ever since Whitevale was invaded by hunters and . . ." He hesitated to swallow. "And vampires."

"Vampires?" I blurted, my eyes huge.

My heart practically fell through my ass having heard that.

Dad quickly shook his head, grimacing. "Never

mind, that can wait. Why don't you stay here with your mother? She'll pour you a drink, and I'll go and make some arrangements." He smiled encouragingly to reassure me he'd make everything better again.

"You better fix this, Dad." I pointed my finger, narrowing my eyes into furious slits.

He sighed and scrubbed a hand over his handsome face. His red hair was messy for a change, no thanks to Mom. He had a scattering of gray through it, but it was more prominent around the sides above his ears. Dad's entire family lineage had bright red hair, which I inherited. Even Gabe had red hair, and he wasn't even related to us. Did that mean all fox shifters had red hair? Had I just made a connection? And Whitevale . . . Austin's dad brought that up during dinner. He mentioned an attack but didn't go into details. And now I understand why.

Mom breezed through the sitting room and went straight over to the alcohol cabinet, pulling out a bottle of pure orange juice and handing it to me.

"Here, do you want a glass and ice?" she offered sarcastically.

She couldn't bring herself to look at me. It was an admission of guilt on her behalf. When I wouldn't take it, she thrust the bottle into my hands. I had my eye on the vodka; that's what I needed. Something strong to take the edge off. Not fucking Tropicana.

"Mom, I'm not twelve. Where's the vodka?" I shoved the bottle of orange juice back at her and poured my own drink.

"But you're pregnant, aren't you?" She glared with disapproval as I downed the clear spirit and I winced as it licked a fiery trail down my throat. "You can't drink alcohol in your condition," she scolded, snatching the bottle from my hand.

I didn't even have the energy to argue back. Dad had been gone for around ten to fifteen minutes. When he came back, he was fully dressed in a black trouser suit, dress shoes, and a white button-down shirt.

"Daddy's taking care of it, princess. It'll all be fine." He held out his arms to try and embrace me, only for his face to flash with hurt when I refused to accept the gesture.

I was glad he was helping to get Austin back, but that didn't mean he was getting off the hook lightly.

"You're angry with me. I completely

understand." His throat bobbed nervously as he swallowed.

"You think? You lied to me!" I snapped. "I know what you are—what I am. Although, I'm not sure if I am exactly like you. I've never felt the urge to, you know? Change. I can't believe you never told me. That was a dick move, Dad, even for you!"

Dad immediately jumped into self-defense mode, deflecting the blame elsewhere.

"Ohh, make me out to be the bad guy. Thanks a lot. It's not easy coming out, you know? Especially when your mate is human. The rejection rate is seventy percent higher. You know what I think? I blame that shrink you hired to brainwash her." Dad's face turned an angry shade of red as he turned to face Mom.

This was Dad all over . . . nothing was ever his fault. Mom wasn't any better. She was just as stubborn.

What a pair!

Mom's shoulders slumped, and she slammed her now empty glass down on the dark wood coffee table in frustration. "Ugh! Bracken, can't you just drop it?! I've said I'm sorry. I thought I was doing what was best at the time, no thanks to you, might I add. You were no help at all. And anyway, she didn't brainwash Riley. She helped her to deal with the trauma."

"Exactly. She brainwashed her into forgetting everything. She can't even remember her first shift." Dad smacked the back of his fingers against the palm of his opposite hand as he spoke.

"Wait! *What?*" I spluttered, feeling dumbstruck.

I remembered all the sessions I had with my therapist; all the nightmares, the anxiety, and only being able to sleep if the light was left on. I think I would know if I'd shifted before. I would . . . wouldn't I?

Ignoring my mother's pleading face, Dad turned to me with rounded eyes that were filled to the brim with compassion. "Honey, what do you remember about that night you got lost in the woods?"

"You want to drag all this up now?" Mom's exasperated voice rang loudly around the room.

"Why not?" Dad's icy glare snapped to meet Mom's contrite one.

There was a wild hint of crazy in his eyes that made him seem quite scary.

"It's all relevant. It'll help her deal with the fact she's not entirely human. Besides, you can't use emotional blackmail anymore, Sasha. Yes, I should have told you about me from the start, but we should've learned from our mistakes and at least told Riley the truth. You denied me that." He pointed at Mom, and her bottom lip trembled.

"Bracken! For God's sake, really? She's pregnant. Go easy on her." Mom looked as if she was gonna burst into tears at any second.

Dad noticed this, and his face instantly softened. His stance relaxed, and his voice adopted a softer tone. "Sasha, there *is no* baby. Don't you think I'd be able to smell the pregnancy hormones?"

"What? Riley? But you said —" Mom's teary-eyed gaze cut to me.

I held my palm up in front of me defensively. "Mom, I just said that to try to pull us out of a tricky situation."

She cut me off. "So, I'm *not* going to be a grandmother?"

I couldn't tell whether it was disappointment or relief, but she placed her head in her hands and bawled her eyes out. It was official—I had caused my mother to have a nervous breakdown. Thank God I was an only child, because if I had sibling reinforcement, she'd probably be six feet under, pushing up daisies.

Dad walked over to her and wrapped an arm around her shoulders, tilting her chin so that her eyes met with his. They were equally matched in height, standing eye level with one another. Which led me to wonder whether all fox shifters were short too?

"She lied to the press, and good thinking, too," Dad told her, appearing impressed with me.

He turned to me as he comforted Mom. "You're astute, Riley. Which brings me back to that night in the woods. You didn't just get separated from the rest of your class; your teacher said she thought you were getting sick. That same teacher, whose silence I bought, said you had a temperature of way over one hundred and four degrees; you broke the thermometer. She said you were convulsing and screaming in pain. And that you were scaring the other kids, so the teachers got them all out of the way."

Mom was uncomfortable discussing the topic. She tried to pull away from Dad, but it didn't look as if he was letting go of her any time soon.

"Riley, honey, it's been a long night. Why don't you just get some rest?" Mom suggested, hoping to sweep this under the rug.

"Wait for just a second," I murmured, remembering a snippet.

Everything Dad mentioned started to filter itself

into my brain, unlocking the vault of my memory bank. Overwhelming memories came flooding back to me, forcing me to relive every painstaking flashback. Before I even had time to think about it, I was telling them things, my mind was reverting to when I was seven, a timid, traumatized little girl who thought she was dying.

"I was getting dizzy. I'd felt weird all day like I was getting sick. *But I never got sick.* I'd never been sick a day in my life. At first, my head hurt like I had the worst headache ever. Then the muscles all over my body started to ache and it hurt to walk. Throughout the day it just got worse and worse until they started to burn. I was so scared. It felt as if I was being burned alive. Like my bones were on fire."

I flinched and jerked away as my father put his hand on my shoulder. I didn't even notice he'd walked across the room to me.

"I'm so sorry, honey, we should have been there." Dad's softened words were laced with remorse.

CHAPTER TWENTY-FOUR

Riley

The second time he placed his hand against my shoulder, I left it there, enjoying the warmth that spread through the fabric of my shirt and warmed my skin. That small gesture of reassurance spurred me to continue.

"I can't remember what happened after that. I don't know exactly when my teacher took off and left me there. But she did. She just left me. I called out for help, but nobody came. I can't remember my body changing. But I think I remember becoming something else. Seeing things differently and all the smells. I ate a mouse and then I threw up. I thought it was a dream, you know . . . after a while."

I felt vulnerable under my father's restless gaze, feeling as if I was seven again, retelling everything for the first time. We should have talked about this. I should have been able to approach them and tell them what happened. But now I know why I couldn't. Dad was hiding a secret, and Mom was in denial. I was collateral. In a flash, I wrapped my arms around my dad's waist and clung to him like a child. Just like the monsters from my nightmares were coming to life, my childhood trauma was real, the memories were real—and I really did eat a fucking mouse!

Dad stroked my hair and spoke softly with reassurance. "It's okay, sweetheart, you've got to let it all out to undo all that psychological hoodoo that the human brainwasher put on you."

I heard Mom force out a breath. "Seriously, Bracken? Hoodoo? What the hell does that mean, anyway?" Mom whined as if she wanted to say, "For fuck's sake."

"It's another word for Voodoo," Dad muttered with distaste.

Mom got all up in Dad's face at the side of me, flinging her arms up in irritation. "I don't know why you didn't just say Voodoo in the first place then." Her pointer finger swiped and landed within an inch away from Dad's nose. His eyes bulged and refocused as they zoned in on it. "And that's your problem, Bracken. Just say what you mean. It's no good passing the blame; you should've told me you were a fox shifter at the beginning of our relationship. Maybe then we could've avoided mentally traumatizing our only child, the messy divorce, the whole shebang." She flung her hands up again, "You're a smart guy. What did you expect would happen?"

"I know that. Don't you think I know that now?" Dad pinched the bridge of his nose and gave an exhausted sigh. "I said I was sorry."

It was as if I'd stepped into a movie theater, and I was watching someone else's life appear on the big screen. My heart thumped like a tribal drum in my chest. It was like someone was hitting it with a hammer—a hammer with nails poking out of it. Everything was such a mess, and for once, I wasn't sure whether money could fix it.

"So, it really did happen. It feels weird saying it out loud. I had my first shift in the woods when I was on my school trip. That's what happened." All the suppressed memories had come back to sock me in the gut, blow after blow like I was standing in the middle of the freeway during rush hour traffic. I was left feeling physically and mentally exhausted.

Dad's soothing voice calmed me. "You were alone, scared out of your mind, and you had no idea what the heck was happening to you. I take full responsibility for that. No one's to blame but me." He pulled me against his chest, and just like that I was a little girl, I wrapped my arms around his waist and squeezed my eyes shut, wanting him to make everything better.

"So, why didn't you just tell me?" I asked.

Dad rubbed my back in small circles. "I wanted to."

"But I didn't," Mom interjected, confirming my thoughts.

Out of the corner of my eye, I saw my mother reach for the brandy and take a swig straight from the bottle.

"So that's why you guys got a divorce? You blamed Dad for deceiving you. I remember hearing part of the argument. You said something about cheating."

Mom wagged her finger while she was

swallowing another gulp. "I said it was just as bad as cheating. I felt lied to; not that I wasn't grateful for the child we had together. You weren't completely human, and I wasn't sure what that meant for you. He should have told me first, but I guess that's history. Your father is right. We should've learned from our mistakes. We are both to blame."

"And if Dad had told you everything, would it have mattered?" I asked, turning to catch her reaction.

A wistful smile ghosted across her lips. "I was crazy in love with him—still am. Of course, it wouldn't have mattered." Her eyes flicked to Dad.

I pulled away, looking between them. There was so much sadness and regret hanging over them. The look of two people who deeply loved each other and had wasted so much time trying to hate each other instead. Who knew mates could be capable of toxic love? Said the woman whose guy kidnapped her while she was sleeping. I guessed when it came to finding a mate, it could make the most rational person do all kinds of crazy shit. The room fell into a somber silence. Moments passed before Mom broke it, pouring herself another drink that made my dad huff with disapproval.

"Sasha, that's not going to solve matters," Dad mumbled sternly.

"It helps me," she replied, then knocked the contents down her throat.

She swatted her hand to try and stop Dad from removing the glass from her.

"So, you and this guy are married?" Mom backtracked as Dad snatched the now empty glass away.

"We're mated, yes," I replied, pulling away my shirt collar to reveal the bite mark on my neck.

Mom's eyebrows raised. "And did he tell you he was a shifter before you mated?"

"Yes," I confirmed. "We passed that hurdle rather quickly.

Dad tugged on his shirt collar as Mom flashed her eyes his way.

"Well—" Mom dragged out the word. "That counts for something. Even if he is just a farmhand from Forest Hills."

"Ranger," I corrected her.

"Right," Mom replied airily.

"Don't be such a snob, Sasha. We've just invested half a billion into building Vixen Hollow. Forest Hills is literally right across the water."

What? My parents are planning to move to Whitehaven? Since when?

Mom's eyes grew wide. "I'm not being a snob, honey. I wasn't. I'm just curious to know more about our daughter's mate. That's all."

I watched the interactions that were taking place between my bickering parents. The comment Gabe made about them reconciling must have a ring of truth to it. Why else would they be hooking up again and diving into business together? Mom would've usually told my dad to fuck off by now, yet here she was, trying to convince him she wasn't being a bitch when she so blatantly was.

Dad didn't look as if he was buying her crap for a second and gave an unconvinced eye roll back in response. He cared enough to stop her from drinking herself into oblivion, and it was evident that he still had feelings for her. Maybe it was true. That my disappearing act brought them back together.

"Since when have you started calling Dad 'babe' again? The last time I checked, you hated each other." I shot her a questioning look, which made her gasp like a deer caught in headlights.

CHAPTER TWENTY-FIVE

Riley

Mom licked her lips nervously. "Well, if you must know, your father and I have decided to try again."

"You're getting re-married?" I looked to Dad who seemed to shrink back even more than Mom did.

Dad choked out, "We're still mated. That still stands. You can't just remove a mating mark as easily as taking off a wedding band. It was the human marriage we dissolved, but that was just for show for the news reporters. We bonded for life."

Mom huffed. "Yeah, the night you bit me I thought you were into BDSM."

Upon hearing that, I almost threw up in my mouth, placing my hand against my now fragile stomach. I decided to switch subjects. "So, what about Grandpa and Grandma, Uncle Dolton and Aunt Celia? My cousin, Sheena? Am I right in believing that they are all shifters too? It's just so I know."

Dad looked to Mom, then back at me, nodding in confirmation. "Yes, everyone on my side of the gene pool. My mate, *your mother*, was the first human to mate into my family." His lips curved up into a lopsided smile as he glanced at Mom. She blushed and pursed her lips. I dropped my tense shoulders and let out a forced breath, slowly feeling myself start to relax. The black leather sofa felt cold against the back of my bare legs as I sat down, curling up into a ball and resting my head on one of the big, furry teal cushions. This was all I'd ever wanted for years. My parents are back together again. Don't get me wrong, I was glad it was happening. I just wished I was here under better circumstances.

"I don't mean to be rude, but are all fox shifters

short?" I spoke the first thing that popped into my head, then saw my dad bristle.

"You know, we may not be the tallest, but we're the smartest race of shifters," Dad defended. "Galileo Galilei the scientist, and Thomas Jefferson the president. Even Bill Gates, he's a—"

"No . . ." I gasped with amazement, jumping up off the couch. "Really? I can't believe it!"

I thought I'd read somewhere that Bill was a natural redhead.

"Yes, they're all fox shifters. Pretty cool, huh?" Dad nodded his head, impressed. "See, you can be proud of your heritage. We're known for our intellect, but our red hair sets us apart from the rest. I know some who dyed their hair or shaved it off, but what's the point trying to hide who we are. We should embrace it."

Mom scrunched her lips as she thought. "What about Donald Trump? He was a redhead, and he's a billionaire businessman. Are you sure he's not a fox shifter?"

Dad flinched back with a look of pure outrage on his face as if Mom had just slapped him. "No, Sasha. No." He shook his head, horrified.

Mom shrugged. "It's only because he was a ginge—"

"Sasha, just shush, please." Dad silenced her by putting his finger against her lips. "I love you, but sometimes, you gotta learn when to keep your mouth shut."

A knock on the door interrupted our conversation.

"Come in!" Dad called out.

Gabe arrived to update us on what was happening. "Alpha White has asked me to inform you he's made the necessary arrangements, just like you suggested, and he should be here in approximately two hours."

"Thank you, Gabriel." Dad gave a sharp nod before turning to me with warmth in his eyes. "You should freshen up and change your clothes. I expect you'll want to look your best when you bring home your mate, won't you?"

He was right. I looked like shit and smelled much worse. Just as I was about to slump away, Dad called out, "Oh, and you'll both need to have a press interview. You know? To smooth things over. You better explain to him that he'll be in the public eye from now on. I hope he's not camera shy?"

Austin + no filter + paparazzi = Oh shit!

"Nah, Dad, he's not camera shy." I chuckled.

I sat on the edge of the tub, mixing a

concoction of bubble bath to the running water. I loved the way the warm steam was infused with all the delicious scents. It licked my skin and filled the room with a warm and fuzzy vibe. As the water reached just beyond midway, I turned off the taps, testing the temperature with my fingers. Then I submerged myself up to my shoulders, feeling it soak away all the stress. I opened my eyes as I lay there, looking around the stylish bathroom that had floor-to-ceiling stone-effect tiles, missing that stupid frog shower curtain back at Austin's cabin. The old cracked bar of soap on the edge of his sink. And all the cobwebs. I finished my bath, feeling refreshed and revitalized. The houses we owned were always stocked full of essentials: hair products, makeup, clothes, so I had everything I needed, but nothing I wanted.

Austin had never really seen me at my best before. He liked my natural look, with my hair scraped back and with no makeup. I wondered what he'd think of me all made up. Maybe he'd be wowed, or maybe he wouldn't care. Either way, I chose a black Christian Dior dress and matching shoes with a golden heel. I styled my hair poker straight and applied tasteful makeup. I'd forgotten just how long it took to get ready. It was such a chore. I was so glad I'd found someone who appreciated me in sweatpants and a ponytail. Just as I was spraying on some perfume, Gabe started yelling from the bottom of the stairs for me to hurry my ass along.

"Mrs. Rayne, your husband's lawyer has arrived," Gabe's husky voice called out in a sing-song manner.

"He better be good, that's all I'm saying," I called back.

We took the limo to wherever the hell Austin was being held in custody. Dad and Gabe seemed to know exactly where he'd been taken. They didn't seem worried, so that made me feel like there was nothing to be worried about.

"Urgh! They're keeping him in here? In this rat-infested hell hole?" I exclaimed as we pulled up outside a shabby-looking county jail. "This is nothing that a wrecking ball won't improve. Let's just get him out of here; he's probably going out of his mind by now." I scrunched my nose in disgust.

I stepped onto the littered sidewalk and glanced left to right and shuddered. I fumbled around in my purse, taking a silk handkerchief out to use to cover my mouth before stepping through the threshold into the pits of Hell.

"Let me handle things. You stay here with Gabriel, and for God's sake, don't touch anything," Dad warned.

Not that he needed to tell me twice. I didn't care that I looked like some freakish germaphobe. The place ought to be shut down by the health inspectors. Rats were running around outside amongst the trash for God's sake. I could practically feel the grime in the air. It was that thick.

While Dad walked over to the reception desk to ask to speak to someone, I stayed close to Gabe, pressing my handkerchief over my face like a surgical mask. It was a pity it didn't block out the smell. The whole place reeked of old sweat, gym socks, and stale tobacco. It was gross. Even Gabe wore a repulsed grimace as he struggled to maintain a steady breathing pattern. Maybe this was a shifter thing, the heightened sense of smell. Nobody else seemed phased. I don't know, maybe they were just used to it.

Every now and then, the doors would fling open, and cops would drag in someone they'd arrested. Some toothless guy spat at one of the officers and grinned, giving me a good look at his mangled gums. I scrunched my nose and looked away. Dad thanked the female at the desk and came back over to where Gabe and I were standing. Like fuck was I sitting on one of those filthy-looking plastic chairs in a designer dress. Dad kept checking his watch while we waited. The anticipation was torture. Somewhere in this building was my husband. My poor baby. He must be clawing at the walls by now.

"Alec's here," Dad announced.

"Where?" I looked around not seeing anyone else.

Dad smirked. "I can smell him. Don't worry. Once you start to shift regularly, you'll pick up on all the different scents. That is, unless you carry on bathing in designer perfume," he muttered teasingly.

"Seriously, I don't know how you can smell anything through the shitty air in here," I mumbled through my handkerchief.

The door to the left of us opened, and a hulk of a guy walked through it dressed like he'd stepped right out of a Men's Health magazine. He was strikingly intimidating. Dad said he was Alpha Alec, and I could see why he was an Alpha. The guy was an Adonis in a suit. There was a pregnant woman with him, incredibly pretty, with a kind heart-shaped face, chestnut hair, and chocolate eyes.

"Alec." My dad raised a hand as if to say hi. "Nice of you to drop by, old friend."

Dad and Alec started discussing something in hushed whispers. The young woman seemed much friendlier than he did, smiling as her eyes met with mine. As she stopped, she placed a hand over her swollen abdomen. Her baby bump filled out the front of her navy suit dress. Gabe told me a bit about Alec while we waited. I learned the guy was a five-hundred-year-old Lycan. Apparently, he was a genius who went borderline insane, and if it wasn't for his mate leveling him out, he would have flipped and gone on a murderous rampage, killing everything that crossed his path.

Well, they do say that genius borderlines insanity.

The beautiful woman extended her arm, offering to shake my hand. As soon as I clasped it, I could feel she mustn't have been aware of her own strength. I started to lose feeling in the tips of my fingers.

"Hello, you must be Riley Rayne. I'm Leah White, the Luna of Whitevale. I'm pleased to meet you. I hope you don't mind, but I've been instructed to act as Austin's attorney. I'm new to this field, but don't let that put you off. I have a way of making people do what I want; call it a special gift." Her smile widened.

My hand throbbed as she let go. "I just want him out of here. It's been hours, and I'm going crazy. God knows how he must be feeling."

"Austin is a good friend of mine, and we owe him everything. Or at least I do. He saved my life not so long ago," Leah said, speaking fondly of Austin.

Alec stopped mid-conversation and pulled a face as if something was bothering him. "Do you hear that, Roth?" He turned to my dad who had now stopped still and was straining to listen.

Only my dad's closest friends called him Roth. He had very few "close" friends. Mostly they were just business acquaintances. That must mean Alec White counted as one of Dad's nearest and dearest, and that honor was very rare indeed.

"Yeah . . .," Dad dragged out the word as he listened. His eyes bulged and shined with amusement. "Is that music coming from the basement cells?"

Alec raised an eyebrow mockingly. "If that's what you want to call it. Sounds like someone is singing an Elvis song—badly."

CHAPTER TWENTY-SIX

Riley

Austin was fully absorbed at the moment, too busy screeching at the top of his lungs and gyrating his hips and strumming on his air guitar. He didn't even notice us enter through the heavy double doors at the far end of the corridor.

He crooned the lyrics to "Jailhouse Rock" amongst the wincing inmates, blissfully unaware of us approaching.

I scrunched my lips, feeling my temper rise. Maybe he was aware—he was a shifter. Couldn't he smell us through all the sweat, dirt, and shit in the air?

How dare he be enjoying himself!

I inhaled a sharp breath through my nasal passages, only to regret it. The air in here smelled vile. Even as I vigorously rubbed my wrist against my nose, my perfume couldn't mask it. The stale, overpowering aroma inside this shitty cell block was killing me, along with the lingering stink of tobacco and alcohol breath. It took everything I had not to run, bolting back through the door to hurl. I needed to breathe clean, sanitary air. After I dragged my hulk of a husband home, I planned to have a Dettol bath and burn this dress outside in the backyard.

I'd like to say I wasn't a snob and that I didn't judge, but fuck that shit! Yes, I was. I was a fucking snob when it came to this. This was a crime against humanity. I'd seen cop shows on TV, but they were nothing like this place. Those cells I saw on TV didn't show all the urine stains up the walls—and the rest.

The slow clack of my heels silenced. I stopped and turned to peer between the ceiling-to-floor bars of cell number three, raising a perfectly sculpted eyebrow. Austin, who was now reaching the crescendo of his strangled cat impersonation, swiveled round on his stockinged feet, eyes widening with shock at the sight of me, mixed with approval. He paused before letting out a low whistle.

"Babe, you clean up well. You don't smell like you, but hey, I'm not complaining." He ran his fingers through his unruly blond hair, his lips stretching into an awestruck grin.

I placed my right hand against my cocked-out hip, noticing his eyes lingering on my exposed cleavage.

"Gee, thanks. Can't say the same about you in that tacky orange jumpsuit," I retorted, casting daggers at my smirking husband.

He pointed his forefinger in my direction. "Are you" — his eyes winced, then he jabbed his finger against his chest — "mad at me?" His brows scrunched questioningly.

I felt my own eyes blaze like two fireballs bulging out of my sockets. He folded his huge arms across his chest, making his biceps bulge as they strained the cheap polyester material to full capacity.

"I was the one who got tased, babe," he replied in an indignant tone.

My eyes flinched as he pulled the emotional blackmail card.

"I could use a little sympathy right about now." He gave a smoldering gaze through the bars, then started singing a verse of another Elvis song, making me glance away, biting the insides of my cheeks, putting all my efforts into not smiling.

He serenaded about being stung by a sweet honeybee, much to my embarrassment. Dad and Alec exchanged amused glances between them, whereas Leah stood alongside me, dumbfounded. Probably thinking the same as me "dear Lord, please don't make it rain."

He wanted me to crack a smile. That way, he'd win, and I'd stop being all moody. This was supposed to be a rescue mission, not some karaoke sing-a-thon. I expected him to be sitting in a corner somewhere, rocking back and forth, mumbling to himself because that's what I would do. My eyes raked all over the grime-covered cell, then observed the nonchalant expression on Austin's face, and I immediately saw red.

"I was worried sick about you," I hissed, swatting away my dad's sudden attempt to hold me back.

I abruptly slapped my satin clutch bag against my dad's chest, forcing him to take hold of it, then gripped the iron bars that separated me from

Austin. Shocked and startled, he passed it from hand to hand like a hot potato.

"Daddy, it's a purse, it won't bite," I huffed in annoyance.

Austin grinned. He seemed highly amused as if this was all one big joke, flashing his perfect white teeth, which only fueled my rage.

"And here you are." I let go of the greasy bars in disgust, jumping back in repulsion, then wiped my palms on my dress. "Having the time of your life!" I pointed my finger at him. "I should just leave you in here if you like it so much."

Austin's grin won out, spreading wide across his face, and creasing his blue eyes as he let out a boyish chuckle.

"These guys are cool." He dragged out his words in a lazy tone, swinging his arm around the shoulders of a dirty-looking biker with a handlebar mustache. "His name is Mike, Mitch . . ." He thought for a second. "What did you say your name was again?" he asked, scrunching his brows together.

The guy mumbled unenthusiastically, "Miguel."

"That's right." He clapped him on the back, causing the tense guy to jolt forward. "Babe, this is Miguel. He tried to hold up a gas station with his finger in his jacket pocket," he laughed as he spoke, then turned to Miguel. "That really was a dumbass move, but you weren't to know the place was full of cops on a training exercise, right?" He chuckled to an unsmiling Miguel.

Austin continued, "That's karma for you. Kicks you right in the balls when you least expect it." He slapped Miguel on the back again, jerking him forward for the second time.

"Lady!" Miguel approached the bars, pleading to me with desperate eyes. "You're not going to leave him here with me, are you?" He shook his head, his brown eyes flaring wide with dread.

An amusing thought popped into my mind. I clicked my tongue and tapped my chin with my finger. "Hmm, I don't know." My eyes narrowed as I dragged out my words with sarcasm. "You boys seem to have made friends, and I'm not one to break up a party." I shrugged.

Dad and Alec both turned to me with their brows cocked in a *what the fuck* look. Leah sniggered as if she understood my joke.

"That'll teach you not to break the law," she chastised Miguel in a whimsical tone while trying to maintain a straight face.

In pure frustration, he tried to rattle the bars

right in front of me. I stepped back, maintaining a safe distance, just in case he tried to reach out and grab me.

"Give a guy a break, and I promise, I will never so much as hold up traffic any more. C'mon, lady, I can't stand Elvis. This guy is killing me here," he whined, revealing his rotting yellow teeth.

Austin took offense at his comment, scrunching his face back as if Miguel had said something insane.

"Leeroy here doesn't seem to mind, do you, Leeroy?" he yelled over his shoulder to a gray-haired African American guy who looked well over eighty.

"What?" Leeroy yelled back, cupping his ear as if he was hard of hearing. "Did you just say something to me, boy?"

Austin sighed, swatted the air. "Ahh, never mind."

The old guy was deaf as a post and hadn't heard a word of what had been said. He turned over on the bench, pulling a gray generic blanket over his head as if to go back to sleep.

Alec cleared his throat to grab our attention. "We need to get him out of here, quickly. We don't exactly have a great deal of time. Leah's influence will only last a few minutes before it wears off," he explained anxiously.

"Influence?" I asked, confused by what he just said.

"Yeah," Leah spoke. "I have a gift that allows me to compel people to do whatever I want." She placed a hand on top of her swollen belly and rubbed it affectionately. "My baby is zapping most of my energy these days, so my power isn't as strong as it could be, but it was enough to get the guard to hand over the keys to the cell. So, we really ought to get moving," she encouraged, producing a set of keys, and jingling them in front of her.

She began trying key after key until she found one that fit the lock. "Bingo." She grinned at Austin. "This almost makes us even, big guy. You saved my ass more than once," she commented.

Austin smiled. "Yeah, well, friends don't keep count."

As she twisted the key in the lock, Alec went to stand alongside her, flashing the cellmates a deadly glare as if to suggest, "stay there and don't even think about moving." None of them looked as if they harbored a death wish, so they either stayed put or backed away toward the far wall. Alec pulled open the cell door to let Austin slip past. The heavy, barred door clinked and clanked as it was closed back over and locked again.

Austin broke out in song once again, gripping me around my waist, twirling me around in circles with my face contorting in a motion-sickened grimace. The words to "Teddy Bear" poured forth before he pressed his lips against mine, then dropped me back down on two feet, holding me steady as I staggered, dizzy and disoriented back down the corridor.

"I'll put a chain around your neck, all right!" I muttered a line from the song as my heels scraped along the concrete floor.

"Now, now, kids," my dad cut in to prevent a squabble. "Act casually as we try and make our way out of here, for goodness' sake."

Alec brushed past us both and peered around the door. He glanced over his shoulder at us and beckoned us forward. "Shh, quickly. Nobody's around."

I pointed to the cameras that were literally everywhere. "CCTV," I hissed, mindful that everything was being recorded.

"Scrambled," Leah whispered smugly. "Perks of having a combined shifter military means we've thought of everything."

Alec's eyes flicked to Austin. "One of Beast's new toys," he mentioned, to which Austin seemed to understand.

Who the fuck was Beast?

A pure look of wonder etched across his face at the sheer mention of this awesome technology. "Maybe I should've joined the military. Especially if you get to play with cool gadgets like that." Then he rolled his eyes with an afterthought. "Ugh! That means the smug fucker will never let me live this down," he muttered under his breath.

"You know" — I eyed Austin with suspicion — "I'm gonna interrogate the shit out of you when we get home. Seems there are lots of things I don't know about you and your friends."

Austin smirked. "Yeah." His eyes narrowed on me as he drank in every detail like I was his favorite dessert. "You're the one with the secrets, babe. I'm an open book. I always knew you were a fox, but I didn't know you were a *fox*," he emphasized his words, flexing two fingers on each hand. "I thought you smelled differently. I just wasn't exactly sure what it was. I thought your dad's name sounded familiar, too. That's what I get for not paying attention to politics," he finished, giving an indifferent shrug.

"Yeah, well, I didn't know either," I admitted, noticing my dad pressing a finger to his lips to silence us. "I'll tell you about it later," I whispered.

Alec ushered Dad and Leah through the door first, then me and Austin. He followed closely behind us, closing the door quietly and dumping the keys on top of the abandoned desk. Gabe, who had been waiting by the front doors, held it open for us, looking nervous and agitated, waving his hand to hurry us along.

"Hey!" A voice yelled from the office behind the front desk. "Where the hell do you think you're going?"

CHAPTER TWENTY-SEVEN

Riley

Leah waddled over to the desk, looking the officer in the eye. "We're going home, and you're not going to stop us."

His angry frown relaxed, morphing to a vacant expression. "I'm not going to stop you," he repeated monotonously.

Leah hurried back toward us. "Quick! Before someone else comes."

We broke into a scrambled run, not wanting to

take any more chances, bolting through the double doors and out into the darkened street. My lungs were appreciative of the cool night air as I sucked it in greedily. Traffic fumes or not, it smelled like heaven compared to what it was like there. Never again was I stepping foot inside somewhere as gross as that. I'd rather have eaten my lunch in a public restroom than spend another second inside that hell hole.

"You look good enough to eat." Austin grabbed my ass, pulling me toward him for a kiss, which I had to stand up on my tiptoes to return.

We snatched celebratory kisses at the roadside, forgetting for a second that we had company. The sound of screeching tires had us breaking apart. A huge, armored truck swerved around in the middle of the road, mounting the curb before bouncing back down onto the asphalt. The brakes screeched as it came to an abrupt stop right in front of Dad's car.

"Here's our ride," Alec announced.

Leah turned to us with a relieved smile. "Don't worry about the human police. There wasn't any time to go through the proper channels, but rest assured, it'll all be taken care of by the morning."

"Thanks again." I returned the friendly gesture, raising my hand to wave. "If there's ever anything we can do to repay you, then all you have to do is ask," I offered.

Alec paused to think as his wife was helped inside the huge truck by a humongous dude with a buzzcut, and was tatted to fuck. The hot giant gave Austin a courteous salute and a grin stretched across his stubble-coated face.

"Austin." His voice was a raw, guttural rumble.

Austin responded with a polite nod in acknowledgment. "Beast."

So *that* was Beast. His name suited him.

There seemed to be an air of friendly rivalry between the two men. Nothing hostile. More like old acquaintances or comrades in arms. I remember Brian talking about his cage-fighting hero called Beast. And Austin had said he fought alongside him not so long ago. This was something I was dying to find out more about.

"Have you asked him again?" Beast asked Alec.

Alec, who seemed to be thinking of how best to address something, glanced between Austin and me with an air of wonder playing on his handsome face.

"You know what I'm about to ask, Austin. I

know you were more than happy to keep your ranger job, but I'm thinking now that you're going to be in the public eye a lot more, that maybe you and Riley would consider a more prominent role. You'd make perfect ambassadors."

It was a worthy cause if there ever was one. If I could use my once conceited social status to do something good for people like us, then I was game.

"Sure," I answered for both of us, ignoring the startled expression on my husband's face. "We would love to. Think of it as a huge thank you for what you've done for us," I added, knowing that Austin couldn't exactly refuse since I had put it that way.

Alec held out his hand to offer us a handshake. "Welcome aboard—finally." He beamed, grasping my hand firmly, then Austin's.

"Thanks again, Alec," Austin responded with genuine gratitude.

Alec beamed. "Don't mention it. You came through for us when we needed help."

He turned to my dad, clasping his hand with a slap. They pulled each other in for a bro hug.

"See you at the next meeting, buddy," Dad spoke with fondness.

"You're buying the drinks, Roth," Alec replied, flashing Dad a wolfish grin.

Alec gave us one final wave, then got inside the truck. Leah leaned across Beast and waved, smiling brightly. I liked her. She wasn't at all what I expected when Gabe told me she was the Luna of the werewolf community. I half expected someone headstrong and cocky, but she wasn't anything like that. She was friendly, decent, and kind. I got the impression she wouldn't stand for any shit, which was good. Just like me.

Beast gave a curt nod and a two-fingered salute, then revved the engine. We watched them pull away as Gabe ushered us into Dad's car. Austin placed his hand on top of my knee. Both of us were sitting in silence in the back of the car, with me squashed between him and Gabe. Dad was sitting in the passenger seat, engaged in a deep conversation with the driver. The two of them were discussing how terrible the road surfaces were and how they thought someone was controlling the stop signs, just for shits and giggles.

"You came for me?" Austin spoke, awestruck.

"Yeah, you're my husband. I wasn't just going to leave you to rot in jail." I rolled my eyes at his stupidity.

Of course, I would come for him. What did he expect? I loved the crass, loudmouthed asshole after all.

"Thanks, babe," he spoke in a softened tone. The twinkle of the streetlights reflected in his blue eyes. "I'm sure as hell glad you came."

For a second, I almost forgot how to breathe. I didn't even realize I was smiling. He had that effect on me. Without even trying, he brought out the best in me.

My fingers laced with his. "About me being a fox," I began, feeling as if I owed him some sort of explanation. "We should talk about what this means for us."

"I should have realized what you were by your flaming red hair, sassy attitude, and ability to manipulate me into bed," Austin commented.

I gasped with horror, flashing my eyes to my dad. "Austin, my dad is sitting right there!" I whisper-hissed.

Austin chortled. "Not that I live under a rock or anything, but I didn't even know who the Fox King was. I knew that fox shifters had a king instead of an alpha, but I never thought I'd be mated to a shifter princess. It just goes to show that opposites attract." Austin shook his head with a boyish smile.

"At least I can say that my wife is a fox." He seemed to like how the words sounded out loud.

All the way home, he harped on about how our children would be hybrids. Fox-bears. Happiness stained his face, stretching an enchanted smile across his lips. Austin wanted more than anything to start his own family. It was written all over his face.

I was and always had been a spoiled, selfish brat. Children never came into the equation. Not once. Not even after my cousin Sheena got married. Not to a shifter. To a douchebag human. He was a good-for-nothing, cheating scumbag, and she had finally seen the light and decided to divorce his ass. But still, we all thought the next step for her would be motherhood. Many of our friends were envious of her when she got married. Whereas I saw family life like a ball and chain, a shackle around my ankles, stopping me from enjoying life. I couldn't have been more wrong. I was thrilled to be Austin's wife. More importantly, I wanted to bear Austin's children. Everything had changed. I had changed. Well, my priorities had anyway. Pregnancy, late-night feeds, diaper changes, the whole shebang. I was ready.

The minute we started driving past mansions in the prestigious part of town, I sensed a change in

Austin's posture. He sat up straight, gripping my hand tighter. Sitting in a shitty jail cell didn't seem to faze him one bit, but the way his body tensed as we drove through billionaires' row, he looked terrified.

"Are you okay?" I asked in a soothing tone. My lips a mere inch from his ear as he leaned across to get a better look at a lavish mansion, slack jawed.

"Yeah," he responded with a sigh that convinced me otherwise.

"Hey, Riley." Dad craned his head around in the passenger seat to talk to me.

"What, Daddy?" I answered, forgetting my present company for a second and sounding like a seven-year-old child. "Dad," I corrected quickly, feeling the blush heat my cheeks.

Dad continued. "When we get inside, you know your mother is going to make a fuss over both of you. Probably want to talk you into having a human wedding ceremony, that she'll no doubt insist on arranging. If you want to avoid an ambush, take Austin straight upstairs. I'll have some refreshments sent up if you're hungry."

Dad's little attempt at pre-warning me was welcome. We both knew Mom would switch to full-on meddle mode and want to micromanage everything.

I leaned my head against Austin's shoulder. "I think I will. I'm beat, and I suppose we'll have the press on our backs now, too. I bet Mom has already arranged for an interview."

"I'll bet you a hundred dollars you're right." Dad chuckled. "Besides, there's no way of avoiding the press, Pumpkin. But you don't need me to tell you how to work the media. You're a pro." His eyes flashed to Austin. "You, however, need a quick lesson on how to handle paparazzi. So, before the gala tomorrow, you be sure to come to see me, and I'll give you a few pointers." Dad gave Austin an encouraging smile.

"What?" I blurted out, releasing Austin's hand as I gripped the back of Dad's headrest. "The charity gala is tomorrow?" My scatterbrain flooded with panic.

I fucking hated that jolt in my heart that I got when I remembered something at the last minute.

"Shit! I have nothing to wear," I exclaimed. "Oh, God, this is a catastrophe," I muttered, feeling completely fucked up the ass by life, once again.

"You're fucking telling me," Austin huffed with anguished sarcasm. "Must be a nightmare, having to decide between Gucci and Valentino. The fuckin' trauma." He shook his head.

Dad scrunched his face. "Aww, you'll be fine, Pumpkin. We can organize last-minute outfits for both of you. It's not like designers won't be tripping over each other for the opportunity to dress you," he commented with certainty. "Austin, you'll have to embrace your new-found celebrity status. You better get used to appearing in the public eye because the press will eat you up, and this charity gala will be a great opportunity for you to mingle and meet some influential people. You're in a position of power now. You better get used to this lifestyle."

Austin blew out a nervous breath through puckered lips. "What if I embarrass you?" He aimed his question at me, his brows creasing with worry lines.

Dad's expression softened, turning back around to give us some privacy. "You won't," I reassured, squeezing his knee.

Austin's jaw locked tight, pulsing as his eyes darted back and forth between mine. "I might say or do the wrong thing."

I stroked my thumb back and forth on his knee, over the cheap orange material of his jumpsuit.

"You could never embarrass me. If anything,

I'm proud to be with you," I told him, meaning every word. "So, think of it as me showing you off to the world."

"Like a fashion accessory?" Austin's tone oozed sarcasm.

I smiled, dragging my gaze from his eyes, down to his lips and back again. "No, like, hey bitches, hands off. He's mine."

The fact that he felt he wasn't good enough bothered me. Austin was awesome. The kindest, most decent person that I had ever met. He just had to realize his potential, and I was hellbent on making that a reality.

A smirk curved across Austin's lips as his eyes flicked up to where Dad was sitting, making conversation with his driver. Austin's silent message said it all. Kissing could wait until we were in private. Like he knew the both of us wouldn't be content with just a kiss. Both of us needed to finish what we started hours ago in our cabin.

I snuggled into him as we drove up to my prestigious family home, feeling so darn lucky I could scream. He was mine. He placed his arm around my shoulders, pulling me close and smelling my hair. Warmth filled my heart, spreading throughout my chest. Nobody could take him away from me. Nobody. Not the cops, especially not that psycho friend of his from Forest Hills.

Which reminds me.

"Austin," I mumbled against his chest, listening to the steady rhythm of his heart.

"Hmm," he responded contentedly.

I hated having to drag this up now and risk ruining a perfectly good moment, but the suspense was killing me. The second he flicked on the TV he was going to see it splashed all over the news. It was better to come from me. And anyway . . . ever since I heard her name, it had been gnawing away inside of me. "Who is Rebecca King, and why haven't you ever mentioned her before?" My heart flooded with dread, feeling Austin's pulse quicken.

There was a long pause before he responded. The torturous wait was like a kick to the gut. Austin wasn't a fuck boy. Whoever she was, she must've meant something to him. It was only natural that I felt a twang of jealousy.

"Someone I hurt," he mumbled sadly. "I've known her since we were cubs. She was my best friend in the whole world. Then when we grew up, she wanted to be more than friends, and I didn't," he concluded. The wistful tone in his voice told me he still mourned their broken friendship. "How come you know about Rebecca?"

"She was the one who called the cops," I informed him regretfully.

Austin didn't say anything. He didn't have to. The flinch of hurt in his eyes spoke a thousand words. One of which stood out the most.

Betrayal.

CHAPTER TWENTY-EIGHT

Riley

Austin followed me up to my room in silence. He hadn't spoken since I told him all about Rebecca King. The atmosphere was tense, but being up here away from my parents allowed us to decompress. Part of me wished I'd kept my big mouth shut. Their friendship meant a lot to him, I could tell. I wanted to tell him from a woman's point of view that she acted out of anger and jealousy. And now she'd had a chance to calm down, maybe she would regret it.

I wanted to say anything that would bring comfort to him, but I didn't want to bullshit him with an excuse if it wasn't the truth. Because Austin deserved more than that. With anyone else, I'd tell them what I thought they wanted to hear and it wouldn't be sincere. In my world, we wore masks just for show. We weren't necessarily nice people; we were a bunch of selfish fakes who wore smiles on our faces while we stabbed our so-called friends in the back.

The difference between Rebecca King and me was not only the money, fame, and power. Those were just the obvious things that separated us. The difference I was talking about was the passion, the emotion, the feeling. She acted out of hurt, whereas we acted out of cold-hearted ambition. Who was better? Me? Her? Or neither of us? If being with a man like Austin had taught me to see the error of my ways and to feel things, then maybe I was changing. Hopefully for the better.

The faintest scent of my perfume still clung to the air from earlier. Austin glanced around as I turned on the lights, dimming them to a soft amber glow. His dull mood seemed forgotten as he gave a low whistle, absorbing the view that surrounded us.

"This place is insane," he commented, shaking his head from side to side in disbelief.

My room was modern, decorated in a chic monochromatic design. Everything was either touch-activated or voice-controlled. There were no photos on the walls, only modern art. There were no trinkets scattered along the dressing table. Instead, the black, high gloss surfaces had white marble sculptures that were presumably worth thousands. Or they were at the time of purchase. Ugly, pointless lumps of stone that, now as I stood with my head cocked to the side in analysis, I decided I fucking hated every single one of them.

"Can I use your bathroom? Or is it just for show?" he joked, thumbing behind him. "Which way did you say it was? I forgot."

"Oh, you can use the en-suite, just through there." I pointed across my room to the door next to my walk-in closet. That was another Aladdin's cave I wasn't sure Austin was ready for yet. The jewelry cabinet alone resembled that of a bank vault.

"A bathroom in your bedroom, huh?" He rolled his eyes. "I bet you have to work out how to use the three seashells to take a dump?" he muttered, sounding as crass as ever.

"It's a toilet, Austin, not a space shuttle." My hands rested on my hips, "Lots of people have en-suite bathrooms. Don't make such a big deal over it."

He fumbled around in the dark, looking for the light switch. "Bathroom light on," I spoke aloud, illuminating the black tiled room he was standing inside. Light bounced off all the chrome and mirrors, giving off a glittering effect.

He seemed awestruck by my elaborately styled bathroom and did an about-face in the doorway.

"You've got a fucking Jacuzzi bathtub as well as a shower cubicle. What the actual fuckery?" His face lit up with boyish glee. I was glad that something as trivial as this entertained his thoughts. It meant I didn't have to bring up our earlier conversation, thank God.

"Yeah . . ." I scrunched my nose. "I've never used the Jacuzzi though. The hot tub on the balcony is by far the better of the two." I shrugged. "It has a minibar." Austin's jaw hung agape as I spoke.

"You've never what? Huh? There's another? Minibar?" Austin spluttered, flabbergasted. "You're fucking kidding me right now?" He ran a hand through his tousled hair, looking at me as if I was insane.

I tossed my satin purse onto the silky black sheets of my four-poster bed. "Well, if it bothers you so much, then why don't you go take a bath in that one to christen it?"

He thought for a second. "All right, I will, but only if you join me right now."

I jerked my head back, cupping my nose with my hand. "Ew, no. You stink of prison sweat," I stated, grimacing with disgust. "I'll shower later. Then maybe some other night we can use the outdoor hot tub."

The paparazzi would be out in force after our little jailbreak. The last thing we needed before the gala tomorrow would be to make front-page news fooling around in the outdoor tub.

Austin's husky laughter trailed off as he closed the door behind him. I heard water running in the shower instead of the bathtub, and wondered why he'd changed his mind, and if maybe he was waiting for me to join him. A few moments later he emerged from the en-suite, naked and dripping wet. "Are you sure I couldn't tempt you to come and join me with this?" He spoke suggestively, shaking his hips from side to side, causing his large manhood to slap against both thighs. "I'll get you all clean and dirty at the same time."

His tone was playful and meant to tempt. I covered my face with my hand, giggling with shock. "Austin, the blinds are wide open."

He gave a disinterested shrug. "So, who cares?"

"Blinds down." My voice came out shrill and desperate. I massaged my forehead knowing he was going to be a handful, "Go get washed and I'll wait for our maid to knock with the refreshments." I spoke without even looking his way, chewing on the insides of my cheeks to prevent a grin.

Austin chuckled as he left to get a towel, and I sat down on the edge of my bed, pulling the shoes from my feet. I pressed my aching soles against the floor as I stood, padding over to the dressing table where I threw down my watch and earrings. I was way too preoccupied, thinking about what would happen come the morning, that I didn't anticipate that Austin would approach me, catching me unawares.

Strong hands gripped my waist from behind, pulling me against his rock-hard chest. His warm breath tickled the side of my neck as he spoke.

"Have I told you how stunning you look tonight?" Austin's tone was different from before. It was confident and seductive, so much more possessive.

My body shuddered in response. "You may have mentioned it once or twice," I replied, hearing the weak tremor in my voice. What was he doing to me? He had me going weak in the knees. My breathing grew shallow with each kiss he nuzzled against my collarbone. My pussy was growing wetter by the second.

"Austin." His name came out breezy and drenched with need. Droplets of water dripped onto my skin from his hair. "What're you doing?" I asked, letting my eyelids flutter closed, giving in to the hypnotic sensations that ran through my core.

His lips curled against my skin. "You like this, huh?" he murmured with confidence. It wasn't a question but more of a statement of fact, because he could blatantly see what this was doing to me. He was much more sexually dominant, so much more self-aware than before. My nipples pebbled behind the scrap of lace that concealed them, becoming prominent through the silk material of my dress.

Austin's chin laid to rest on my right shoulder, his fingertips traveled from my hips to my globes, caressing them with the palms of his hands.

"You're so turned on," he stated the obvious, gripping my nipples through my clothing.

My chest heaved as unevenly as my pattern of thought, unable to find the right words through the tangle of pleasures that consumed me.

"What about if I did this?" His fingers trailed to curve around the hem of my neckline, snapping my eyes open.

I managed a single gasp, feeling the material pull taut, then an almighty tear filled the room as he tore my dress in half. I shrieked with shock.

"Austin? What the?" I yelled out, flustered. I didn't care about the dress. I was more shocked by his actions, not that I was going to complain much.

I turned abruptly in his arms. The damp, manly scent of his body sent a pool of moisture rushing straight to my core.

"What the fuck are you doing?" I pulled back, pressing my palms against his clammy pectorals.

A slight smile flickered across my lips as I struggled to maintain composure. He'd surpassed all my expectations, proving himself to be the sex god I knew him capable of being.

A carnal hunger blazed in Austin's blue eyes. His expression tensed like an animal done playing with its food. His movements were swift, tearing away the scraps of lace that covered my modesty and using all of his pent-up frustration by sweeping my legs from beneath me. My back hit the floor, gently, with one of Austin's arms snaked around my waist and one cupping the back of my head.

The ability to breathe left me for a second or two, startled by the unexpected action. "Fuck! Prison changed you," I panted, impressed already.

Austin flashed a roguish smirk. "Nah, you did that."

CHAPTER TWENTY-NINE

Riley

We held each other's gaze for a moment, until the sexual gravity pulled us together, kissing one another with raw, savage hunger. He knew what I wanted, and I knew what he needed, wrapping my legs around his hips, stroking my pussy against his impressive length. He may have been the one in charge tonight, but that didn't mean that I'd refrain from teasing him.

He second-guessed what I was trying to do and pinned my limbs still. Sucking my flesh into his mouth, leaving the faintest little marks behind. The sound of someone knocking could be heard on the other side of the closed door.

"Just leave it outside and I'll come get it," Austin called out, turning his attention back to me. We listened as the sound of footsteps trailed away.

I understood his intentions perfectly. Tonight, I was his to devour like the submissive little vixen he wanted me to be, and I would let him have his way with me, over and over again until the both of us were spent.

Austin's kiss was scorching. His lips branded mine as his tongue fervently made love to my mouth. Every kiss before his had been mediocre in comparison. I'd never known what I was missing until our lips touched for the first time. Never knew just how perfect falling in love could be. This kiss, unlike his earlier, hesitant kisses where he lacked self-confidence, was rough and demanding. His lips battled mine with a voracious passion, hungrier than ever, his arms coiled around me possessively as he poured everything he had into it.

"You're so fucking sexy." His voice was a rough, husky growl. "I want to see your perfect body." He leaned back, eyeing my naked body with approval. A delighted flush heated my skin, and I lay still, just as he commanded. My eyes were giving their seal of approval of his perfectly sculpted torso. So completely drunk on love, I traced my fingertips across his sinewy muscles, watching how they rippled and flexed with each ragged breath.

Austin was watching me like a starving man, his eyelids drooped low, his gaze shadowed with lust. His fingertips skimmed my skin, rough and calloused, serving as his natural aphrodisiac, leaving a trail of goose flesh in their wake. His jaw clenched, pulsing as his fiery blue eyes darted between mine, no doubt plotting his next move.

I shivered as the cool air caressed my heated skin, and my nipples pebbled to hardened peaks. I liked this newfound sexual dominance in him. He was a natural, and he had me completely at his mercy. He ran the pads of his fingers over my stiffened buds. I gasped, arching into his touch, craving more. A deep, rumbling sound of pleasure left his chest, and he cupped my breasts fully. His giant hands, fully encompassing them as he massaged.

"Austin, please," I begged, needing more.

I leaned into him and clutched his huge biceps. He withdrew his touch, and I gasped in protest.

"Shhh, baby," he breathed. "I'm not finished

with my business here." He crawled to his knees before me, his eyes riveted on my sex as I compliantly spread my legs before him.

It took several seconds for him to regain composure, not wanting to rush. I used a small amount of time to shift my position, making myself more comfortable on my cool, wooden floor.

He leaned in, close enough that his hot breath teased across my clit. Without thinking, I dropped my knees to the sides, craving his touch. He pressed his lips just above where I needed him, trailing kisses across my mound.

"I love the way you open yourself like a pretty flower, just for me." The words vibrated against my flesh as his lips brushed across my skin.

"Please, Austin," I begged again.

He lifted his gaze and shot me a wicked grin. "You want me to show you how much I love you. Is that what you want?" His carnal gaze was dripping with lust, and I fell deeper into his thrall, intoxicated by his desire for me.

All I could do was nod my head hastily, desperate to feel him caress the bundle of nerves that pulsed with each teasing breath. His large hands smoothed across my skin, cupping the globes of my rear, and lifted my sex to his mouth.

"God, Austin! Yes!" My head reared back with abandon, arching my back off the floor, writhing my hips in his grasp, matching with every stroke of his punishing tongue.

Austin snarled as he lapped, feasting greedily as if thoroughly enjoying the taste. My legs quaked, my sex clenched, and my stomach tightened. "Oh, God," I chanted, over and over, seeing stars. His tongue softened as he lapped up my essence, his hand holding me still as I tried to wriggle my ass, pulling my highly sensitive clit away from his touch.

"Mine," Austin growled, his hulking frame crawling over my trembling body like he was coming forward to claim his prize. His knees splayed my legs apart, his rough, masculine, worker's hands sought out my wrists, dragging them above my head, pinning them there. He nestled his powerful hips at my center, positioning his cock at my slick entrance, nudging its way home.

He held me right there at begging point for several torturous seconds. Never before had I ever begged a man to fuck me. Never had I wanted someone as much as I wanted Austin. But he had stoked the embers of my passion, breathing the flames back to life.

"Please," my needy voice pleaded. If he didn't

do something soon, I thought I would die of frustration.

Austin lowered himself so that his lips were a mere hairsbreadth from mine, and in doing so, he sheathed the full length of his cock deep inside my loins. His blue eyes locked onto mine with an ocean of love that completely swept me away.

With every gentle stroke of his organ, he made love to me, mind, body, and soul. I knew right there and then I would die for this man. And no matter what life was to throw at us, we could get through anything as long as we had each other. My fingers clung to his muscular shoulders as he rocked me into sweet submission. Rather than wake the dead with the sound of my cries, I sank my teeth into the groove of his neck, leaving behind a claiming mark of my own.

CHAPTER THIRTY

Riley

Our romantic bubble was fit to burst the second the sun came up. We both knew our peace would be short-lived. At least Austin and I managed to bathe and grab a quick breakfast before Mom hammered down the door. The minute she caught up with us, we were ambushed with orders. She had us styled, dressed, and camera-ready by half-past six in the morning.

Mom had set up an interview with *Good Morning America* as well as arranged a photoshoot for *OK*

Magazine. Our living room had been transformed into some kind of television studio overnight. Cameras were angled at the sofa, people bustled about behind the scenes, handling the situation with so much professionalism that even I felt like I was out of practice. Even the way we sat together, posed on the sofa like two lovesick teenagers was choreographed by a member of the team.

"Lean a little closer to Mr. Rayne." The woman in charge fluttered her hand as if to signal him to edge closer to me. "And Mrs. Rayne, angle yourself toward your husband. You have to let the nation believe that you're in love," she advised.

Austin snorted, and my gaze snapped to him, barely able to suppress a laugh.

"Look like you're in love, please," he muttered with sarcasm. "We could always give them a recap of last night as proof enough," he mumbled, low enough for only me to hear.

I giggled. "Just go along with it," I replied, maintaining a poker face. "The sooner we get this over and done with, the sooner we can . . ."

Austin finished off my sentence. "Sit through hours and hours of photoshoots." He let out an exhausted exhale.

I turned to him, cringing apologetically. "I'm so

sorry. It comes part and parcel with our lifestyle, babe. And I know you're not looking forward to the gala tonight, but I promise, I'll make it up to you afterward." I flared my eyes with lustful intent.

Austin's eyes shimmered with excitement. "Hot tub sex?" he whispered seductively.

I blinked rapidly, feeling the heat creep up my neck. "Yeah, sure, whatever you want." I flashed an embarrassed smile, making sure no one overheard that comment. "But what I meant was, we could have ourselves a honeymoon before we go back home. It's not like we're going to be left alone much after today, is it?"

I saw the curiosity brewing as his brows scrunched with intrigue. "What have you got in mind?" he asked.

"Focus, please." Mom clapped her hands together. "You go live on-air in under three minutes."

Both of us snapped our gaze forward, regaining our composure. Speaking from the corner of my mouth, I managed to give him a little clue to keep his spirits up. "While you were in hair and makeup, I booked two tickets to Graceland."

Austin stiffened beside me, gripping my knee. I smirked triumphantly, knowing I'd just pleased my husband. Because one thing I was fairly sure of was this: Austin had never been at a loss for words in all the time I'd spent with him.

One of the crew made an announcement. "We're going live in, three, two." He then pointed a single finger to signal number one, then the interviewer, a pretty brunette in her mid-twenties began the introduction.

I spared a glance at my husband, who was still basking in the euphoria of the prospect of visiting the home of his idol. At least my little reveal took away some of his nerves. He seemed perfectly at ease as the cameras started rolling.

"Riley, what was it about Austin that first captured your attention?" The interviewer, named Carmen, asked.

My lips pressed together as I processed her question, thinking how best to answer. I could see my parents behind the cameras, both waiting anxiously to hear the big love story everyone thought it was. How could I ever tell people the truth, and would they ever believe it if I did?

"Um, we met unexpectedly," I began to explain, watching Carmen lean forward in her seat, resting her chin on her hands.

"She almost ran me over," Austin cut in, making her sit up straight with raised brows.

"Hey, you just walked out in the middle of the road," I responded with a quick comeback.

Austin rolled his eyes, then told Carmen, "I bet the tire marks are still visible on the road where she spun off." He flicked his finger up to point across the room as if to accentuate his statement.

I scoffed, folding my arms across my chest defensively. "Excuse me? You removed the glow plugs from my car, practically stranding me at the guest house." I nodded to Carmen who was staring at us both, open-mouthed.

My parents looked on with shocked expressions, their eyes darting back and forth between Austin and me like a game of ping-pong.

A dreamy smile stretched across Carmen's face. "You did that so you could buy some time to talk to her. How romantic." She sighed dreamily.

After chewing the inside of my cheeks, I turned to Austin. "And his little plan worked, didn't it, honey?" I looked straight into his sparkling blue eyes as I spoke.

He grinned. "It certainly did," he replied, holding my gaze.

People didn't need to know the sordid little

details of how he carried me off back to his cabin in the woods; how I woke in his bedroom with him sleeping naked beside me. Those memories were ours, even if they were as creepy as hell.

When it came to questions regarding my pregnancy, or fake pregnancy, we asked for a little discretion. I wasn't sure how we were going to claw our way out of that hole, but eventually, we would have kids. It wasn't like they were completely off the agenda because they weren't. I just wanted to leave it a while so we could enjoy one another first. We hadn't exactly been careful last night, so who knows? Perhaps we'd conceived during our sex marathon. Only time would tell.

Carmen spoke to us privately when we came off air. "You two are the real deal, aren't you?" She held that knowing look in her eyes that could see straight through the bullshit; probably because she saw enough of it all the time in her line of work.

Austin held my hand as I spoke. "When you meet the one, you just know," I told her. He brought our entwined hands up to his lips and kissed the back of my hand gently.

CHAPTER THIRTY-ONE

Riley

"Your dad is eyeing us, babe." He jerked his head toward the far right-hand corner of the living room, to where my parents were waiting.

"Excuse me, Mr. and Mrs. Rayne, it was such a pleasure meeting you." Carmen shook both of our hands as she excused herself.

We made our way over to where Mom and Dad were waiting, and Mom held out a clipboard with a schedule attached to it.

"I know you've only just finished the interview,

but from now until three, you'll be having a photoshoot. They're going to ask you some questions throughout so be mindful of your answers," she advised. "There will be a short break for lunch, so make that count because it'll be a while until we have dinner."

"We're having dinner at the gala?" Austin asked, trying to make himself sound nonchalant, but he didn't know what to expect.

Mom turned her gaze to his. "Yes, dear, fifteen courses."

Austin choked on thin air as he spluttered, "Fifteen courses?"

Mom's eyes pinned him where he stood. "It's à la carte, dear. I've no doubt you'll manage."

Dad held his hand up, curling his finger and thumb to form a small circle. "The portion sizes are teeny tiny little bite-sized amounts. More like miniature, edible works of art than anything else." Dad shrugged.

"Why bother going to all that effort?" Austin responded with a confused frown. "What a waste of dishes." He turned to me. "At least we're not on wash-up duty."

Dad found his comment amusing; whereas Mom flicked her wide-eyed gaze to me, then back to Austin. "Um, Austin dear?" Mom spoke, choosing her words with care. "If at all you find tonight overwhelming, please don't hesitate to come to us at any time."

He placed a hand over his heart. "Oh, I promise, I will be on my best behavior." The volume of his voice dipped low. "I don't want to cause you any embarrassment."

Mom placed a hand on his shoulder, speaking in a gentle tone. "Nonsense, nothing you say or do will embarrass us. I'm not worried about that, Austin, I'm more concerned for you."

Her comment surprised me. She turned to face Dad. "Are we feeding the poor boy into a pit full of lions, Bracken? Some of those people can be vicious," she voiced, showing concern for how they'd treat Austin as opposed to being worried about Austin's behavior itself.

"Mom, he can handle himself," I assured her. "I'll be right beside him all night, so just let 'em try." I scowled, folding my arms in front of me.

"Your mother is worried that our family has been the topic of gossip, just lately. What with your disappearance, sudden marriage announcement, baby rumors, and our recent reconciliation," Dad explained. "Not to mention what your poor cousin,

Sheena, has been subjected to. Especially with all the malicious rumors that good-for-nothing ex-husband of hers has been spouting off to the press."

"We're used to living in the public eye. We can handle whatever people throw at us," I assured him. "Will Sheena be there tonight?" I asked, feeling nothing but sympathy toward my scorned cousin.

"Your uncle Dolton has insisted, considering we're representing the five charities. Sheena loves children, so I'm sure she'll change her mind and come to show her charity some support," he revealed.

Sheena was the only daughter of Dolton Roth, my dad's little brother. She was older than me by four years. Uncle Dolton married a lot earlier than my parents did. I knew this meant that Sheena was also a fox shifter like us, but I couldn't believe she never told me. We were incredibly close when we were kids.

"Please excuse me for a minute. I want to give her a call. I don't want her to feel like I'm rubbing her nose in my happy marriage when hers has broken down," I explained. "Mom, Dad, look after my husband for a minute and try not to scare him off while I'm gone." I winked at Austin, giving him a playful smile.

Reconnecting with my cousin was something I needed to do, and I was ashamed that I hadn't reached out to her sooner. Over half an hour later I returned with my mobile phone still hot in the palm of my hand.

"I've managed to convince her to come, but she said she'll only stay for an hour or so," I told Dad, whose eyes crumpled with sadness.

"Oh dear," he muttered under his breath. "It's still early days, and I can only hope that one day she's as lucky as you've been with finding her mate. Human emotions can be so very fickle, indeed."

Mom coughed to clear her throat. "And what exactly do you mean by that?" She shot Dad a pointed look.

Dad immediately jumped into defense mode. "I'm not implying anything about you, darling. You're my mate, not just some human woman that I became infatuated with." As he returned her a smoldering gaze, I witnessed my mother melt before him, blushing like a schoolgirl.

"Anyway, I'm glad you two have patched things up," I commented. "But if you're going to suck each other's faces off, please do it in the privacy of your own room." I pulled Austin's arm. "Come on, you. We've got a date with the wardrobe department." His muscular shoulders drooped as he sighed in defeat.

During the next few hours, Austin and I endured outfit change after outfit change, being ushered around different rooms in the house, both indoors and outdoors. But what would've been a boring, life-ending, tortuous stint, Austin turned into something out of some hilariously funny comedy sketch.

"Shit, were these meant for her?" He gestured to the white feather boa and clip-on earrings he was wearing. The cluster of stylists exchanged a mixture of shock and horror between them. I gave a rather unladylike snort as I roared with laughter, unable to catch a breath.

"What do you think?" He pulled one of the long-stemmed red roses from a vase and held it between his teeth as he posed, batting his eyelashes.

I curled my finger and thumb as a sign for okay.

"Oh yeah . . ." I nodded in approval. "That'll start a new trend."

I hurried away, only to come back wearing the

suspender britches that were meant for him, tucking the oversized shirt into the waistband.

"How about these?" I asked as I drew on a fake mustache with black eyeliner.

Austin applauded. "Bravo . . . You should wear that tonight," he encouraged, trying his best not to laugh.

"And . . . we're all done here." One of the girls conducting the shoot announced, probably because we had lost all interest.

"Thank God." I threw my head back as I gave a relieved sigh. "Any longer and I'd piss my pants."

Never had I ever goofed around like that before; never had I ever spoken so uncouth before either. Austin gave a hearty laugh as I twirled him around.

"Don't miss me too much," I said, rising on my tiptoes to kiss him.

No sooner had I come back from the bathroom, we were summoned once again.

"Riley, it's almost time to get ready for the gala."

Mom barged her way through the cluster of people in the sitting room with what looked like a small entourage trailing behind her.

"Austin," Mom addressed him directly, using her pen to point with. "This is Mai Lue, your stylist." She gestured to a tiny, immaculately dressed Japanese woman. "She's America's number one fashion guru. Listen to her because she knows what she's talking about."

Mai craned her head up to look at him, blinking twice before muttering with sarcasm, "That's right, give me a weird-looking mountain to dress." She then cast Mom the stink-eye.

Mom tucked her clipboard under her arm and slouched all her weight onto one leg. "Oh, come on, Mai, you can handle the challenge. That's why I chose you," she buttered her up using flattery. Something Mom was good at.

"Fine —" Mai Lue dragged out the word. "But you pay me extra for dressing an extra-large man."

Mom blinked, shaking her head, and not wanting to argue. "Whatever." She then turned to me. "Honey, I had to pull a few strings with Daddy's pilot, but I managed to get Serge over from Sicily."

Sergio wasn't only my stylist; he was probably the one person in the universe I could count as a real friend. He stepped out from behind Mom, dressed in a colorful fitted suit with golden stitching.

Serge greeted me with open arms, air-kissing

both sides of my face noisily. "Riley, apart from the fake mustache, you're looking radiant, darling."

I spoke in hushed whispers, "I'm not pregnant, Serge. These baggy clothes were supposed to be Austin's."

"Meh." He swatted the air, then placed a hand on his hip. "Shall we get started?" He over accentuated the action of checking his diamond-encrusted watch, giving a fake gasp. "We only have like four hours to get ready. Ohmygod!"

Austin did a slow turn, pleading with huge, wide eyes. "Four more hours of torture?"

Just as I was about to answer, Mai got there first.

"If you don't get a move on, I'll show you torture," she promised, prodding his stomach with her index finger.

Austin's brows furrowed as he glanced down at her fierce expression. I could tell he was trying to figure out whether to laugh or not.

"Be nice to Mai, Austin." The warning was there in my voice. "You wanna look your best tonight, don't you?" I nodded, eye signaling him to play nice.

Mai's eyes twitched, silently daring him to sass her.

"Follow me, Mr. Rayne," she muttered, turning to exit the room. Austin trundled behind her apprehensively.

"Phew," Sergio mumbled. He swiped his hand over his brow dramatically. "I'm glad she's gone. One minute alone with her makes me thankful I'm gay."

I threaded my arm through his, then smiled at Mom as we passed. "I'm so glad you could make it, Serge. After the couple of days I've had, I want you to make me look like the Belle of the Ball."

The camera crew was packing away equipment in the hall as we rounded the stairs. "Oh, honey, relax. I know what you want. You wanna make that ex of his jelly? No?" Sergio winked. "I saw the news." His expression melted with sympathy.

"She's not his ex," I corrected.

Sergio cast me a doubtful look, and I stopped halfway up the staircase, causing him to halt in place right alongside me.

"Fine, amiga then," he huffed with amusement.

"Yeah, she was his best friend," I revealed.

"You know I love to tease, I'm sorry, Bella." Sergio's tone was sincere, calling me beautiful. "Don't be intimidated by a girl that he friend-zoned years ago. You made a point of dating your way through the world's rich list, and you don't think that your sudden marriage to a poor guy isn't gonna raise some eyebrows tonight?"

He was right; all focus would be on Austin tonight. Judging him, sniggering at him, whispering spiteful comments that his shifter ears would pick up easily. I was ready for it, but was he? Of course, he wasn't. He'd never experienced the snobbery of the high-class elite before. This night could end up being disastrous. Especially if he shifts and tears them all to shreds.

"If you want my advice, you're leading your boy, Austin, straight to the shark tank at feeding time." Sergio only confirmed what my parents and I already feared. But keeping him out of the spotlight would also set tongues wagging. I'd be accused of hiding him away out of shame, which wouldn't be true at all.

I resumed climbing the stairs, bringing Sergio along with me. "I can handle myself," I reminded him.

"Yeah, you can, but can he? He's a long way from home, Riley. He seems so ..." Sergio circled his fingers as he searched for the right word.

"Nice?" I answered.

We made it to the landing, hearing the distinct

sound of Japanese curse words coming from my room. I half chuckled, wondering what the heck Austin had gone and done now.

"Yeah, nice," Sergio agreed with me. "I was going to say a different breed, but nice fits too."

Serge didn't know how close he was to the truth, but he was talking about class differences, and not DNA. I could never tell him about us and that saddened me. It would be too dangerous.

"He brings out the best in you, I can see it already. And someone so good is shark bait for people in your world. Don't let them destroy the happiness you've found," he advised, waving his hand around flamboyantly and added, "It takes someone with a strong backbone to handle celebrity status and stardom. I hope for both your sakes your guy can handle it."

"He can," I replied, sure about that. "Just you wait and see . . . we'll be the next Hollywood power couple. I thought of our ship name, Rilstin."

Sergio's pitiful grimace told me I should keep that name to myself.

CHAPTER THIRTY-TWO

Riley

Austin gripped my hand, lacing his fingers with mine as we stepped from the car and onto the red carpet. He was nervous, but he wouldn't admit it. For me, this was second nature, but to anyone who wasn't familiar with this lifestyle, it was incredibly overwhelming.

The champagne-colored gown I was wearing cascaded around my ankles. The millions of Swarovski crystals that had been fixed onto the fabric glittered as they captured the light. My hair was pinned up in an elegant style, which complimented my delicate features. Drawing attention to the sweetheart neckline was a daisy chain diamond necklace that my dad gifted to me.

"Cast your eyes to the ground," I forewarned Austin because the onslaught of camera flashes was blinding. "Focus straight ahead and don't stop until we reach the step and repeat."

"The step and huh?" Austin looked completely bamboozled, not knowing what the heck was what.

There was a promotional backdrop where the attendees stood to pose for the photographers.

"Just relax and follow my lead," I reassured, bracing my shoulders back to straighten my posture.

Despite him not feeling it, Austin oozed power and masculinity. He was dressed like a dream in his tailor-fitted black tuxedo, Armani shoes, white pleated button-down shirt, and bow tie.

His blond hair had been styled to one side and his clean-shaven face only emphasized his insanely handsome looks. He was every ounce the sex god shown in cologne commercials, but he was a real manly man beneath the suit, not just some actor who pretended to be one.

Lights glittered from left to right amongst the

sea of faces that blended like one unfocused blur. Journalists called out our names, but our advice was to ignore them for now, having given exclusive rights to a certain news channel that made me wonder if it was owned by fox shifters, or if the name was purely a coincidence.

My parents walked straight ahead of us, followed by my Uncle Dolton, Aunt Celia and my cousin, Sheena, who held onto her father's arm. The seven of us walked proudly along the red carpet, putting up a united front. Amongst the questions that were fired at us, the harsh accusations that were flung at my cousin made my blood boil.

"Sheena, is it true that you tried to siphon funds from your charity and deposit them into a private, offshore account?"

Both Dad and Uncle Dolton shot them down with thunderous glares.

"My daughter is the victim of a ruthless opportunist. Justice will prevail when we get our day in court. No further questions, please," Dolton growled as Aunt Celia quickly ushered my devastated cousin away.

Austin bowed his head to speak beside my ear, "Are you all right? You're trembling."

I was angry. No, even worse than that, I was livid. Byron Valentine was a sleazy snake who weaseled his way into my cousin's affections, lived lavishly on her wealth, and used her to feed his expensive habits. His "doomed to fail" real estate company was just a smokescreen. The guy was a conman who faked his way into her heart, then smashed it into a million pieces. Earlier in the day, Sheena told me everything during our telephone conversation. How he had cheated on her with his so-called secretary. How they had embezzled money from her personal bank account and tried to do the same with the charity funds.

When I say tried, I meant that Sheena had found him out before he could finish his plans. Only after she filed for divorce, with claims of his infidelity, did he come forward with a counterclaim of his own, accusing her of conspiracy to theft. Sheena was sinking deeper and deeper into despair, and it wasn't over for her yet. Not by a long shot.

"I'll be fine. It's Sheena I'm worried about," I told him, flashing a composed smile to confuse any onlookers.

We reached the backdrop of the step and repeat, stopping to pose before the shine-free vinyl. The five separate charity logos were printed in a repetitive sequence in shades of green, red, blue, purple, and orange. Our family founded charities that supported the homeless, terminally ill patients, children in the care system, young entrepreneurs, and victims of domestic abuse.

"You're a natural," I complimented Austin as he struck a pose that could've given a sports model cause for concern.

"It finally paid off, having to watch my three sisters hog the mirror every morning," he muttered, all in good humor.

The press lapped him up like he was a free dessert from Serendipity 3. This was my night to show him off to the world, and boy, did I extract every opportunity. Even to the point of flashing my wedding finger so they got a good shot of his grandmother's ring. Austin bit close to the bone when he patted my flat abdomen, thus, reinforcing the baby rumors. Instead of discouraging him, I let him continue. He was having fun, God love him, and so was I.

Dad held back and waited for us so he could escort us both to our table. We were seated right at the front of the stage in the Beverly Hilton function hall. The ceiling was concealed with a black cloth that glittered with twinkling lights to give the effect of a night sky. Blue neon lights lit up the ice sculptures that had been carved into elegant swans. Each table and chair had been covered with white silk cloth and blue organza bows were added to give a splash of color to the chair backs. Round mirrored tiles were placed beneath the crystal vase centerpieces and were filled with faux diamonds and bunches of white and blue peonies.

Austin's name plaque was placed between mine and Uncle Dolton's. Sheena sat beside me, whereas Mom, Dad, and Aunt Celia sat facing us. Austin's eyes scanned the room, searching amongst the hundreds of well-dressed bodies that filled each table. Curious eyes practically scorched holes into the back of my head, but I was too proud to care. My man was worth a billion of them, so I reached my hand over to his and took hold of it.

"Now it's my turn to ask whether you're okay?" I checked, noticing him begin to fidget.

He flashed me a nervous smile. "I'll be all right. Just give me a minute."

A waiter placed down two ice buckets containing four bottles of champagne. Then he began to fill each of our glass flutes with the pale, effervescent liquid.

Uncle Dolton caught Austin's attention. "Knock

back a few of those to take the edge off," he advised, noticing how tense Austin was.

I was thrilled by how welcoming my family had been toward Austin. He was one of us now, and we would take good care of him because that's what we Roths did best. We protected what was ours at all costs.

CHAPTER THIRTY-THREE

Riley

"Do you see anyone you recognize?" I asked Austin.

He glanced around with narrowed eyes, scanning the room with keen interest. "Is that —" He lightly pointed, then held his chin in an observational pose as if deciding it wasn't who he originally thought it was.

"Who?" I press further, following his line of sight.

"I thought I just saw Han Solo," he mumbled, squinting, now that he wanted to check for sure.

"Oh, you mean Harrison Ford? He was invited, so it's possible," I mentioned.

It was rude to point, but I managed a discreet head jerk to the left of us. "Don't make it obvious, but Sly Stallone is sitting right over there."

Austin sat bolt upright in his seat as he searched.

"Whoa, so it is! It's Rocky Balboa in the flesh! I gotta get his autograph for Beast."

That made me chuckle. "I'll introduce you later," I promised.

"Yes, please!" His expression brightened. "And Han Solo. Don't forget him, too."

I couldn't help the genuine laughter that came out of my mouth, sounding more like an ungraceful cackle. "Austin, you do know that those aren't their real names, right?"

His brows bunched together. "Yeah, I knew that." He picked up his champagne flute and drained the contents in one go.

His awkward behavior was telling me otherwise. Maybe that's why he referred to Kain as the "Galactic Space Orc from Mars" the other day.

My dad waved to his brother from across the table.

"Dolton, give Austin a top-up," he encouraged.

He then leaned forward to speak to Austin. "I

want you to enjoy yourself tonight, son. The auction is coming up after the announcement. Bid for whatever you want. It's on me."

Austin's face paled. "Oh, I couldn't."

Mom swatted the air in dismissal. "Nonsense. Have fun. Choose some wedding gifts to brighten up your cabin."

I tapped Austin's knee under the table, and he flicked his shocked gaze to mine. "It's all going to charity anyway," I reasoned.

He let out a nervous exhale. "Um, all right. If they're sure."

Even though I was blatantly aware of the intrusion of prying eyes, I ignored it. Instead, I engaged in a conversation with my cousin.

"So, you haven't shifted yet?" Sheena mouthed discreetly.

"Nope, have you?" I directed the question straight back at her.

She winced her eyes in an apologetic grimace. "Yeah, of course, I have. It wasn't me with the human mom and the forest phobia."

I rolled my eyes at her comment. "Well, duh! You still could've told me. We used to tell each other everything, and I thought I could trust you to always be straight with me."

She recoiled back in her seat, looking more downtrodden and remorseful than before. "Sorry, I wanted to, but Uncle Bracken made me promise because Aunt Sasha didn't know about the likes of us. He bought me a pony to shut me up."

My eyes rounded on her accusingly. "Unbelievable. A freakin' pony was all it took to buy your silence?"

She gave a small gasp, clutching her chest. "I was only a child, and I loved Butterscotch! He was adorable, not to mention loyal. At least I could trust him not to run off with the filly from the paddock next door."

The sadness in her words felt like a stab of pain in my chest, and it was moments like these when I wished that I owned a Byron Valentine voodoo doll and an extra sharp pin. Austin pressed his lips together in a sympathetic smile as if he didn't feel like it was his place to comment.

I picked up the champagne flute by the rim as I pointed, using the same hand in a dismissive gesture. "Ah, forget about the past, and forget about Byron fucking Valentine. It'll all work out. You'll see."

"Yeah, I hope so," Sheena muttered grimly.

"It'll be fine," I told her. "It will. What did you

just say to me earlier? That you're selling your apartment here in the city and moving to Whitehaven?"

The chances of her meeting her mate will increase if she relocates to the shifter state. Then it would be Byron who?

Sheena nodded. "Yeah, I'm doing some house hunting next week. I'm viewing a property in Lakewell."

Dad flicked his gaze to us. "Well, keep in mind that Dolton and I are collaborating on a project called Vixen Hollow. We always talked about branching out into real estate, and now we're putting our long-awaited plans into action."

"We sure are," Dolton agreed.

"These are exciting times," Celia commented. "I can't wait to take a look at the plans."

"Yeah, we get to look at them next week," Mom added. "The two of you always wanted to collaborate on something, didn't you?"

Dad nodded. "What matters the most is family," he expressed sincerely. "Our community has forgotten that just lately, and if we're not careful, we'll go the same way as the cats."

Dad's tone wasn't loud enough to be overheard from anyone who wasn't sitting at our table. We were careful when speaking about our community.

Uncle Dolton agreed. "That's right, Bracken." Like Dad, he kept his voice low as he spoke. "Fox families rarely have more than one cub at a time, and because we live in dangerous times, some don't even bother having children at all. Our population is dwindling, so by building our own safe haven, we're hoping to increase the numbers by over seventy-five percent."

Austin

As Dolton delivered his comment, I felt the temperature in the room jump up a couple of notches. The unforgiving suit jacket became stifling, especially under the watchful gaze of Sasha Roth, the mother-in-law. I pulled at the collar of my shirt as if it held me in a chokehold.

"Seventy-five percent, huh?" My voice sounded abnormally weak for a man of my size.

Dolton cocked his head with an assured smirk. "That's what we're hoping for," he added confidently.

Sasha's eyes narrowed as she thought. "Speaking of which," she cut in straight after Dolton.

I closed my eyes in a momentary pause, feeling the dull, throbbing, pound of dread flow into me the second Sasha made her comment with all the subtlety of a brick.

"When should I expect to hear the pitter-patter of tiny feet? I assume you are trying, right?" All eyes landed on Riley and me, and the room seemed to shrink to the size of a matchbox.

My words got jammed in my throat, and I coughed, choking on air. The silence only lasted for a second, but it was one painstaking, God awful, "I'd rather cut a nut off and roast it for supper," kind of silence.

A nervous laugh came out of Riley. "Mom." Her voice was sweet, but her eyes were throwing daggers.

Sasha shrugged. "It's a valid question." She then grasped the stem of her champagne flute, knocking back a large gulp.

Bracken cleared his throat subtly. "Uh, Sasha, honey, we work a little differently in that respect."

Both Sasha and Riley cast doubtful frowns. "Dad, I'm fairly certain that our anatomies work in the exact same way." She chuckled as if he had said something completely ridiculous.

Even Sasha rolled her eyes, then gave him a look of mock pity. "Don't listen to your father. He's talking through his ass. I'm a human, and I conceived you naturally." She looked at Riley as she spoke.

A trickle of sweat ran from my hairline and past my ear. Fuck. Goddamned awkward social situations. That was precisely the reason I stayed in the woods. I wasn't good with people, always saying or doing the wrong thing. I glanced down at the array of cutlery, all fanned out in size order and felt more anxiety bubbling.

"Riley hasn't shifted in years. And as any shifter knows, a female who doesn't shift regularly will find it impossible to conceive," Bracken explained, much to Sasha's horror, not to mention Riley's.

CHAPTER THIRTY-FOUR

Austin

"Oh," Riley's brightened expression faltered. She flashed her eyes to mine momentarily, then down to the table. I noticed the light-hearted humor extinguished from them. "Well, that's just awesome." Her voice trembled as she spoke.

I knew we hadn't known each other for long, and the prospect of having kids someday hadn't exactly been the topic of conversation. But if there was ever a sign that Riley had thought that far ahead and wanted to bear my children, it was written all over her face. Right now, the distant sadness in her eyes was grieving for something that she couldn't have. Something that all the wealth in the world couldn't buy.

There was only one person I knew of who could help Riley with this problem. It wasn't my mom with all her medical knowledge. She could fix anyone inside or out, but not this. Not something deep-rooted as Riley's childhood trauma was. She needed therapy, and the human therapist she sought help from wasn't the right kind of person to make contact with the animal within. After everything that happened recently, I was fairly certain that the person she needed would rather rot in Hell before she would agree to help us. That only made me feel more helpless.

"Um, Riley, why do we need all of this?" I asked, pointing at the cutlery to change the subject for both our sakes.

Her glossy red lips formed an O. "Work from the outside inward," she said as if it was as simple as that. I glanced over my shoulder, hearing a guy snigger after my name was mentioned. Heads snapped away the second my eyes met with theirs.

My brows furrowed, hardening my gaze into a

pissed-off scowl. "The fuck you looking at?" I muttered, agitated.

Neither one of the fancy-ass, trust-fund jerks turned to answer. It was just as well they weren't within grabbing distance. The dark-haired one, who snorted first, muttered something else to one of his pals, and they all began chuckling amongst themselves like a gaggle of geese. I wasn't in the mood to be dealing with assholes like those. They'd been sniggering at me ever since I got here.

Riley's soft fingers fanned out across the top of my clenched fist, and I relaxed my shoulders and returned her a placated smile.

"Ignore them, babe," she spoke with resolve. "They're not worth your time or effort."

That was true, but it was easier said than done. With my ears twitching like radars picking up mashed-up bits of conversation from different areas in the room, it was impossible to block it out. By the time I downed my fifth glass of—*shit*—I couldn't even pronounce it. It was Dom—something. It sounded like Celia called it Dom Perry Nom. But without snatching up the bottle to read the label, I couldn't be sure. Well, anyway, I was able to drown out all the background noise with alcohol.

Course after course of microscopic portions

came out. Tiny little morsels on humongous plates. I needed a magnifying glass to find them. I can honestly say I'd flushed bigger turds compared to some of the stuff they served me.

My shoulders dropped with a heavy sigh, scooping up the smudging of crushed green stuff and a cube of meat, then chowed it down in one, scrunching my nose as I watched Riley cut hers in half, then half again. It looked barely fucking visible as she brought the curved side of her fork to her mouth. Once, twice, thrice, she chewed. All the while, I stared at her, flabbergasted. She then dabbed her napkin against the corners of her mouth that was already pristinely clean. My stomach yelled at me from within, screaming out for some nourishment, and I drowned it with another mouthful of the fizzy liquid. After fifteen courses, I was still hungry as fuck and half thinking of hauling my ass to the kitchens to ask whether or not they had any leftovers.

The room grew brighter, and I glanced up and around me. "Oh look, the auctions are starting," Riley announced, nudging me. And then I recognized the guy who walked onto the stage.

It's him. The space dork. Kain Cox.

My eyes hardened as they followed the smiling

jerk as he took to the stage in some kind of goofy dance, stopping at the microphone and giving Riley finger guns. I recognized him all right, and my heart plummeted, knowing that Riley knew him well enough to sail across the ocean with him in a fancy yacht. That was the guy from that shitty space movie. The one Riley had passed out drunk with. She blushed, rolling her eyes in embarrassment.

"Ladies and Gentlemen; on behalf of Roth Corp, I want to thank you for coming tonight," he spoke humbly, placing his hand over his heart. I hated him already.

The sound of applause filled the room, and I felt obliged to join in, giving a begrudgingly slow clap. I watched through narrowing slits of fury as he kept glancing down at my wife. I saw his gaze flick to her chest and his throat bobbed as he swallowed. Hell-fire raced through my veins, and I imagined leaping on stage and ripping his head clean off. The pounding pressure in my ears drowned out the sound of his voice, and all I could hear was a rhythmic *thump-thump* as the bear inside me fumed.

"Babe?" Riley whispered, tapping my forearm.

"Huh?" I snapped out of my murderous trance,

not realizing that my expression was twisting with rage.

Riley chuckled. "Babe, did you zone out? If you want to outbid these guys, you have to focus."

I gave a disgruntled nod, making a disinterested face. "Fine."

After another bottle of fizz, and a couple of ugly paintings later, things started to look a whole lot better. I was not just talking about the double-vision. The next lot had my eyes popping out on stalks.

"Ladies and gents, what we have here is a beaded fringe jumpsuit, owned by The King of Rock and Roll, Mr. Elvis Presley," Kain announced.

"Holy shit!" I spoke my thoughts out loud.

Riley tapped my arm excitedly. "You got this, babe," she encouraged.

I picked up the number thingy that looked a lot like a spanking paddle I found in Riley's bed stand, and held it up.

"Austin, wait for it to start," Riley muttered, pushing my arm back down.

Kain muttered, "Someone's keen." Then pointed at me, grinning.

I rolled my eyes, anxious to get on with it. I forced a half-assed smile that was gone in a flash.

"I'm starting the bidding at twenty-five," Kain announced.

My brows lifted with surprise. "Twenty-five dollars? What a bargain." I raised the paddle in the air.

Riley subtly scratched her nose, leaning into me. "Not dollars—thousand," she muttered.

My eyes bulged out of their sockets. "Shit a brick!" I coughed, trying to conceal my involuntary outburst.

There were polite smiles given from all around our table, while I wished the ground would open up and swallow me whole. Before I knew it, there was an all-out bidding war for the jumpsuit. Especially when it was announced that it still had Elvis's sweat patches under the arms and crotch.

"Who will give me one and a half?" Kain yelled into the microphone.

Riley forced my elbow up and the paddle almost flew out of my hand.

"Going once, going twice — Sold! For one and a half million dollars. To the abnormally huge guy sitting at the front!" he announced, pointing at me.

There were victorious cheers from around our table, and I was left panting for air the moment I heard the price.

"Congratulations, babe!" Riley expressed with an ecstatic grin.

Air forced its way through my throat in place of words, making me sound like a punctured squeaky toy. I didn't even notice the A-lister jump down from the stage and approach our table.

"I believe this belongs to you." He produced the jumpsuit, and I turned suddenly as if startled.

"Thank you very much," I joked, in an impersonation of my idol.

I held the soft material between my fingers as if frightened it may disintegrate. This was a precious artifact to me, and I intended to treasure it forever, even though I was tempted to try it on for size. It was stretch fabric, after all.

Captain Dork leaned into Riley with puckered lips and the world seemed to slow right down. My eyes flared as wide as saucers, and I thrust my hand out with the jumpsuit clasped firmly within it, to where Mr. Frisky inadvertently planted a smackerooney straight against Elvis's sweaty crotch stain.

In my head, angels flew down from the heavens and sang Hallelujah harmoniously, having thwarted his plans. Kain grimaced, spluttering, and picking the fluff off his tongue.

"Riley, long time no see." His eyes dropped to hers in a smoldering gaze, having chosen to bring her hand up to his lips instead.

Riley's other arm snaked around my waist. It was a subtle reminder that she chose me above all else.

"Oh, you know me." She shrugged playfully. "I've been busy."

"Too busy for an old friend?" He wiggled his eyebrows suggestively. "You had a lot of fun on my yacht, if I remember correctly."

Riley laughed off his comment, whereas I saw it for what it was. He was trying to mark his territory —with my wife!

In the animal kingdom, that would've been deemed as a challenge. Cats would spray their pheromones all over the place and claw each other's eyes out. Dogs usually pissed up trees and would rip one another limb from limb, but bears . . . we did more than snatch your picnic baskets and chase you through the woods. We'd have ourselves a five-star banquet, then we'd pick our teeth with your bones. And there I went again, thinking about food.

I didn't have the energy to fight tonight. My stomach was slowly digesting itself from the inside out. That only made me more and more cranky, and when I got cranky, the sarcasm only intensified.

"Listen here, Kain, you really wanna crash into this planet?" I tapped my fingertips against my chest. "Your yacht didn't just sail. It sank faster than that crappy space movie." I jabbed my finger at him, hating how the smug fucker was still grinning at me.

"What are you talking about?" he asked, finding my reaction highly amusing.

I scowled like a petulant kid who was guarding his favorite toy. "You can't have her," I growled. "I've already licked it, so it's mine."

Riley's face turned an abnormal shade of crimson as I used a food metaphor to describe what I meant.

"Austin." She eye-signaled for me to shut up. "You're misreading the situation. Kain and I never had *sex*. We're just friends."

My left eye twitched as I considered what she said.

"I see there's been a misunderstanding here," Kain replied, giving an exaggerated blink. "Riley, please excuse me. I didn't mean to offend your beau." He flashed a humble smile. "But since we've been friends for quite some time, I wanted to introduce you to my fiancée."

I gave a double-take, feeling the air rush back to me in abundance. "S'cuse me? Did you just say, fiancée?"

Right at that point, a tall, leggy blonde walked over to him and attached herself to his side. It was at that moment that I excused myself to go in search of the bathroom.

"Idiot," I muttered under my breath, having just humiliated myself once again.

He was probably a nice guy, and now it would seem that I was the jerk. I hated having to apologize, but I guess I'd take a moment to recover and swallow my pride before doing the unthinkable.

CHAPTER THIRTY-FIVE

Austin

The staff, who were dressed in black and white waiter uniforms, hurried back and forth with trays of drinks. I snatched a glass of scotch that was probably meant for someone else and chugged it down in three fiery mouthfuls.

Another waiter looked at me with utmost disgust as I placed the empty glass down on his tray.

I still had Elvis's jumpsuit draped over my arm as I swaggered down the hall, placing one foot in front of the other, not knowing where the hell I was going. A one-and-a-half-million-dollar suit. I stopped dead in my tracks, pinching the corners of my eyes and chuckling to myself.

What the fuck am I doing here?

"Austin?" I heard a voice in front of me that made my heart stop dead.

My eyes opened in an instant, and I slowly moved my hand away, uncovering my face. I wasn't imagining things. It was her, all right. My so-called best friend, Rebecca King. She was dressed in a waiter's uniform and looked just as out of place as I felt.

"You look good," she commented, fidgeting awkwardly and barely able to look me in the eye.

The remorse was evident in her puffy, watery eyes, and I detected a stab of hurt in her strained voice.

"Can't say the same for you," I replied coolly.

She looked down at the badly fitted uniform and shrugged. "I borrowed it so that the press could sneak me inside."

My eyes darted around, shocked. "The what?" I flinched back as if burned. "Haven't you done enough?" I eyed her accusingly, livid that she was in cahoots with the press of all people.

She stumbled toward me, only to hesitate.

Rebecca's eyes glanced at something behind me, then flared wide. Her lips quivered as if finding it difficult to speak, and that was when I felt a hand at the base of my back.

"Babe, I was worried you'd gotten lost," Riley spoke, keeping her voice controlled, but her gaze was fixed firmly on the sheepish brunette in front of us.

There was a momentary pause where time stood still. Riley was like a coiled snake, just waiting for an excuse so that she could spring to attack.

Rebecca took a deep breath, placing a trembling hand against her chest. "I begged them to sneak me in here because I just wanted to say that I was sorry," she explained regretfully. "I'm not asking for your forgiveness. I was jealous and selfish, and what I did was awful. But what I'm really trying to say is that you deserve to be happy. You're a really good guy, Austin. You won't hear from me again. Take care, okay?"

Rebecca turned on her heel and bolted for the door. Riley turned to me, rubbing my shoulder in a comforting gesture.

"You should go after her," she encouraged.

I scrunched my brows, turning to her with a

frown. "Huh? You what?" I asked, hardly believing what she was saying.

Riley seemed to understand something that I didn't. "She fell in love with a great guy, who didn't reciprocate those feelings. She's broken-hearted. I could see it as clear as day." She took hold of the jumpsuit. "I'll hang onto this. You can't just go running around with a million-dollar suit."

"Even after all she's done?" I asked, surprised by her compassion. I knew that the answer to our future lay in whether or not Rebecca would help Riley to shift, but I was shocked more than anything by how much Rebecca's actions hurt me. Seeing her face-to-face only made things seem much more real.

Riley sighed. "Austin, do you want the chance to save your friendship or not? I saw how much she hurt you, and I saw the look on her face when she let you go just now. Maybe you could salvage a lifetime of happy memories or maybe you can't. But at least you can say that you gave it your best shot."

I lowered my face to hers and stole a kiss from the most amazing woman in the world. "I love you," I told her with everything I had.

She twisted her lips in a sappy half-smirk. "I love you, too."

I braced myself for the ambush of camera flashes as I chased after Rebecca. I saw her flee past the press, covering her face from view.

She got as far as the edge of the red carpet, then hesitated like a deer caught in headlights.

"Mr. Rayne, what's your relationship with Miss King?" a reporter asked.

I glanced back to answer, just as Rebecca turned around, distraught.

"We're not in a relationship!" she yelled back in response, answering for me.

"She's my best friend, and she's pissed that I didn't invite her to the wedding." I spun them a line, in the hope they bought it.

Rebecca sniffed, wiping her tear-soaked face. "What are you doing out here, Austin?" She stared at me defeatedly.

"We need to talk," I told her straight, holding out the olive branch.

The camera flashes were coming at us from all angles, so I ushered Rebecca into a waiting limousine, thinking that it was the same one we arrived in. Only, it wasn't.

"Sir, I'm going to have to ask you to vacate the vehicle," the chauffeur spoke through the window divider.

I held a relaxed palm in front of me. "I'm sorry, this will only take a second." I looked at him pleadingly. "Those guys are like vultures."

"Fine . . . you've got two minutes, the clock is ticking," he replied in a warning tone.

"Can you give us a moment of privacy, please?" I asked.

The chauffeur huffed and rolled his eyes, then raised the dividing panel between the back of the Limo and the driver's seats. Rebecca wiped her eyes on the sleeve of her shirt, leaving a streak of black mascara along the crisp white cuff. Now that we were alone, we could talk openly.

"I'll go first," I volunteered.

Her gray eyes flicked to mine, and she quickly nodded. "Okay."

"I never meant to hurt you," I told her sincerely. "You're like a sister to me."

Rebecca's expression was penitent as she held my gaze. "I'm sorry that I tried to kiss you, okay? It was a dumb move, and I wish I could take it back," she blurted out in a contrite tone.

"I'm talking first," I reminded her, tapping a finger against my chest. "You always do that when I'm talking. Call yourself a therapist."

Rebecca exhaled with a forceful huff, allowing

me to continue. Whenever she asked me a question, she always answered it for me, not giving me the chance to answer for myself. She complained that I was too vague and that she could read me like a book.

"You know I love you, right?" I picked up her hand and held it in mine. "But just not like that." I held her gaze, taking a candid approach. "We talked about this, remember? I hope that we can put things back to how they were."

We'd been friends ever since we were cubs. She was the girl next door. The one with whom I used to make mud pies, camp out in my treehouse, name the worms we collected, and pull pranks on my sisters together. We used to ride our bikes to school together every day since we were old enough to travel to school alone. We were inseparable, like two halves of the same whole, but just not in the way that she hoped.

But cutting a long story short, she was my best friend. One who I could talk to about anything. Even when I woke up at three a.m., struggling to sleep, we would talk via the string telephone that ran from my room to hers. I could look out of my bedroom window, and she would be there, waving back at me. We used to tell each other all our secrets, and ever since we let things come between us, this emptiness would never go away.

"I know," she replied softly. "I guess I was scared that I was going to lose you. But then I messed it all up and lost you anyway," she admitted, flicking her gaze to mine.

"You didn't lose me," I scoffed, rolling my eyes.

"Yes, I did," Rebecca disagreed, adding emphasis to her words. "You took up that ranger's post out of town. You wouldn't have taken that job if it weren't for me."

I winced my eyes, feeling the truth sink in. I did run away from my problems. After I came back from Whitevale, the severity of what had happened there hit home. It made everyone anxious about the future and what it might hold.

"I did what I thought was best at the time. You were acting all crazy, talking about biological clocks and shit!" I shrugged.

"Austin!" Rebecca jerked back, offended. "I was scared, and acting irrationally. I wasn't thinking straight, and I panicked."

The dividing panel rolled down three inches, and the chauffeur's face appeared in the gap. "Your time's up!" he announced.

"One more minute," Rebecca pleaded. "Here, here's fifty dollars for your trouble."

"Fine," he conceded, reaching his hand through the gap in the divide to accept the cash. He then closed the privacy screen so we could talk some more.

Rebecca turned back to me. "I know what I did ruined things. I was scared that you weren't gonna make it back after the hunter invasion, and when you did, I was so relieved. Then it made me worry about the death toll and the fact that we hadn't found our mates yet. There was a strong possibility that they could've been killed, and I panicked. I wasn't thinking straight. Then when I saw you had found your mate, and I hadn't." Rebecca's eyes downturned, brimming with tears.

"You were jealous," I answered for her this time.

"I was—stupidly," she admitted. "But I had no right to be. I acted impulsively when I called the cops. I regretted it as soon as I did it. My feelings for you were confused, and those lines were blurred even more when I worried about your safety. I see that now. I just hope that it's not too late to put things right again."

"He's out there somewhere," I reassured in an attempt to console her.

Rebecca chuckled doubtfully. "I don't think so. Look at me. I've got absolutely nothing to offer anyone."

I half snorted. "And you think I do? Hell, I'm not worth shit, and I bagged a billionaire for a wife."

Rebecca's eyes bulged.

"And you wanna hear something else? This is the guy who doesn't spend more than ten bucks on a shirt, and who has owned the same pairs of jeans for almost eight years." I pointed to myself. "Tonight, I just bought one of Elvis's costumes for one and a half million dollars."

"Holy shit!" Rebecca choked on her words.

"I know, right?" I agreed.

"Do you think your wife hates me?" Rebecca asked out of the blue.

I winced my eyes, scrunching my nose. "Nah." I swatted the air, hardly convincing myself with how I answered.

Rebecca ran a hand down her face. "Yes, she does. I called the cops to try and get rid of her. All because I thought I was jealous and wanted you back."

"So, you don't think of me in that way anymore?" I checked, wincing my eyes.

"God, no!" Rebecca shuddered. "The cops showing up to arrest you was a wake-up call."

I struggled hard not to laugh at that comment. This was what I hoped to hear: that she no longer harbored a romantic desire for me whatsoever and that the idea of us being intimate was just as repulsive and gross as it was for me.

"Well, I think you really ought to apologize. I think that would help," I urged, straight-faced.

"Okay," Rebecca said as she attempted to open the door to leave.

"Not to Riley . . . to me!" I glared, with an air of indignance. "It was me who got tased to the ground, and it was my ass that got thrown into jail."

"I'm sorry!" she pleaded. "Whatever you want me to do—to prove, just say it, and I'll do it." Her eyes widened with sincerity.

I folded my arms, trying to remain composed. The look on her face was priceless, and I wished I could've taken a photo for proof. "Well, it's funny you should say that, Becca, because I do have a favor to ask. And with you being a therapist, I was kind of hoping that you could help me out with something."

"Uh-oh, what is it?" she asked, bracing herself for the worst.

"Riley was traumatized during her first shift and hasn't shifted since. Do you think you could help with that?" I asked, getting straight to the point.

I saw the understanding begin to settle within her eyes, and I could tell that she understood the importance of what I was asking.

"Of course, but we're in the city, Austin. My kind of therapy only works best in our natural habitat," Rebecca replied with a keen response, although, pointing out the difficulty we were in.

"The woods?" I asked, cocking my head to one side.

"Yeah, the woods. Why? Is there a problem?" she asked, shrugging her shoulders, completely oblivious to the challenge I was about to present to her.

I narrowed my eyes questioningly. "How sorry are you?"

CHAPTER THIRTY-SIX

Riley

After the night we had, I lounged with my legs up on the patio chair while staring distantly out at the brochure-perfect garden. The gentle morning breeze fanned my face, contrasting with the hot steam of my coffee as I brought the mug to my lips to take a sip. Hot versus cool, just like the atmosphere that creates thunder up in the clouds. It mirrored my mood, sullen and irritable, having spent the night facing outward in bed, while my husband tried relentlessly to butter me up. I figured creeping had never been Austin's forte. And the way I was feeling last night, he could fuck off to Graceland all on his lonesome. *Suggesting I accompany Rebecca King to a forest retreat.*

Who the fuck gives him these ideas?

The mental image alone makes me want to piss my pants with terror. *Shifting in the forest.* That repetitive nightmare had been branded into my subconscious, and Mom paid a therapist to slap a big fat Band-Aid on top of it. For a hefty price, may I add! And now, Rebecca King wanted to rip said Band-Aid off, without so much as a count to three.

"You gonna sulk out here all day?" Austin's deep baritone voice floated past my ear from behind.

I released a heavy sigh, hating having ignored him since he suggested the outrageous idea.

"I haven't decided yet," I answered, still staring ahead, noticing all the dead crickets that were floating around the edges of the pool.

R.I.P Jiminy. Where the fuck were you when I needed the voice of reason?

"About what?" he asked, testing my turbulent waters to see if it was safe to dip in a toe.

I rolled my eyes and took another sip of my

coffee, figuring he could wait a little longer for me to dignify him with an answer. "About whether or not I'm going to stay in this mood," I replied eventually.

He made a huffing noise, which suggested he was getting frustrated with my snappy behavior. "Baby, it's like I told you. If you want to have a family, you have to learn how to shift. Mother nature just needs to give your hormones a kickstart. That's all."

I let that thought swim around my head again, not that it ever floated away, not really. It was so typical. The one thing I never wanted was now the only thing I craved, and all my wealth and power couldn't buy it for me. I was ruthless when I wanted to be. Shrewd and then some. I could strut my stuff in a boardroom full of trust fund jerks and come out on top of the food chain, having them eating from the palm of my hand. But this . . . what if it didn't work? We would both be disappointed, and how would we recover from that?

"I'll think about it," I offered, being the best answer I could muster right now.

Austin paused for a moment before he replied. I couldn't see his face, but I thought I heard him exhale a little sigh of relief. "Well, don't think too long. Your flight leaves tonight."

That grabbed my attention like an ice blast. I whipped my head around to see him leaning casually against the doorframe. All he had on was a pair of my dad's lounge-shorts, and a "just rolled out of bed look" . . . damn it. It was like he didn't even have to try.

"My flight?" I reiterated, needing a little more clarity. "As in, just me and not you?"

He raised his brows, looking pleasantly surprised by my display of interest. "Not exactly," he added, scrunching his nose.

I internally groaned, figuring that there would be a catch.

"You and Becca will be traveling together." He saw my face flood with horror and added, "It'll give you two a chance to bond. She's a lot like you in some ways," he remarked. "She's smart, is what I meant," he finished with a nice save.

"So, it's Becca now, huh?" I muttered, attempting to conceal the jealousy in my voice. "Yesterday, it was Rebecca, and now you've shortened her name. That means you've mended your little rift, I take it?"

He chuckled, dragging his fingers through his

hair. "Well, that all depends on whether she can help you," he threw in casually. "Then all's square between us, and I'll be willing to forgive and forget."

There was an unmistakable look of longing hanging over him, like everything hung by a millimeter-thick thread. Austin wasn't a pushover by any means. But I could see he was desperate for this to work in his favor. He couldn't allow Rebecca to walk away from her actions scot-free, commanding a certain level of respect from his friends because he showed them the same level of courtesy. *Shit!* There it was again . . . another reason why he was a better person than me.

"Do you *want* me to try?" I asked, like the coward I was, needing him to be the one to reinforce my choice.

"Do *you* want to try?" He deflected the question back at me.

I winced, expecting as much. "I'll do it for you." I delivered a heartfelt gesture.

I would willingly walk over hot coals for this man. I would dive headfirst into a pit of snakes or donate all my clothing to charity and wear potato sacks from now on—not that I would ever tell him any of this, out of fear that he would expect me to follow through with it.

"No, if you're going to do it, then you'll do it for *us*," he corrected me.

I nodded, and he smiled a genuine smile, one that reached his eyes and sparkled there. Austin was a good man who deserved better. He deserved a mate who would go to the ends of the earth just to keep that glint in his eyes.

I held out my hand, making a grabbing motion for him to come to me. He obeyed, not taking a second longer than he had to, to think it over. "I'm sorry," I apologized as his fingers clasped with mine. Remorse blazed like a ball of heat in my chest, burning its way up my throat like a fiery trail.

He scooped me up, then nestled down beside me. "It's okay," he responded, seeming to understand, not that it made my guilt lessen any. It just cleared the distance between us, meaning we could draw a line under last night's fiasco.

"I'm just scared," I admitted, resting my head against his bare chest. I could feel the rhythmic thumping of his heart, beating out a languid pattern as if nothing ever fazed him at all. "What if I can't learn how to shift, or what if I do and it makes no difference? The damage might've been done, back when I was seven."

He removed the mug from my hands and set it

down on the ground. I fidgeted with my hands now that they had nothing to do. Austin curled his body around mine, wrapping his strong arms around me. Such a simple token of support was enough to make me feel safe and loved. I felt his lips pucker against my cheek, then he dragged in a lungful of air through his nose. I knew that he, too, thought this was a possibility, but the fool's hope was all the encouragement he needed to give it a shot. I owed it to him, and myself, to at least try.

"She's good at what she does, babe, or else I wouldn't have asked for her help." He sounded genuinely sincere about that.

So, who knew that the shifterverse had its own answer to Dr. Phil? Maybe Rebecca King was a good person beneath all the proprietorial shit she pulled, or maybe she intended to murder me in the woods. Who knows? I guess there was only one way to find out.

"I guess I better go and pack," I responded, grimacing through lack of enthusiasm.

"And I ought to do the same," Austin mentioned, piquing my interest once again.

"Where are you going?" I narrowed my eyes with an air of spousal suspicion.

Austin made an excited chuckling noise in the

back of his throat, which made him sound like a kid that'd been let loose in a toy store. "I'm not letting those tickets to Graceland go to waste," he protested.

"You're going on your own?" I scoffed.

"No," he dragged out the word. "I have a traveling companion. One who appreciates the king and his creative legacy."

I frowned. "Who?" I spat out the word, wondering who on Earth was insane enough to accompany him on his fanboy tour.

"Beast," he answered straight-faced.

I blinked, waiting for the punchline . . . which never came.

"The big scary, tattooed guy who looks as if he eats fully grown men for breakfast? That guy is a shifter version of The Hulk!" I blurted out in shock.

Austin found that analogy amusing and chuckled. "You think he's like The Hulk, huh?" I detected a hint of envy in his voice. "He used to be as skinny as my little finger." He held it up as evidence. "But all those years in the Cage made him bulk up some," he explained, leaving me clueless as to what the fuck he was on about.

"The Cage?" I questioned, narrowing my eyes. "As in prison?"

Austin shook his head, widening his eyes. "Nah-ah, not the type of prison you're thinking about, but you're not far off," he stated, turning his posture so that we were sitting comfortably. "The Cage is a fighting arena in the Lakewell underground. You see, Whitehaven has its good points as well as its bad. We have drug lords and cartels the same as anywhere, only, they are the shifter kind."

I listened intently as he continued. "Kian, or Beast, as everyone else knows him, was once caught up dead center of it. It took him a while to get out, but when he did, he wasn't the same guy anymore. He was different. He'd become . . ."

"The Beast," I interjected, figuring that much for myself. "So how come he landed a job with the United Shifter Council?" I asked, unable to connect the dots.

Austin told me about them fighting side by side in Whitevale, but I struggled to understand how an ex-underground cage fighter became a legitimate fighter, only to wind up as a gun runner in some criminal biker gang, then somehow manage to end up as a general of the combined shifter military. That was some life journey. It just went to show that anyone could change their fate. Life was full of opportunities and choices. It was ultimately down to us to choose the right path.

"Yeah, he thought he'd forfeit his soul to the devil himself the day he took a man's life," Austin explained. "He got himself into a mess, and he got himself out of it. If you could call joining the Roughnecks motorcycle gang any better. Then there's the deal he made with the Reaper."

"Death?" I gasped. "He made a deal with Death?"

Austin exhaled a dark chuckle. "As good as," he replied. "The Reaper Cartel runs Whitehaven's underground. He's not a force to be fucked with, babe." There was not a hint of amusement flickering within Austin's eyes, which meant that he was being deadly serious. "The only one strong enough to keep him down in the dirt where he belongs is the Alpha Dog, Alec White."

Austin gave me a brief summary of what happened in Whitevale, which wasn't pretty. Alpha Alec was the target along with his mate, Leah.

"What was stopping the Reaper from teaming up with those hunters who wanted to take down Alec?" I asked, trying to put together some sort of mental imagery around this new and disturbing news.

"Because Reaper is an alligator shifter, and hunters hate shifters in all shapes and forms. For once, the Alpha dog and the cartel were singing from the same hymn sheet. The Alpha needed weapons, and where do you suppose he obtained them from?" Austin tilted his head as he delivered the question as if to say, "it's not exactly rocket science." He continued, "The Roughnecks Motorcycle Club rode into town with an arsenal of weapons, but they came gift-wrapped with a big fat bow on top, courtesy of The Reaper Cartel. Alec may be a genius, but even he should've figured that Reaper would come to collect someday. I dread to think what it'll cost him."

I took a moment to think about that. "If I were a crime lord, forced to live a covert life in a state where human rules don't apply, then I would want to conduct business out in the open."

Austin's lips twitched up in a half-smirk. "That's what we all anticipate. But on the flip side, if he promises to comply with how things are done around those parts, then he stands a good chance of putting a case before the council."

I shook my head. "But a guy like that can't be trusted," I voiced vehemently.

Austin agreed wholeheartedly with me. "No,

love, he can't. Which is why you have to get your shit together pronto and get your cute, intelligent ass on that seat at Town Hall."

I swallowed hard, feeling bile creeping up my throat. My parents were right. Life wasn't a party. It was about time I started to pull my weight, grow up, and take some responsibility.

CHAPTER THIRTY-SEVEN

Austin

Telling Riley about the underbelly of Whitehaven wasn't the smartest idea I'd ever had. But now that she would be returning home without me, I figured it would serve her better to have a heads-up. I didn't want her to think she could go about town, prancing around in Prada and not draw some unwanted attention to herself. The last thing I needed was for the Reaper Cartel to learn that Bracken Roth's only daughter was living all alone, out in a remote ranger's cabin in the woods.

Rebecca owed me for what she did, but I didn't want her risking her life. They would be heading back to Lakewell by private jet, courtesy of the Fox King. Before we knew it, Beast and Rebecca had arrived, and the time had come for my wife and I to part ways.

"Time to go, babe." I nudged my wife gently.

Her parents would be joining us in a couple of weeks after they finish tying up loose ends here. They mentioned something about a quick stop via a courthouse, reinstating those nuptials that only mattered under human law.

"Behave yourself, Austin," Riley warned, pointing her finger at me. Her gaze bounced between Beast and me as if she couldn't decide who was worse.

"Scout's honor," I joked, holding my fingers up in a salute.

Beast snorted, shaking his head. Figured he would be better off staying mute through experience. Gianna, his mate, had trained him well. She was the reason the Beast of a bear shifter was now a reformed character. Well, semi-reformed. Fatherhood looked good on him and gave him a purpose in life. I was surprised Gia let him off the leash so he could come on this road trip with me.

"Like you were ever a Boy Scout," Riley scoffed with her signature eye roll.

Little did she know, I had been—still am. Those of us who wanted to train as Rangers were sent up into the mountains and learned to live off the land. We had to familiarize ourselves with our territory, get to know it inside out. That way, any foreign scents were picked up in a heartbeat, keeping the danger away from town.

"Play nice," I returned, pointing my finger at Riley, and then at Rebecca. "I don't want to have to rush back because you girls have gouged each other's eyes out."

Riley crossed her arms in front of her tits as if she resented that comment. Becca feigned innocence, like how dare I suggest she was capable of committing such an atrocity. They were so alike it was freaky.

"Are you ready?" Beast spoke in a voice that sounded like thunder rumbling across the sky. The kind of tone that sent all the ladies into a hormonal flurry. My sister, Stacey, could vouch for that, but that's another story. One that sent a cold shudder down my spine when I overheard her talking with her girlfriends.

I flashed my eyes to my wife, noticing how her

gaze was trained solely upon me. Once again, I thanked my lucky stars for the mate bond . . . and the fact that my comrade was a happily mated male.

"Are you kidding?" I turned to him with a shit-eating grin. "This is like a home away from home for a guy like me."

"Well, don't get too comfortable," Riley commented, uncrossing her arms so that she could give me a farewell embrace. "Or else you'll come home to find the cabin knocked down and a condo in its place."

That wouldn't surprise me in the slightest. Riley would stamp her mark on it somehow. My humble abode wasn't exactly the Four Seasons. So, if she felt the need to drag it by the balls into the twenty-first century, then she could be my guest. Interior design wasn't exactly my strong point. It couldn't hurt to add a few feminine touches here and there.

"Try to relax and listen to what Rebecca tells you," I advised, enjoying one last squeeze of her ass as we hugged.

Riley squeaked, and then pulled back so she could kiss me. Beast cleared his throat, and I got the hint that he was itching to get a move on.

"Bye, babe, have fun!" Riley chimed, putting on a brave face.

I slung the suitcase full of clothing that Bracken had put together for me (probably by a member of his entourage) and climbed into the army-style truck alongside Beast.

Both doors made a loud crack as they were pulled shut. "Was surprised to get a call from you so soon," Beast rumbled in his gravelly rough voice.

"I knew you missed me, honey," I joked, earning an amused chuckle from him.

He fired up the engine, which roared like a jungle cat, and I watched Riley's reflection in the side mirror get smaller and smaller as we took off down the drive.

"Mated life looks good on you," Beast remarked.

He was never one for small talk, so that stirred a whole load of curiosity right there.

"Thanks," I responded, unsure what to make of that.

"I'm glad you saw some sense and agreed to fight for the cause," he drawled, throwing the USC out into the conversation just as I anticipated he would.

And I was expecting that. Just not within five seconds of pulling out of Riley's street.

"Well, I figured trouble has a habit of finding me whether I go looking for it or not, so what the hell? Why not face it head-on instead?" I reasoned, staring out through the windshield.

"The Alpha Dog isn't blind. He knows what's coming," Beast mentioned as if he knew something I didn't.

But then I had been left out of the loop just lately, and that was mostly my fault. It wasn't exactly compulsory for me to live like a hermit, licking my wounds in that dingy wooden hut all on my lonesome. I chose to stay away from all the whispering and scaremongering. Ignorance was bliss after all.

"But he has been sidelined, and that doesn't exactly bode well for the rest of us," Beast added.

"He's still going ahead with that?" I asked, pausing to blow a forced breath through puckered lips. "That could take years. Even centuries."

Beast made a grunting sound in the back of his throat, which suggested that he agreed.

The Alpha was a man of science, an Einstein of his time. He had five long centuries to train that superb brain of his, absorbing so much knowledge that even someone as brilliant as Stephen Hawking could've learned a thing or two. The Alpha had succeeded in inventing a serum that was potent enough to reduce a pureblood vampire into dust. After the battle for Whitevale, he now had a legion of turned vamps wanting him to come up with a remedy that would cure them of their affliction. Sure, he could've sent them on their merry way or turned them into a pile of smoldering ash. Only, they had him by the balls. If his mother and sister hadn't been turned, then the Alpha Dog might have declined the challenge. Blood was, after all, thicker than water. Not even a man as powerful as Alec White could live with the guilt of turning his back on family.

"And that means that he's going to be spending a great deal of time away from Whitehaven," I deduced, figuring as much. "Shit!" I exhaled a stunned breath as I collapsed back in my seat.

While the dog was away, the gator would play.

"Shit indeed," Beast reinforced.

Riley

Rebecca King and I stood side by side in

awkward silence, watching the truck crawl away down the gravel drive.

Both of us waved our goodbyes with forced smiles plastered across our faces. The minute the truck veered out of sight, I rounded on her.

"Look, I'm a straightforward, level-headed person. Whatever you want to say to me, just come out and say it." I held my palms out at the side of me.

She smashed her lips together, placing her hands on her hips. "Fine," she muttered, then dragged in a lungful of air. "I'll start by saying that I'm sorry," she said while maintaining direct eye contact.

I was unprepared for that and it made me soften my approach. "Thank you," I accepted her apology.

She was a proud person; I could tell. An apology like that must have tasted like acid on her tongue. Still, she apologized nonetheless, and if I slapped away the olive branch, then that would make her the bigger person and me a spiteful bitch.

We both held our stare for a moment too long. Sensing the uneasiness between us, Rebecca began to talk about the treatment she was proposing.

"I know this seems a little rich coming from me, but I need you to trust me," she said, cringing at the end of her sentence. "I want you to know that I take my job seriously, and my level of commitment will be none other than impeccable. As of now, you're my patient, my responsibility. When I cure your mental blockage" — she described it as if it was like some sort of clogged drain or something like that — "it'll allow your natural instinct to come through."

I imagined her pulling out a sink plunger and clamping it down over my mouth, sucking out all the shit that festered away down there. I was curious to experience how it felt to shift, but then again, I was also apprehensive. I really did eat a mouse that night. A little furry mouse that I put in my mouth, chewed, then swallowed.

"Riley, it sounds a little daunting at first." She assumed it was the therapy that bothered me.

I wrinkled my nose. "Nah, I'm good." I shrugged it off as no big deal.

"But don't think it's all going to be mind-grueling psychology," she promised, smiling brightly. "The point to all of this is to make you feel comfortable in your fox form. Before you know it, you'll be racing through the forest, hunting down your supper."

That's what I'm worried about.

I forced a smile as if I'd been threatened to do it at gunpoint. As she turned away with a spring in her step, my cheeks dropped back down. There were pros and cons of being able to shift. And right now, Rebecca fancied herself as Florence fucking Nightingale, expecting me to haul my ass onto Dad's plane so that she could fix me. Something feral snarled from within me and made me wonder if I had completely lost my mind.

Grudgingly, I followed her onto the aircraft. It was a pity Gabe wasn't able to accompany me back to Whitehaven to prevent me from committing a felony. If Rebecca King thought for one second that I was going to chow down rodents during our time together, then she was dead wrong. We boarded the plane, and I did my utmost to ignore her. Almost an hour rolled by before Austin sent me a text. I opened it and saw it was a goofy selfie he had taken in a service station diner, with him about to devour a big, juicy burger. My stomach growled in protest, wishing I had eaten more than a chicken salad for dinner. I regretted not packing any snacks for the journey, searching through my purse to see if I could find a stick of gum or a mint imperial or something. No such luck.

"Is that your stomach I can hear?" Rebecca

inquired, chuckling at the gurgling sound coming from within me.

"I'm fine," I downplayed it. "Just a little hungry, that's all."

She pulled out a candy bar and snapped it in half for us to share, and I swear, I almost orgasmed at the sight of it.

"Thanks, you're a lifesaver," I expressed, cradling the chocolate-coated calorie stick with reverence.

Any ill will I harbored for the curvy bear shifter vanished in an instant. She was now the Messiah of all things tasty and wholesome. That was until my hunger struck again.

"I'm glad we have this opportunity to become friends," she said, making me feel guilty as sin. "Maybe when I find my mate, he and Austin can become friends too. Then our kids can grow up together and we can all laugh about this someday." She sounded genuinely hopeful about that.

Come on, Riley, you can do it!

"Yeah, I hope so too," I replied, thinking it might not be as far-fetched as it seemed.

You see . . . the bigger person. Who would've ever thought it possible?

CHAPTER THIRTY-EIGHT

Riley

The cabin felt empty without Austin around. Even though we were a couple, I still felt as if I was trespassing by being here without him. Rebecca seemed to know her way around Austin's home like the back of her hand. Not that she had been here before, but she had known him all her life. This made her able to navigate this space almost fluidly. Jealousy boiled within me like a bad case of stomach flu. I'd never had something I was afraid of losing before, which was setting off my natural defense mechanism. But I trusted my man. Mates were faithful. I had to stop all this jealous nonsense and try harder to make her my friend rather than my enemy. It took ages for me to get to sleep, but when I did, I slept like the dead.

The sound of the birds chirping their early morning song prevented me from sleeping past my mobile phone alarm. Sunlight seeped in through the threadbare curtains and flooded the room with a hazy yellow glow. I exhaled a heavy sigh, knowing I would have to get up and face Rebecca, who was sleeping downstairs on the sofa.

Reluctantly, I slumped out of bed and stuffed a pair of brown Gucci flip-flops onto my feet. Austin's T-shirt hung down to my knees as I stood and stretched. I could hear movement downstairs and knew my houseguest was already awake and mobile.

Great, let the fun and games begin.

I wasn't looking forward to this therapy and learning how to shift. I wished there could be some other way to jumpstart my ovaries, but apparently, there wasn't. Austin would be back in a matter of days. Hopefully, we would make substantial progress before he returned. My fingers gripped the smooth wooden banister rail as I descended the stairs, each step creaking in protest like an old geriatric riddled with arthritis.

"Would you like some coffee?" I called out, making friendly conversation.

I stopped dead in the doorway of the kitchen upon witnessing Rebecca maneuvering herself fluidly around Austin's humble domain. She let the utensil drawer close over with a soft rattle and then spared an over the shoulder glance my way.

"I was just making some," she mumbled, holding a teaspoon up as evidence.

A twang of jealousy twisted my insides as if her touching his things was a form of territorial sabotage. Austin told me about their conversation in the limo. He mentioned that she divulged her feelings for him, but he also told me that she had accepted that those feelings were unrequited. In the short time that I had known Austin, he never gave me any reason to doubt him. I knew I had to fully trust Rebecca King for this therapy of hers to be a success. But it was in my nature to be suspicious. This was another one of life's obstacles I would have to overcome all on my lonesome. Austin couldn't help me with this. This was between Rebecca King and me.

"Here," she said while pouring some freshly brewed coffee into two mugs. "Let's have breakfast, and then we'll make a start."

I guess the first test would be to drink the coffee.

"Thanks," I replied, bringing the mug to my nose to sniff the contents.

The smokey aroma caused my parched mouth to salivate, prompting me to give in to the velvety taste. I blew away the steam before taking a sip.

"Don't worry, I haven't poisoned it," she mentioned, causing me to splutter.

A wry smile spread across her lips as I wiped my coffee splattered mouth with the back of my hand.

Bitch! That's totally something I would say.

I reached for a dish towel that was hanging over the oven door handle and used it to mop up the rest of the moisture. Rebecca turned from me, chuckling to herself as if that was the highlight of her morning. She sauntered over to the kitchen sink where she rinsed her empty mug and left it to drain on the metal dish rack. My eyes raked around the simple oak kitchen, making a mental note of how we should redecorate. I wondered whether Austin would mind if I changed a few things, maybe add some matching appliances, and get rid of the salt and pepper shakers that were designed to look like a pair of tits. Rebecca spared an over the shoulder glance after grabbing a fresh dish towel from the cupboard under the sink.

"According to the weather report, it's likely to rain this afternoon. If we want to kickstart the treatment, we ought to leave now." She turned to face the window and pulled back the red gingham curtains, using the hooks on either side to pin them back.

"All right, just let me go and change," I replied, tipping the remnants of coffee down the drain and setting the mug down in the washbowl.

I figured that while she was playing hostess, she could wash my dirty mug out too. Her face scrunched with outrage as I flounced back upstairs, leaving her to it.

As I sifted through my luggage to find some suitable outdoor leisurewear, I could hear Rebecca huffing and puffing downstairs, muttering about why it was taking me so long to get ready. It was all right for her, little miss organized. I was in a tricky predicament. My wardrobe didn't exactly accommodate outdoor activities. The best I could find at such short notice was a pair of Gucci sweatpants and a matching hoodie, and a pair of sneakers that had the logo stitched into the sides with glitzy golden thread. I finished the look with a Khloe Kardashian sweatband in Aztec gold. Rebecca came up the stairs to spy on me as I was fixing it into place across my forehead, then paused in the doorway.

"What the actual fuckery is all of this?" She eyed my outfit choice with scrutiny. "J. Lo called. She said she wants her old look back," Rebecca quipped, then covered her mouth with her French manicured fingers as she chuckled.

I turned to face her, placing my hands on my hips, and inhaling a long intake through my nose.

"This is the best that I could find at the last minute," I replied, ignoring the amusement that highlighted her face. "Not all of us can pull off the 'sponsored by Nike' look as well as you do," I retorted, regarding her gym bunny attire.

She looked like some plant-eating Yoga instructor, the way she was dressed in three-quarter-length leggings, a bright green vest top, and colorful training shoes.

Rebecca responded with an exaggerated eye

roll, then walked away from me with an amused smirk on her face.

Were we bonding? Was it me, or was this considered an exchange of friendly teasing?

I'd never experienced this before. Not in the cut-throat world of the high-class bitch elite. Women generally spat venom at one another before plotting their social demise behind their back. This face-to-face brutal honesty was nothing new to me, but the fact that there was no malicious intent lingering behind those words was like a whole new level of communication.

Rebecca led me out past the small plot of land that Austin had claimed as his backyard. The blade of his ax was buried deep into the tree stump where he had flung it the last time he was here. The cool morning breeze held moisture from when it rained during the night. I could feel the soft pattering of dampness tickle my face. The ground was still wet but drying in patches where the light kissed the ground. The fast-moving clouds that hovered overhead looked ominous with patches of angry gray swirling amongst them. Rebecca was right. At some point during the morning, we were in for another heavy downpour.

I filled my lungs with a fresh intake of clean

forest air, almost tasting the earthy loam and wet pine at the back of my tongue. It reminded me of the time where I thought those tree-shaped car fresheners actually smelled like the forest when in fact, they were nothing in comparison. It was this forest scent that I associated with Austin: the scent of fresh pine, wood, earth, and the great outdoors.

CHAPTER THIRTY-NINE

Riley

"Are you feeling all right, Riley?" Rebecca inquired, giving the top of my arm an affectionate pat as we walked.

"Yeah," I replied with a weak, breathy smile.

The anxiety began to churn the contents of my stomach, but thanks to the memories that Austin and I had made down at the falls, it managed to placate it and hold it at bay. I clung to the image of him swimming naked in the cool, rippling waters.

The sight of him floating on his back, his wet hair brushed back off his face, his vast masculine body bathed in the silvery rays of the moon, and the way the reflection of the stars imitated diamonds as the water cast their reflection back up at them.

I could remember exactly how I felt that night, ready to give my heart and soul to the man I barely knew, but a man I was born to love no less. Whether some people understood it or they didn't, soulmates were real, and when you managed to find the one the universe paired you with, you don't always stop to question logic and reason. It made me feel bad for Rebecca King because I knew what she was missing out on. Everyone deserved to be happy. Austin and I had stumbled upon one another by chance, back when neither one of us was looking. Maybe that was how fate worked its will.

"We don't have to go far," Rebecca explained while we walked, stepping over the fallen branches and loose bark chippings. "We just have to surround ourselves with the beauty of nature, preferably without any distractions."

She went on to advise that I calm myself with some easy breathing techniques: in through the nose and out through the mouth. I could feel it already start to take effect. My anxiety had faded into nothing, and I started to appreciate the calming atmosphere that swaddled me with comfort. I was not saying I was ready to sit around a campfire, toasting marshmallows, and singing "Kumbaya", but I was at ease with taking a chaperoned walk through the forest without the need for a GPS tracker and a flare gun. I wasn't knocking this progress. Not at all. I only wished I had thought to bring a bottle of water along for the trip because my mouth was feeling as dry as the Sahara Desert.

"This looks like a good place to start," Rebecca suggested, looking around the dense forest that surrounded us. "You won't have to worry about prying eyes because there's nobody around here for miles."

I wrinkled my nose as I recalled something that Austin once told me. "Isn't there another cabin out here?" I vaguely remembered. "I'm pretty sure that Austin said that a wolf family was living out here." I thumbed behind me as if I knew exactly where that was, which was funny because I couldn't even tell which way led back to the cabin. Without Rebecca, I would be so screwed.

Rebecca almost choked on thin air. "Wolf family—that's the understatement of the century," she spluttered, then swatted the air in dismissal. "They won't be bothering us. The Bennetts are practically a whole pack of their own," she mentioned, then gazed dreamily into the thicket. "But to think, having four gorgeous men at your beck and call, waiting on you hand and foot and worshiping you in bed each night. That mate of theirs is one lucky bitch. But don't ever let her catch you saying that. She's territorial over her mates."

I flared my eyes wide as I replied, "Don't worry. I'm fully content with what I have at home, thanks."

Rebecca made a face that suggested she wished that she had something in comparison. "Maybe one day, perhaps," she mumbled, trying to instill a level of optimism in her voice.

The girl needed reassurance. That was my cue to step in and say something to reinforce that thought.

"It'll happen when it happens," I told her, nodding my head as if I was certain of it. Rebecca smiled a sad smile that was gone in a flash. "Look, if it can happen to me, then that means there's hope for everyone," I added, coaxing a genuine smile from her.

An awkward silence fell around us where neither of us knew what to say next, then Rebecca clapped her hands together and suggested that we make a start.

"Okay so, I need you to focus," she coached, placing her hands on top of my shoulders, and looking me level in the eyes. "You have to clear your mind of all thoughts and picture yourself standing amongst the forest in the form of a fox."

I gave a sharp nod of my head to indicate that I understood. Rebecca took a few steps back to maintain a safer distance, then I exhaled a forced breath, rolling my shoulders and giving a little motivational bounce to psyche myself up.

"All right, clear my thoughts," I muttered to myself as I closed my eyes and mentally erased everything that didn't belong in there.

"That's it," Rebecca praised, assuming I had followed the instructions correctly. "Now picture yourself as a fox."

Now that was the tricky part, picturing what I thought I would look like as a fox. The image of coarse red fur with a dash of white beneath the chin, tip of the tail, and paws sprang to mind. In my mind's eye, I began to envision two pointed ears and a thin snout, sharp teeth, and amber-colored eyes. I could feel my skin beginning to tingle as the strange sensation migrated through the current of my veins, gradually reaching the tips of my fingers and toes, spreading warmth that seemed to emanate through the pores of my skin.

"Easy," Rebecca warned, obviously witnessing something that I was oblivious to. "Just take it a little bit at a time."

It only lasted for a couple of seconds before the feeling was snatched away like a snapped elastic band. The overwhelming feeling of nausea hit me, and my knees gave way, forcing me to brace myself against the damp, earthy ground. I opened my eyes to the distorted image of dancing ferns and tree trunks that blurred in and out of focus. It wasn't enough to reunite me with the toast that I had for breakfast, but it was enough to put me out of action for a little while. Rebecca rubbed the center of my back as I struggled to grasp a steady breathing pattern. The first attempt had proven too much for my suppressed genes, leaving me feeling weak and lethargic. I knew I couldn't push myself any further today.

"This wasn't going to happen overnight," Rebecca soothed.

She then placed her hand under my arm to help me stand.

"I said that it was going to take time before you see anything substantial," she reassured with logic.

I wasn't disappointed. If anything, I was impressed that the first attempt helped me to feel something. I couldn't wait to call Austin and share the good news.

"It's a start, right?" I groaned, wrapping my arm around her shoulders for support.

Rebecca took most of my weight while we walked back across the rugged terrain.

"It is, and to celebrate, why don't we hit one of the bars here in Lakewell?" she suggested, making me an offer I could hardly refuse. A night on the tiles with an endless supply of alcohol and no paparazzi.

"I need a nap first, then a long soak in a warm bath," I replied, fighting hard not to yawn.

Yikes! I had barely been awake for a few hours and already I was itching to crawl back into bed. Whatever happened back there had drained me of all my energy. All I could think about was sleeping for a week, then ordering everything from the take-out menu that was stuck to the side of the fridge.

We arrived back home just as it had started to

rain. The patchy lawn that spread around the cabin was soon flooded with a river of rainfall. As I glanced through the kitchen window, I watched how each droplet bounced off the muddy ground like scattered pebbles.

I filled a glass of water from the tap and brought the rim to my lips. I had never taken a drink straight from a tap before. My usual choice of water came from a mountain-fed aquifer from the southern region of Argentina. That particular spring was five hundred meters below the ground and was surrounded by twenty acres of untouched forest. I prefer it to be chilled between forty-nine to fifty-five degrees. It was the equivalent of drinking heaven in a bottle and came with a price tag of six dollars per 750ml. The thought occurred to me that my old habits seemed utterly ridiculous right about now, especially as I guzzled down the cool, fresh liquid that was filtered straight from the mountains of Forest Hills. Water was water when you were thirsty. To be honest, I couldn't even taste the difference.

Rebecca claimed the small kitchen table as her temporary workspace during her stay. She opened her laptop and began replying to some of the emails that pinged through while she was making a fresh pot of coffee. The stress lined her face as she read some of the comments, and it let me see that her clients' problems weighed heavily on her mind. Rebecca cared about the people she helped. I could see that she took her role seriously, and that was why she had earned the solid reputation that Austin spoke highly of.

"Shit," she muttered, getting annoyed with the dongle that was plugged into the side of the device. "I wish Austin had Wi-Fi," she grumbled something we both agreed on. "I keep losing signal, and the attachments won't fucking load."

"Do you mind if I go lie down for a bit?" I asked, not wanting to be rude and just leave her there.

Her eyes cut to me, her frown lines leaving deep divots across her forehead. "No, not at all, but if you hear a smash, it'll be me throwing the laptop through the window," she half-joked, saying something else that was totally like me.

I left her to it and went upstairs to lay on Austin's bed, cocooning myself in the comforter because it still smelled of him. I wasted no time in calling him, just like I promised him I would. I was tempted to let my fingers wander south as I listened to the deep, husky tones of his voice. The only thing that was stopping me was the fact that Rebecca was downstairs and could no doubt hear and scent everything that took place. So, I resisted the temptation and kept the conversation clean.

For now.

CHAPTER FORTY

Riley

"You'll never guess what happened!" Austin couldn't contain the excitement in his voice. "Beast let the tour lady touch his biceps, and we got tickets to the exclusive VIP tour around Elvis's private collection," he gushed, and I heard Beast grunt from somewhere in the room, which confirmed what Austin just said was true.

"I'm so glad that you're having a great time," I replied, feeling pleased for him.

"What about you, honey? How did the first

therapy session go?" Austin asked, sounding a little cautious. "You two are getting along, I hope?"

"We haven't killed each other yet, if that's what you're asking." I kept my response a little vague, just to mess with his head.

I heard an ominous chuckle from Beast rumbling down the line, no doubt having just heard me mention the one thing that Austin had been fretting about during their trip. Austin's pause let me know that my assumptions were right.

"I like her. She's nice," I told him, hearing him exhale a huge sigh of relief.

"Thank God," he mumbled, sounding as if that took a load off his mind.

"We're going out tonight to celebrate," I mentioned before telling him how the first session went.

Austin took the news positively, telling me this was a great start, and I shouldn't try to force things. He also made me promise not to wander into the sketchy parts of town, telling me where all the ruffians hung out and how they'd devour a peach like me.

"Just stick with Becca and you'll be fine," he counseled. "As for the treatment, it's all good news."

Our conversation diverted back to today's progress. "The last thing you want is to suffer a forced shift."

I cringed at the thought.

"Austin?" My voice came out a strangled whisper. "Does it hurt while shifting?" I asked, unable to recall every single detail when it happened to me.

Maybe it hurt so bad my brain decided to block out the trauma.

"A little," he answered honestly, but from the dismissive tone of his voice, it indicated that it wasn't as bad as it seemed. "Mom always says it's like childbirth; she describes it as a bearable sort of pain that you can handle again and again without being put off by it. I mean, if it were to hurt so bad, then we would only shift once, right?"

I guess he had a valid point.

"Just like if childbirth was so excruciatingly painful, then people would only have one child?" I thought about the woman who had given birth to quadruplets and wondered if she had birthed them naturally or whether they were delivered by cesarean.

I found myself mindlessly crossing my legs under the comforter with sympathy.

"I can't wait until you're pregnant with my

cub." Austin lowered his voice to a low rasp, sending a tingling sensation straight to my clit.

Oh, fuck it!

The bedroom door was closed, and the window was slightly open. The pattering sound of raindrops formed the background noise. I could be quiet, and it wasn't as if Austin were here to pound the headboard against the wall.

"Babe?" The husky tone of my voice gave him a subtle hint of what I was thinking about.

"Are you thinking dirty thoughts while you're lying in our bed?" he asked, sounding thrilled about that.

"Maybe," I hinted, "Can you go somewhere where you can be alone?"

Austin chuckled. "Beast just left to buy beers. He will be gone for about ten to fifteen minutes . . . why?"

"I want you to talk dirty with me and touch yourself at the same time," I told him, hearing his breath release with surprise. "I'm completely naked in bed, and I'm brushing my fingers over my pussy, imagining you're touching me. I'm getting wetter and wetter just thinking about it."

Austin's breath caught in his throat. Then I heard the jingling sound of a belt buckle being released, followed by the sound of a zipper being pulled down, and the loose change jingling in his pocket as it hit the floor. I almost forgot that he was used to pleasuring himself while living the lonely life of a bachelor. He must've been a dab hand at whipping his pants off in record timing.

"Go on, give it to me, baby," he replied in a breathy moan. "I was hard the second I heard your voice."

The fact that he jumped at the opportunity almost caused me to laugh out loud, but then I heard the distinct pounding of flesh and knew that he was jerking off to the sound of my voice. My pussy clenched at the thought.

"Tell me what you want to do to me right now?" I asked, delving my finger into my center to moisten it, then dragging it around the engorged nub at the height of my arousal.

The electrifying feeling caused my toes to curl as I played, remembering how good I was at delivering myself a decent service. Our conversation was filthy and breathy, both getting lost in the moment.

"I want you to swallow my cock down your throat and let me empty my balls inside you," he rasped, his voice sounding desperate and full of need. I heard the crack of a lid, followed by the wet sound of liquid as he jerked himself.

"I'm pretending that this hotel body lotion is your juices sliding down my cock," he groaned, spurring me to work my clit faster.

"Imagine me sliding down onto it and seating myself on your lap, arching my back slightly as I bounce upon it," I encouraged, giving him a visual. "Fuck, Austin, you're so big!"

"Oh yeah, I love the way your tits bounce, lookin' all perky and waiting to be sucked," he breathed, sounding close to cumming by the way he rushed his words.

Lights danced in my vision, my finger hitting the detonator button of my pleasure center, "Austin, fuck me harder!" I begged, needing one final filthy word to tip me over the edge. "Take control and fuck me however you want."

"I'd pull you off me and flip you over so that you can suck my cock while I eat your pussy at the same time, because you're my filthy little cum-slut, and you love to be fucked like a dirty whore, don't you?" By the vehement tone of his voice, he had lost all self-control.

"Yes! Oh God, that's it!" I panted, my pussy clenching into tight spasms as I flooded the bottom sheet with the essence of my climax, lights flashed behind my eyelids as I came fast and hard.

Austin roared a strangled cry as he chased his release, then his heavy panting rattled down the other end of the line, followed by his satisfied groan.

"Fuck, woman, what have you done to me?" He chuckled breathlessly.

My body trembled beneath the softness of the comforter, coming down from my euphoric high.

"Awoke a sexy beast, I hope," I replied as equally spent as he sounded.

"Speaking of a Beast, I think he just pulled into the parking lot," Austin informed, sounding as if he needed to hurry to hide the evidence. "Gotta go, babe. I need to spray some cologne and haul my ass to the shower before he gets here. I'll call you tonight."

"Bye, honey," I returned, ending the call so that I could roll over in seventh heaven and sleep like a log.

Rebecca showered and changed before I woke, which left the bathroom free for me to use at my disposal. By the time I had finished, the room had filled with the sweet scent of fruit-infused steam. I brushed my teeth, then set my long red locks into heated rollers.

"Hey, does this look okay?" Rebecca asked as she came to my room, wanting some advice on the outfit she brought with her.

She turned from side to side in a white belted shirt dress and brown leather boots.

"You look great," I complimented her truthfully.

The black and gold embroidered catsuit and golden twist heels I had chosen to wear were both one-of-a-kind designs, but after I saw how Rebecca was dressed, they seemed way over the top for a quiet meal in town. It made me think about what Austin said about trying to fit in. I would stand out a mile in a flashy, designer outfit. What was I thinking?

"Have you decided what to wear yet?" she asked.

I scrunched my nose and stood in front of where my catsuit was laid out on my bed to hide it. "I'm just gonna finish my hair and makeup and then I'll decide."

It wasn't just the outfit. I would need to rethink my entire life. I couldn't wait to become part of the community here at Whitehaven and begin my role as an ambassador. Accepting a seat on the council alongside my father was not only a pleasure but an honor. Tonight, I wanted to go out and get a feel for the place and mix with some of the locals, but it was more than that. I wanted to fit in around here. I wanted people to like me. This was my fresh start, and I wasn't going to blow it. The locals wouldn't necessarily know about my checkered past in the human world unless they took an interest in human current affairs, and as far as I was aware, the country folk around these parts couldn't give a rat's ass because they had bigger things to worry about. They were farmers, builders, carpenters, and rangers. Outdoorzy types who didn't much care for watching television. I wondered whether they were all as accommodating as Austin's family had been, and the Whites who I had briefly just met.

"There's just one minor detail that I have to warn you about." Rebecca cringed, baring her teeth in apology.

I retrieved my makeup bag and tipped it onto the bed so that I could find the blasted eyeliner that always found its way to the bottom.

"What's that?" I muttered, not paying much attention because now my fingers were covered in glitter from the eyeshadow that had crumbled and spilled everywhere.

Fuck my life!

"It's been announced all over the Whitehaven news that you are Bracken Roth's daughter and that you have been appointed a seat on the United Shifter Council," she mentioned, grabbing my attention because I knew that this was more important.

I huffed a defeated sigh. "Great. I bet they're making a meal out of it."

"Don't worry. It's nothing bad," she reassured me. "If anything, they're singing your praises. And for a good reason, too. Our people need strong leadership." She took a seat on the edge of the bed while I dusted the glitter from my fingers. "I've always been a loyal supporter of Alpha Alec and the order he's enforced across the state, but he's not been around much lately. That's when the Reaper will come out to play. And with you being the Fox King's daughter, and Alec's goddaughter, you're like bait to him."

I felt the color drain from my body as all the blood seemed to rush to my feet. Those were two big enough reasons to paint a target on my back. Not that I knew I had a godfather until now.

"Me?" I gulped hard, "You think he'll try and hurt me?"

Rebecca made a face that suggested she didn't know for sure.

"I highly doubt that he would go as far as to hurt you, Riley. Not when he's trying to get into the community's good graces. He wants a seat on the council. That's all he's ever wanted. And as the reptile community is borderline extinct, there's a loophole which allows him to be seated by default."

My jaw hung open as I struggled to process everything she just said.

"He befriended the Luna of Whitevale a couple of years ago, which Alec wasn't too thrilled about. She's all for giving him a chance, but all he needs is for one more member to back him, and he's home and dry," she revealed, her words somber and foreboding.

I felt my shoulders drop as I spoke. "He thinks that I'm easy pickings because I haven't grown up in the community?" I started with an aggravated huff because I was sick of men underestimating me.

Rebecca shook her head timidly. I could see she was worried, and that frightened me a little. "He's pissed because you've been welcomed in with open arms." She hesitated, struggling to find a diplomatic way to say what she wanted to say. "Every minor discretion, scandal, public fuck-up of any kind, and he's going to either exploit you as an unsuitable candidate, or he's going to blackmail you with the leverage."

She stood to her feet, her eyes swamping with sympathy, "He can't know about your current situation, Riley." She applied pressure to her statement as if that were of huge importance. "Or it's game over."

Rebecca's expression darkened. "I'm scared that if he gets in, Whitehaven will be screwed."

CHAPTER FORTY-ONE

Riley

Rebecca and I had been rehearsing the plan over and over as I put on a pair of stonewashed jeans and a pair of brown tassel boots. I finished tying my pink plaid shirt at the front, leaving my belly button exposed. I was toying with the idea of getting a piercing, but perhaps I should talk to Austin first. He might not like it.

Rebecca put away her hairbrush and turned to me. "Like I said: baby steps. You show your face around Forest Hills first, then venture into the hot spots of Lakewell at a later date," she advised, wanting to snuff out all the gossips. "It'll stop people from making their assumptions about what Bracken did or didn't disclose to you."

This was necessary to avoid any bad press and damaging rumors that could slur my father's reputation on the council. My seat could be challenged if people knew about my furry little problem or lack thereof.

Dad called an hour ago to inform me that I would need to go to the United Shifter HQ within the next few days to formally accept the role. I needed to be officially sworn in, just like a human government official. This was one of the biggest responsibilities of my life. My first real job. I wasn't sure how I would feel about that, but since coming back here, I was ready to undertake the role. I wanted to learn more about my kind; most of all, I wanted to make a difference. Austin had rubbed off on me. I was shedding the layer of selfishness that had encapsulated me all my life. Coming here to Whitehaven had awakened the women inside, and like a beautiful butterfly who had burst free of her ugly restraints, Riley Roth was now laid to rest so that Riley Rayne could step up and take her rightful place.

"Shall we have another glass of wine while we wait for the cab?" I suggested, deliberating whether it was such a good idea.

"Yeah, why not?" Rebecca didn't need to ask twice.

We probably shouldn't. I needed to maintain a level head if I was to remember the plan without a hiccup. Pun intended. The last thing I wanted was to be accosted by the Reaper and slur my words in an act of feeble retaliation. The guy was an alligator shifter. I was a fox. I vaguely remembered the story about The Gingerbread Man: the one where the fox managed to trick the Gingerbread Man into riding across the lake with him, then later devoured him as he stepped onto his nose to avoid the rising water. The more I heard about this Reaper guy, the more anxious I was about meeting him. He wasn't some naïve little cookie; he was a mob boss. He was the bad guy in the story, and I was the novice fox.

"You're overthinking things again," Rebecca pointed out. "I can tell, I'm a therapist."

I was. She was right. "I know," I admitted. "Let's go through it one last time."

Rebecca nodded. "We're just two girlfriends going out for dinner." She shrugged simply. "We let people see that we're friends and that everything's peachy." She winced her eyes as if she had jumped ten steps ahead. "If that's okay with you?"

I swatted my hand in dismissal. "Sure, you're my BFF now. Austin has Beast."

Both of us chuckled at that. Rebecca dropped her shoulders with relief. "That means a lot to me." We both paused to take another sip of wine to avoid any awkwardness. "Okay, we show our faces during dinner. Nothing swanky, just a casual restaurant. You're going to mingle with the locals and win them over with your charming personality."

"Right. And if the Reaper just so happens to rear his ugly head?" I asked.

"Then you politely explain to him that if he wishes to discuss matters, then he has to arrange an appointment just like everyone else. He isn't going to want to talk about his garbage collection dates or issues with his taxes." She chuckled to herself. "He can't take a shit these days without Alpha Alec being notified about it, so don't worry. He's not stupid enough to try anything. Rumor has it that he's trying to win the affections of his mate, so be prepared for him to try to sucker you into a sob story," she warned, taking on a foreboding tone.

"He's one of your patients, isn't he?" I asked off the bat.

Rebecca blanched. "Huh? I . . . I," she stammered, not knowing what else to say.

I gave an assured shrug. "I could tell by your aggressive body language when you were talking about him, and the sarcastic tone in your voice."

"I'm not allowed to discuss it! Doctor-patient confidentiality!" she squealed, placing one hand against her chest. "But that doesn't mean that I can't warn you about him. That guy gives me the creeps. His mate is better off without him, that's for sure. Thank goodness she's tucked safely back in Whitevale where his scaly claws can't reach her."

The way people used reptilian characteristics to describe him made me form a monstrous image inside my head like one of those alien lizard guys from the 80s movie franchise, V. Just the thought of that sent a cold shiver down my spine. It was at that point a car horn honked outside the cabin.

"Drink up, the cab is here," I urged Rebecca. "There's no need to waste good wine that costs a whopping five dollars a bottle," I joked sarcastically.

Rebecca spluttered with laughter. "You know, after a couple of mouthfuls, all wine tastes the same.

I lived on this shit during my college years," she muttered while screwing the cap back onto the bottle.

I had never seen a wine bottle with a screw-on cap before. I raised my brows as I thought about that. My wine had always been handed to me in fine-cut crystal, so I would never know.

The cabs around here were all Jeeps. I suppose they had to be, considering this was a hilly town. Most of the dwellings were high up in the mountain range. Rebecca tried to persuade the cab driver to accept the fare, but he wouldn't take our money. I guess it paid to have a mother-in-law as treasured as Eliza Rayne was. Money wasn't the only thing that gave you status. Having a caring and considerate nature went a long way too. I realized that now.

We were dropped off at the familiar town square of Forest Hills. I had been here once before to sign the mating license. The whole place screamed old country and reminded me of the old western movies my dad used to watch. I was glad to have taken Austin's advice and dressed more like the locals.

"You're going to love it here." Rebecca's voice rang with excitement. "Rosie's pot roast is to die for."

"Pot roast?" I said, cringing. "If it's as good as Eliza's stew, then I'll give it a try."

The sound of music and friendly chattering greeted me as I stepped into the rustic establishment. A smoky, meaty scent wafted from the kitchen door as it opened. The atmosphere was laid-back and homely, a place to sit back and relax as well as fill your stomach.

My eyes were never still. All I could see was red and white gingham everywhere. The curtains, the table cloths, the seat cushions, and even the staff wore it in the form of aprons, shirts, neckerchiefs, and scrunchies. They even had a stuffed squirrel on the bar next to the tip jar, and it was wearing a pair of gingham dungarees. Each time the waitresses put their tips into the jar, they'd pat the squirrel's head.

I shot Rebecca a side glance, and she responded with a stern eye signal. "Act natural," she hissed from the corner of her mouth. "Just remember, each shifter community has different customs that may seem a little weird to you."

I fluffed my hair as we waited by the door to be seated. People looked up from where they were sitting, giving me their full evaluation. I knew they could smell me and knew exactly who I was. The judgment had already started, and now it was a matter of proving to them that I wasn't a stuck-up bitch. They could approach me. I was super approachable.

Rebecca huffed. "Scratch that, just copy me. Your fake smile is scaring the children."

CHAPTER FORTY-TWO

Riley

My cheeks relaxed and I shot her the stink-eye. One of the waitresses noticed us and smiled. She grabbed two menus from the counter area and made her way through the maze of tables to get to us.

"Welcome to Rosie's! Table for two?" she asked cheerfully.

I glanced between Rebecca and the pretty waitress, wondering whether it was a trick question. "Uh . . . yeah, there's two of us."

She chuckled, scrunching her nose. "I hope you like it up here. I know it is a little different from what you're used to in the city."

"It's fine," I answered quickly. "I love Forest Hills. Everyone here is super nice. I feel so welcome."

There were a few raised mugs as a gesture of cheers, and a couple of guys returned a welcome home as we were escorted to our table. I found myself smiling back, completely unforced this time. Now all I needed was for my husband to come home and my mind could finally rest. Being apart from him was pure hell. I wondered if he felt the same way about being so far away from me, or whether he was enjoying the peace.

The waitress gave us a few extra minutes to peruse the menu, then returned with the drinks we ordered. She flipped open her little notepad and pulled the pen out of her ponytail.

"Have you guys decided what you want to order?" she asked.

Both Rebecca and I answered at the exact same time. "The pot roast."

Rebecca looked back at me, impressed. The waitress scribbled that down before walking over to the counter. She tore off the square piece of paper and impaled it onto a spike on the countertop. As her hand slammed down on the bell beside it, an enormous bearded guy came sauntering through the saloon-style doors and snatched it up to read. He then sniffed the air, his eyes snapped to mine, and his brows disappeared beneath his floppy fringe. I would have to get used to being the center of attention, but all I wanted to do was to blend in and eat my dinner. More than anything, I wanted these people to see me as a regular person, doing everyday, mundane things. I wasn't a socialite any longer; I was a wife and soon-to-be council official.

Rebecca's gaze lifted above my head as a shadow loomed across the table. We had company.

"Hi, I was wondering if you could spare me a moment of your time, Councilor Rayne," a young-looking woman asked as she came to stand at the side of our table. She had a small boy tucked against her side.

"Yes, of course. Although, I'm not yet official," I pointed out.

"But you will be taking the role?" she asked hopefully.

Her enthusiasm humbled me. "I . . . um . . . yes, of course."

She breathed out a relieved smile. "Good. I'll be

glad to see another female on the council. Will you come down to the community center and take a look around? The volunteers would love to share their ideas with you."

She spoke so passionately about helping others that it struck a chord in my heart. I was shocked to learn they had to fundraise for everything and that their Council of Elders barely gave them a cent. Apparently, Forest Hills was divided into class categories that were not dissimilar to the human world. The council threw money at the wealthy areas and left the poorest to claw around in the dirt. It made me realize just how privileged I had been having never had to worry about money, paying bills, or where my next meal came from.

"I would be honored to help in any way that I can," I promised wholeheartedly.

And I meant that. Having listened to the struggles they faced, I found myself caring for people I had never met and wanting to make a difference in their lives. I only had to look into the eyes of that small boy huddled at her side and my heart clenched with emotion. These people needed a voice, and there was no one in the entire state of Whitehaven louder than me.

"Do you mean it, lady?" a stocky bearded guy

asked from where he was slouched at the adjacent table. "We rely on that center for everything. It really is the beating heart of our community."

His comment was rather abrupt, but I could tell by the genuine look of interest on his face that it was well-intended.

"Certainly I do. I want to help make a difference in every shifter town. Every issue that is brought to the table ought to be taken seriously, however big or small. My role is to be the people's advocate, and I intend to fulfill that position to the best of my ability."

The guy gave a satisfied grunt in response.

"Thank you," the young mom replied, bobbing her head in a grateful nod. "I guess I'll be seeing you at the community center," she asked hopefully.

"You can count on it," I assured her.

I watched them as they left the restaurant, saying goodbye to a few other people as they went. This town was close-knit. I figured everybody knew who everybody was. Rebecca and I chatted casually as we ate our dinner. Our evening was going so well, we decided to stop off at a quiet little bar across the street. Rebecca held open the door for me, which closed over with a loud creaking sound. I swear, it was like something out of an old cowboy movie. The music ceased to play, and everybody turned to stare in our direction. By the time we took a stroll toward the bar, the Dolly Parton song resumed playing and everyone continued to talk amongst themselves.

"We'll just have the one drink, then we'll call it a night," Rebecca suggested.

We had accomplished what we set out to do. I had shown my face around town, eliminating all cause for suspicion. Rebecca ordered two glasses of Merlot, and we carried them over to an empty booth for some privacy.

"Ugh, I need to pee," Rebecca grumbled, scrunching her face in a grimace.

"Well, go on then. I'm not holding your damn hand." I chuckled.

I gazed through the window as I sipped my wine, completely unfazed by the bustling bar around me. The next song to play was a Carrie Underwood song about cheating. I found myself smiling as I hummed along to the lyrics.

"S'cuse me, ma'am, but I'm gon' need to borrow your cellphone to call animal control. Seems we have a fox in the buildin'," some guy with a Cajun accent drawled.

I didn't even notice him approaching, too engrossed in my thoughts.

"How original." I rolled my eyes with a turn of my head, then they bulged wide. "Holy shit!" I muttered as the sheer magnitude of the guy had me spluttering for air.

My eyes raked up and along his intimidating frame, from his silver-tipped cowboy boots, right the way up to his vivid-green eyes. I could tell by the tattoos that peeked from the collar of his shirt and his rolled-up sleeves that he was completely inked from the neck down. Maybe beyond that, I could only speculate. Despite his gorgeous exterior, there was something dangerous lurking behind his reptilian eyes. It was like staring into a soulless, black chasm. At that moment, I knew exactly who he was. The Reaper. I could tell by the ominous vibe that made the underside of my skin itch. Death didn't follow this guy . . . he was death.

"I'm mated?" I flashed him my wedding ring as evidence. " If you're here to hit on me, then you're shit out of luck." I chose to play ignorant rather than show any sign of fear.

And anyway *"there's a fox in the building"*. Was that the best line he could come up with? That was almost worse than that cheesy Tennessee pick-up line about being the only ten I see.

I didn't much care for jerks who used lame pick-up lines. They only sounded cute when Austin used them sarcastically.

He placed a hand over his heart in a sincere gesture. "I apologize. I was just tryin' to be friendly."

I fidgeted uncomfortably in my seat. Trust Rebecca to choose this precise moment to empty her bladder.

"Friendliness is acceptable." I managed a chaste smile.

"Did ya mean what ya said 'bout bein' the people's advocate? Ya won' be discriminatin' against any particular species?" he asked, narrowing his eyes in a way that made me feel cross-examined.

How the hell did he know that I said those exact words?

I placed my glass down in front of me as he slid into the opposite side of the booth and propped his elbows on the table. From this proximity, I could see my reflection in his black vertical-shaped pupils. I thought I would be more scared when confronted by him, but at this moment, I felt fierce. He had been spying on me, and that pissed me off.

"I'm going to go out on a limb here," I said, not

giving a shit how sarcastic it sounded. "I take it you're the Reaper. I have to say, your reputation doesn't do you justice. I thought you'd be taller." I decided to maintain a cool facade, raising my hand way above my head to measure a greater height.

He studied me as I lounged back, casually sipping my wine. I didn't know if he was impressed by my feisty attitude or not. I was all out of fucks to give. Maybe the wine was giving me courage, or maybe he wasn't all that scary. I was cut from the same cloth as my father. We Roths didn't show weakness to our opponents. That was bad for business. The Reaper would have better luck trying to squeeze blood from a stone.

"That's me," he replied in a casual drawl. "You didn' answer my question though." He wagged his finger mockingly.

I sat up straight in my seat. "You were listening to my earlier conversation. Didn't anyone tell you that it's rude to eavesdrop?"

From the corner of my eye, I saw Rebecca freeze as she returned to our table. Her face paled as she noticed who was sitting in her seat. Her horror-stricken expression told me she had not orchestrated this. He had taken it upon himself to confront me here in town. To be honest, I preferred that he had chosen a public place rather than to turn up unannounced at the cabin.

"Ya got me." He held his palms up. "I'm guilty as charged." He flashed a million-megawatt grin that could've swept the panties off many girls. Thankfully, I was immune to assholes. "But I was intrigued by what ya said." He scratched his bottom lip with his thumbnail. "Ya really gon' give everyone a fair chance, withou' discriminatin'?"

There was a hopefulness in his voice I couldn't help but notice. He wasn't demanding, he was asking, and that surprised me. He didn't seem like a man who had to ask for something he wanted. He struck me as a man who took what he wanted and to hell with the consequences.

"That's the consensus," I responded pointedly. "Look, if you want to raise issues, then you'll have to schedule an appointment, just like everyone else. I highly doubt you'll manage to sway the council in favor of organized crime though." I hit home with the truth, noticing the flash of anger in his eyes.

There you have it, Crocodile Man. Take a number and stand in line along with everyone else.

"Yeah, but when ya take away the 'organized', you're just left with crime," he spoke in a warning tone that could've been mistaken as threatening.

"If I tell you that I'll get you a hearing, will you go away?" Our eyes were locked in a heated battle across the table.

"I'll leave ya alone, for now. But you make good on your word, or I guarantee y'all be seeing more of me." His harsh words delivered a deadly promise.

"Riley, come on . . . we're leaving," Rebecca interjected.

"You don't scare me." I continued to glare at the Reaper as I slid from my seat and bent down to grab my purse.

"Afraid of nothin', huh?" he muttered lazily. "Everybody's afraid of somethin'."

I could feel his seedy eyes on me as we left the bar. Rebecca must've been holding her breath because when she stepped outside, she began gasping for air.

"Oh my god! Are you okay?" Her voice was strained as if she had been close to tears. "What did he say before I came back?"

"I'll tell you once we get home," I assured.

I just wanted to get out of there as quickly as possible.

Rebecca hailed a passing cab. It barely had the chance to stop before we threw open the door and piled in. I whipped my phone out to reply to Austin's latest text, typing, *"I love you too. Everything is all under control here."*

"Aren't you going to tell him about what just happened?" Rebecca seemed incredulous. "I think that he would want to know about this."

"And worry him while he's miles away? No." I shook my head, stuffing my phone back inside my purse. "I need to concentrate on our therapy sessions, now more than ever."

Rebecca pursed her lips as she slouched back in the seat. She may not like this, but my main priority was Austin.

Not myself, for the first time ever.

CHAPTER FORTY-THREE

Austin

"Something's wrong," I grumbled, scowling at the vague text Riley sent.

Beast grunted, showing interest. He was busy focusing on the road and scowled through the windshield.

"Did she say as much, or have you just got a hunch?" he probed further.

Beast spared me a fleeting glance, cocking an eyebrow.

"It's more of what she's not saying," I answered,

seeing his face scrunch with confusion. "I got a strange feeling, a little while ago, like she was scared of something. I don't know . . ." My voice trailed off.

Beast exhaled a long breath and flared his eyes. It seemed my comment baffled him. "I'll never understand women," he muttered under his breath.

"Yeah, well, my woman can talk for hours without coming up for air, but now she's suddenly gone radio silent. That ain't right; something's wrong." I could feel it in my heart.

Beast sucked in a sharp intake through his nostrils, then released it as he spoke. "A silent female is a dangerous one. It means she's overthinking things. Either something's happened, or it's likely to. When a man falls silent, he's procrastinating. When a woman falls silent, she's plotting something big. Good thing we're on our way home so you can find out what that is."

My eyes flinched. "But then why would she feel afraid?"

"How the fuck should I know? She's your mate. What does your gut tell you?" Beast bounced his shoulders in a shrug.

Right now, my gut was telling me that the spicy beef tacos I ate for lunch were a really bad idea.

Every couple of minutes hot gusts of air escaped through my ass cheeks and I was sweating profusely. I rolled down the windows to blast some fresh air into the cabin of the truck.

"I'll feel a whole lot better when I get home, talk to Riley, and take the shit I've been holding onto for the last hour and a half," I told him.

Beast flung me a side glance. "Do you need me to pull over so you can crack one out in the bushes?"

"Nah, just step on it. I'll wait until we come across a gas station." I muttered, preferring to sit on porcelain in my human form than to squat and purge at the roadside.

We traveled through the night, passing the boundary of Whitehaven by dawn. Beast dropped me off at the edge of my drive, giving me a chance to check out the scent around my cabin. As soon as I was satisfied that the girls were safe and sound, I crept in through the back door, not wanting to disturb Becca as she slept on the couch. I toed off my boots and shucked off my jacket, draping it over one of the chair backs at the kitchen table. Everywhere looked clean and orderly, a clear sign that my absence had been taken full advantage of. The cabin was spotless. With a slight cringe on my face, I crept up each of the creaky stairs, hoping to surprise my wife with my early arrival. Only this surprise was on me because when I tiptoed into our room, the bed was made, and there was no sign of Riley. Her scent was everywhere. It sent me into a dumbfounded state of confusion. I tail-assed around and thundered down each step, only to find a vacant sitting room.

"Riley? Becca? Are you guys home?" I called out.

Silence filtered through the cabin as the sound of my voice cut off.

"Where the fuck?" I muttered under my breath, searching around for an obvious clue of their whereabouts.

Their purses were placed side by side at the foot of the couch. Two mugs were upturned on the sink drainer. Someone had eaten turkey bacon for breakfast, and the other opted for French toast. I could tell. The scent of failed cookery still lingered in the air because neither of them could cook for shit. Just as I spun around to face the back door, I saw that someone had taped a note to the back of it. I covered the space in three strides and snatched up the note. My eyes scanned across the words: "Austin, if you're back home before me, come and find us in the forest. My therapy is going great. I have a good feeling that today is the day. Love you, babe. Riley."

I exhaled a relieved sigh, knowing she was safe.

"She's fine," I mumbled, chuckling to myself.

I had myself all worked up over nothing. Not wanting the bother of putting my boots back on, I shed the rest of my clothing and shifted in the backyard. Maybe seeing me in my bear form would help Riley's animal side to come out of hiding. I had no idea if it would work or not, but anything was worth a shot.

Running on four paws was much faster than sprinting on two feet. I was able to cover twice the distance in half the time. The sound of feminine laughter chimed through the woodland . . . then I saw them. My wife and my best friend were getting along as though they'd known each other forever. The swell in my heart was almost powerful enough to lift me off my feet. The girls were smiling, sitting face-to-face and cross-legged in a meditational pose.

Do I just go on over and interrupt or . . .?

I hung around, unsure whether I should just wait for one of them to notice me. Rebecca muttered something from the corner of her mouth that made Riley's eyes fly open.

She whipped her head in my direction. "Austin! You're back!"

I walked like a klutz in my bear form, somewhere between a hop, skip, and a lumbered step until I came to a stop alongside her.

"We're emptying our minds," Riley informed me before going back to her meditative state.

"Sit and join us, Austin. The forest is peaceful this morning," Rebecca muttered, keeping her eyes closed.

Peaceful in the morning?

There was nothing peaceful about this forest during the early morning, I should know. I'd spent long enough out here, all alone, to memorize every chirp, squawk, croak, rustle, and all other early morning calls of the wild. What I found alarming was that I could hear nothing but the sound of the breeze rustling through the trees. It even looked calm out on the lake today, with barely a ripple on the glassy water. My sharp ears pricked up to full alert. The girls had no idea what this meant. Any ranger knows that a quiet forest was a deadly forest. It meant that all the wildlife had gone into hiding because a predator was lurking around. I reared up on my hind legs, stomping my front paws back down on the ground as a way to warn them. Both girls flinched back with shock, their eyes wide with fright.

"What is it, Austin?" Rebecca's voice was frantic.

As they scrambled to their feet, three gunshots blasted out through the air. I managed to lunge in front of the girls as sharp pains seared through my thigh and shoulder. A roar tore through my throat as another bullet pierced my chest. Then darkness snatched me before my body hit the ground.

CHAPTER FORTY-FOUR

Riley

The world slowed down as Austin's body hit the ground with a sickening thud.

"Austin!" My anguished scream reverberated off the trees.

Oh my God, he's been shot!

His brown fur darkened where it absorbed the flow of blood. I pressed my palms against the wounds, alternating between his thigh and shoulder, not knowing where the fuck to put my hands first. He was bleeding out like a punctured blood bag. I didn't dare to remove my hand from his chest, praying that the bullet had missed his heart because I could still feel it beating beneath my palm. It was faint, but it was there. My wedding ring disappeared beneath a river of crimson liquid, and I bawled over his body like a terrified child. There was so much blood and not enough of me to stem all the bleeding.

"Stay with me, please," I sobbed.

Rebecca rushed to my side, her trembling hands covering the exposed wound on his thigh. Another gunshot skimmed the ground by my feet, sending dirt flying up in the air. I didn't care about me. If he died, then I wanted to die with him.

"Fuck off back to where you came from!" Rebecca roared, her eyes wild with fury. "Riley, we have to get out of here."

"I'm not leaving him!" I cried.

Rebecca's torn expression told me that she felt the same way about leaving him, but this was a hopeless situation, which meant that staying here would be suicide.

"Those are hunters," she exclaimed. "They'll kill us."

"Help!" I screamed.

Who would hear us out here in the middle of the forest? Where are all the rangers?

This was Austin's post . . . and Austin hadn't been here for a week. He hadn't been patrolling the woods like he was supposed to have been, and now hunters had encroached onto his territory. This wasn't the perfect haven people thought it was. Hunters had come here once, and now they were back again. They'd never stop coming. It would take a miracle to keep them out.

Rebecca took off her T-shirt and started tearing it into strips.

"Tie this around his thigh, and I'll tie one around his shoulder. Quickly!" She handed me a scrap of material, and we set to work frantically.

More shots rang out through the forest, but they sounded as if they were firing in another direction. We seized our chance to try and drag Austin to a safer distance. He was heavy, so we didn't get very far. There was no chance in hell that Rebecca and I could get him to the cabin without being shot at. Whoever had surprised the hunters in the forest was doing it to give us a chance to run.

But I can't just leave him here.

As I glanced up, I saw two hunters standing at the edge of the lake, firing shots into the water. It churned and spit back at them with each bullet fired. Then, just like something out of a nature documentary about lake monsters, an enormous alligator broke through the surface and snatched one of the men in its deadly jaws. I wasn't prepared for it, and my heart jolted with shock. Bile rose up in my throat at the sight of his body being severed in half, blood bursting onto the gator, and splattering over the embankment.

A barrage of gunfire bounced off its scaly body as if it was made from bulletproof armor. Another hunter went down with a gargled cry. I looked away as his lifeless remains were flung into the lake. The powerful reptile charged into the forest amidst the sound of more gunshots and blood-curdling screams. My god, it could move fast.

"Now you know why he's called the Reaper," Rebecca breathed through skittered breaths. "Even Silvertips can't take him out. The guy doesn't just defy death; he *is* death."

I swallowed fast. "Well, for what it's worth, that guy just saved our asses," I expressed gratefully.

Austin's body began to convulse beneath our fingertips.

"Shit! He needs help," Rebecca said. "We need

to call Dr. Rayne. He's not healing because of the silver in his bloodstream."

I contemplated running to the cabin to retrieve my phone, but before I did, the Reaper stalked out of the tree line as naked as the day he was born, his huge cock bashing against his thighs.

"One fucker got away," he announced, thumbing behind him. His green eyes darted to Austin, and he wasted no time in offering some assistance. "We gotta get those bullets out," he ordered.

Rebecca cleared the tears from her eyes with the back of her hand. Her palms were covered with Austin's blood, and her sports top had turned from white to red. As I looked down, I saw my clothes were soaked in it too. I was no doctor, but I knew he was losing way too much too quickly.

"I can't lose him . . .," I chanted over and over, my teeth rattling in my mouth.

I was more than scared. I was completely fucking terrified.

"Hold him still," the Reaper advised. "This is gon' hurt like a son of a bitch, but I gotta get the silver out. Once it's out, he'll start to heal by himself."

We did as he said, listening to him because he

seemed to know what to do in an emergency. Austin shuddered as the Reaper plunged his finger and thumb into the wound on Austin's chest, so close to his heart.

"Come on . . . slippery little fucker . . ." the Reaper muttered as he struggled to get a grip.

Movement from the tree line drew my gaze toward it, and just like a movie frame slowing down, I saw the hunter who evaded the Reaper. He kneeled and peered through the telescopic sight of his rifle. That was when all hell broke loose.

Anger boiled in my veins, fueling my body with a fiery rage. I didn't realize that I was running toward him, dodging bullet after bullet as if I was as agile as the wind. He exhausted his rounds in the time it took me to cover the distance, then stood as if to turn and run. Why the fuck long grass was whipping me in the face, I'd never know, but then it dawned on me that I'd shifted! I had paws instead of fists. I might not be able to land a punch on that scrawny fucker, but I had a razor-sharp set of teeth.

And I used them.

His high-pitched scream was deafening, but as my mother always said, the best way to bring a man down was to attack their most sensitive part: his dick. I didn't let go, shaking my head from side to side. The more he tried to pull me off him, the harder I bit down. I tasted blood and knew that it was pretty much game over for hunter junior. Rebecca was beside me in a flash and grabbed the rifle, knocking him out with the butt end.

"Let's go. The rangers will find him," she urged before heading back to Austin.

Even if he woke, he was unarmed. He wouldn't get far now the scent of his blood was thick in the air. Someone would find him and finish the job. I padded alongside Rebecca, still drunk on adrenaline with the foul taste of blood on my tongue. Reaper hauled Austin onto his back so he could carry him to the cabin. My chest swelled with a newfound respect for the guy. He may be a dark stain on society, but at this moment, he was a hero.

"Gotta hurry." The Reaper's tone was strangely benevolent. For a guy who flipped the bird to the world, he seemed to care more than we gave him credit for. "The bullet next to his heart won't budge. I gotta cut in deeper. You might wanna call his momma. Gon' need somethin' to help with the pain after I'm done."

"But he's going to be okay, right?" Rebecca asked, keeping up with his strides.

"Not promisin' nothin'," he rumbled. "He got shot up pretty bad."

We reached the cabin within minutes. Each passing moment was vital. All I could think about was whether or not Austin would make it. He had to make it. I would trade places with him in a heartbeat. The Reaper would want something in return for helping us. I knew that. But right now, I would sell my soul to the devil if it meant that Austin would live.

Whatever the price.

CHAPTER FORTY-FIVE

Riley

The Reaper set Austin down on the kitchen floor, then started rummaging through the utility drawers for a knife. When he pulled out a bone-handled butcher's knife, I almost choked on my own heart.

Why didn't I go to medical school and do something useful with my life?

Rebecca's hand was shaking as she held the phone to her ear. And when Eliza answered the call, Rebecca rushed her words in a frenzy. My anxiety of being two feet tall and covered in fur set my nerves on overdrive. I was no use to anybody like this, especially if I had to perform CPR. Unfortunately for me, there wasn't a reboot button attached to my ass cheeks, so I had to solve this problem alone.

Okay, so how does this work?

Rebecca said that to shift, I had to focus on becoming a fox. So to shift back I just had to channel all of my thoughts into becoming human again. I squeezed my eyes shut and willed myself to change, thinking about my physical appearance, my arms, and my legs, hoping all my fingers and toes were intact when I was done. The transition was agonizing, but thankfully, it was a success.

"Austin!" I croaked, scrambling up to my feet.

I grabbed the nearest garment I could find: Austin's naked lady apron. I used that to cover my modesty, hiding my nudity with the image of a porn star's body, complete with pink nipple tassels and a heart-shaped bush. Personally, I couldn't give a shit what I looked like, but I knew Austin wouldn't appreciate me being naked in front of another man. All this, from head to toe, belonged to him now.

"Hey," I murmured, taking hold of Austin's heavy paw. "Baby, I'm here. You're going to be fine."

His fur was rippling across his limbs as if his body was trying to shift back. I couldn't tear my eyes away from his gigantic bear head as it morphed into a part-human, part-bear face like some grotesque horror movie prop.

"What's happening to him?" I flicked my terrified gaze to the Reaper.

The Reaper had already managed to pick out most of the shrapnel from Austin's shoulder and thigh. Now he was turning his attention to the gaping hole in his chest.

"Hold him steady," he instructed. "His body is fighting the fragments of silver in his bloodstream. He's gonna get as hot as Hades with a fever, so I need your help to hold him still. I got one chance to get this right. One slip and he's a goner."

That comment was enough to put the fear of God in me. Rebecca paced into the kitchen with the phone still pressed against her ear, having heard that too.

"Eliza and Brian are on their way," she informed us, her expression pained and anxious.

The voice on the other end of the line belonged to a man. Austin's dad, Brian. Rebecca's voice trailed off as she took the conversation back into the sitting room. I heard her reassuring them that he was stable and that she could hear his heartbeat loud and clear.

I pressed my weight against Austin's shoulders, careful not to touch his injury.

"It's okay, baby," I cooed, making soft shushing sounds as I bent forward and let him nuzzle into the crook of my neck. My scent calmed him. The convulsions settled into a tense tremor.

"Steady, big guy," the Reaper muttered while he worked, sliding the tip of the knife into Austin's chest wound. I couldn't look, but I could hear the sound of cutting flesh as he made a careful incision. Austin's bear whined softly, and my heart clenched with sympathy. A clean dish towel caught my sight as the Reaper used it to stem the blood flow, turning from white to red in seconds. I closed my eyes, breathing unsteadily. God, I felt sick. My stomach spun, churning up everything I ate for breakfast. I didn't want to see Austin bleeding. Wet sounds let me know that our tattooed savior had inserted his finger and thumb into Austin's wound and was trying to fish out the bullet by hand. I just had to keep breathing in through my nose and out through my mouth, or else I was going to toss up my French toast.

The Reaper let out an intense gasp, making me look. *Goddammit! Damn him to Hell.*

"I've got it!" he exclaimed triumphantly.

"Hm-hm," was my response because I was fighting with my gag reflex.

I would be fine as long as he gave me a minute. I kept my eyes closed and continued to breathe. There was a light thud against the linoleum that told me that the bullet was out. My eyes flew open, assuming that the healing process would be immediate, but Austin's convulsions only seemed to worsen.

"What's happening?" I rushed my words desperately.

I heard the sound of a car engine tearing up the dirt track, followed by the loud crack of doors being opened and slammed.

"We need some help here!" The Reaper yelled out to Rebecca.

The door burst open, and Austin's mom's voice filtered through the cabin, making my heart leap with hope. Eliza Rayne rushed into the kitchen, letting her doctor's bag fall to the floor with a thump. Her blue eyes were glazed with maternal anguish, the haunting look of a mother who was facing the loss of her youngest child. Her only son.

"Sweetie, can you hear me?" she soothed, dropping to her knees and cradling Austin's head between her hands. "Momma's here."

I noticed the Reaper shuffle back from where he was kneeling. The sight of my husband's blood coating his inked body was too much to bear. Brian was already rolling up his sleeves as he entered the room, eyeing the Reaper with distrust.

"If I find out that you orchestrated this, so help me, Goddess," Brian muttered scornfully.

"Brian! Your son needs your blood. Give me your arm, now!" Eliza barked at her husband, setting up a contraption that siphoned blood from one person to the other.

Austin didn't so much as flinch as his mother injected him with a pale blue substance. His labored breathing began to even out, settling into calm, relaxed respiration. Within moments, he had completely transformed back into his sexy nude self.

"Is he going to be okay?" I asked Eliza.

"I sure as hell hope so," she replied, bouncing her gaze from me to the Reaper. "I want to thank you for what you did for my boy," she choked, her words full of gratitude and raw emotion. "I don't care about ulterior motives. You could've just passed them by instead of stepping in like that. If you hadn't shown up, they would all be dead. In my eyes, you were a hero today."

"Aw, Eliza, he probably set the whole thing up just to worm his way into the USC," Brian argued, and then he turned to scowl contemptuously at the Reaper. "You stay where you are. You're under arrest!"

I half expected them to start brawling in the middle of the kitchen, but the Reaper remained composed despite the fury on his face.

"Figured as much," Reaper mumbled under his breath. "I went for a swim the same as you fuckers go for a run. The last time I checked, that wasn't a felony. I heard gunshots and decided to go see what was going on. This is my home too." He pushed himself up from the kitchen floor, glowering with anger. "I don't want hunters sneaking around in my backyard any more than you do. I can't stand the fuckers. It was me who supplied the Alpha dog with artillery to defend this state not so long ago. Did I receive a thank you card?" He curled his fingers around his chin in a sarcastic pose. "Nope, it must've gotten lost in the mail."

"So, you're not going to try and coerce my daughter-in-law to support your application to the council?" Brian cast him a doubtful look.

The Reaper huffed an amused sigh, turning from him to me. "I wish your ranger a speedy recovery. Congrats on the new job, by the way. I guess I'll see you around."

We all got a clear view of his tattooed ass as he stalked out through the back door—a green reptilian eye on either side of his ass cheeks as if he had eyes in his rear.

"Hey! Didn't you hear me? *I said* you're under arrest!" Brian yelled, his face reddening with outrage.

CHAPTER FORTY-SIX

Riley

"Let him go, Brian!" Eliza berated her husband. "What's done is done. Our boy is still breathing thanks to him. Can't you just be grateful for that?"

"I am, Eliza, but . . ." He dragged a hand down his face, then jabbed his finger in the direction of the back door. "But there's just something about that guy." He sucked in a breath, clenching his fist against his chest. "Call it a cop's hunch, but he's not to be trusted. He's a criminal, not someone who runs to the rescue like some heroic Boy Scout."

I could see Eliza getting more and more frustrated, so I stepped in to diffuse the situation with the art of distraction. "Why don't you boil some water and make us all some sweet tea? I sure as hell could use some."

Jesus Christ, I sounded like my grandmother.

Eliza practically yanked the line out of her husband's arm. "I wouldn't say no to that. My nerves were shot to shit on the way over here."

Brian tore his glare away from the back door and dropped his shoulders with a sigh of defeat. "Fine, I'll make the damn tea."

Eliza tapped his arm affectionately. "And while the kettle's boiling, you can help me get this big naked lug up to bed."

Brian and Eliza lifted him without breaking so much as a sweat. "He's hurt badly," Brian muttered. "You're going to need to keep him dosed up to get him through the night. Our boy is strong, but he's not out of the woods yet, excuse the pun."

"What does he mean, 'not out of the woods?' He's started to heal, hasn't he? That's a good sign!" I blurted out, my mind flashing with panic.

I waited at the bottom of the stairs as they carried Austin to bed, pacing the hall and chewing my thumbnail. And when they returned, I was ready with more questions.

Eliza's expression crumpled with uncertainty. "Honey, he's stable right now but the next forty-eight hours are critical. The bullets are out, but there's still silver floating around in his bloodstream. That's the thing about silver tips. The tips explode upon impact. His body has to fight back and burn off the silver."

"I'll make the tea," Brian muttered in an exhausted tone.

The next forty-eight hours were pure torture. Austin's sisters stopped by with their mates and cubs, each taking turns to sit and talk to him as if for the final time. I'd never had something that I'd been afraid to lose before, and I knew that if Austin died, my heart would never recover from it. My parents flew in on their private jet. They comforted me while Austin's friends went into his room one at a time to say whatever they wanted to say. Beast told an unconscious Austin that a ranger called Lincoln killed the hunter we left behind. Now they were all dead, I could relax more. I didn't intend to eavesdrop on him, but when he started mumbling about them as kids, I couldn't help it.

I watched as Beast sat hunched on the edge of

Austin's bed, his head bowed, brows pinched, and his hands clasped together.

"You're the luckiest son of a bitch I've ever met, do you know that? I envied you growing up, the kid that had everything I ever wanted. A stable homelife, a kind momma, and a dad who never missed a single one of your games. Even though you spent more time on the bench than anyone else on the team." He chuckled fondly. "And if there's one thing I learned about you, it's that you hate to sit on the sidelines and watch the action. You prefer to be right in the thick of it making lame-ass jokes, which is where you belong, front and center, and annoying the shit out of me. So, wake the fuck up and quit scaring me, will you? There's still so much work to be done around here and I can surely use your help."

I ducked out of sight as Beast glanced at the door. It was a private moment that I shouldn't have intruded on, but I'm glad that I did. The cabin soon filled with people I had met through my short time knowing Austin. He had more friends than I could count. Real friends. Ones who wanted nothing from him, but who came anyway.

"Why don't you get some rest?" Mom suggested

as she helped Eliza clear away all the mismatched coffee mugs from the sitting room.

My eyes felt scratchy and raw, but I was too afraid to sleep in case I missed something. What if Austin passed away when I was sleeping, and I was not there to be by his side?

"I'm fine, Mom." My eyes watered as I yawned.

"You're not fine," Stacey, Austin's youngest older sister, told me. "People are getting ready to leave now anyway. Why don't you scootch up alongside Austin and take a nap. It'll help him to heal faster."

She ushered everyone out of our bedroom and left me to change in peace. Eliza had kept the curtains closed to block out the harsh glare of the sun. The temperature in the room would've been way too hot for comfort, but thanks to the tall office fan Brian borrowed from the station, cool wisps of air were able to blast back and forth across Austin's human form.

Needing some peace of mind, I lifted the gauze on Austin's chest wound. The other wounds seemed to have healed completely; it was just the one over his heart proving stubborn. This was typical Austin, stubborn through and through.

"Babe, it's just me," I murmured, reassuring him

that I was here and not knowing if he could scent me in his weakened state.

I snuggled beside him, taking care not to apply too much pressure to the mattress. His brows creased, and his lips mashed together as he moistened his lips.

"Riley?" His voice was hoarse and gravelly.

"Austin, you're awake," I said, startled to see him waking. "Are you in pain? I'll go fetch your mom."

His hand reached out and snared my wrist in a sudden movement. Even with his eyes closed, he could anticipate my proximity.

"Stay. Just stay here with me for a little bit," he rasped, gently tugging on my arm.

With a relieved sigh, I placed my head beside his on the pillow, and he turned to me, his blue eyes cracking open for the first time since he blacked out.

"What happened?" he croaked. "Are you all right?" he checked, his expression turning tense with concern. "Is Becca all right?"

"We're both fine," I reassured him.

His breath played tug-of-war in his throat.

"Thank God," he replied, scrunching his eyes closed.

They cracked open again slowly. He held my gaze as if figuring out what he wanted to say, or maybe he knew what to say, but he was just working out how best to say it.

"How?" is all he managed.

I could see the confusion swamping his features. He didn't know how we managed to survive the hunter attack and how Rebecca and I managed to get him back to the cabin.

"The Reaper," I informed him. "He took out the hunters and then carried you back to the cabin. You lost a lot of blood, and you had a silver bullet lodged in your chest."

Austin gave a gentle nod of his head as he blinked his eyes. He didn't say anything else; he just parted his lips to breathe. I didn't want him stressing unnecessarily. It was my job to worry about the Reaper and whether he would or wouldn't want any favors in return. Strike me down dead for thinking things, but maybe Cyrus Theriot wasn't all that bad.

"It all happened so fast," he murmured. "The hunter who took the first shot was aiming for you," he said, his eyes wincing as he remembered that. "I saw at least two take aim and lock you in their sights."

A sudden chill raised the hairs on my arms.

Were they after me?

I was far too exhausted to dwell on that right now.

"There's nothing to worry about. I injured one of them, and the Reaper took care of the rest. Beast came to tell us they're all dead," I said, stroking my fingers along his forearm.

"Promise me that you'll check in with the USC first thing tomorrow?" Austin urged. "Once you're sworn into office, you'll have ample security around you at all times."

There was no stopping him from worrying about my welfare, so I had to settle for distracting him, instead.

"Fine, I will. But guess what I can do?" I grinned.

Austin's brows lifted with intrigue. "What's that?"

I freed myself from his grasp and stood at the side of his bed. Within moments, I clambered back onto the mattress as a beautiful red fox. Austin could only look on, slack-jawed as I snuggled beside him and drifted off to sleep.

CHAPTER FORTY-SEVEN

Riley

It had taken a little over two weeks for Austin to make a full recovery. During that time, he had several fevers as his body fought to burn away every last fragment of silver. He was granted another two months of sick leave before enlisting into the United Shifter Military alongside his pal, Beast.

In the meantime, I began my role as a council official. The USC consisted of eighteen members. My father. Alpha Alec White. His wife, Leah. Alpha Rafael Ortiz. His wife, Danielle, who were both from the cat shifter community. And twelve elderly bear shifters, with one being the newly elected Clan leader, Zeke.

I glanced up at the office clock on the wall, conscious that it was almost lunchtime. My stomach growled in protest, desperate for nourishment. Since shifting, my body needed to consume a ridiculous number of calories to sustain me. It meant I could eat whatever I wanted without putting on an ounce of weight. Which made me think back to all the years I suffered in vain when I could have pigged out with zero regrets. And my god, I was making up for lost time.

The dull clomping of Doc Martens boots stomped across the hall, making me breathe a sigh of relief because my lunch date had arrived, and my mouth was salivating at the idea of stuffing my face with something deep-fried and smothered in chocolate. Then right on cue, a loud, confident knock let me know it was time to grab my purse.

"Leah, you know you can walk right in." I chuckled.

The wolf Luna opened the door and peered around the varnished wood, making sure the coast was clear.

"Oh, I thought you might have company. I can

smell ... uh ... I can smell Austin," she stammered awkwardly.

My face flushed red hot with embarrassment.

Fuck! I keep forgetting they can smell stuff.

Austin had been here earlier. He came to bring me the bagel that I accidentally left on the kitchen countertop this morning. However, he ate it as he sat in my chair. So, I ate him for breakfast instead.

I know . . . I was such a filthy bitch.

I clicked my tongue. "Darn it, I keep forgetting that my dad's office is just three doors down, not to mention, my bodyguard is stationed right outside."

Leah chuckled. "Well, at least it's a great source of protein, but sucking dick isn't going to get you pregnant, just so you know."

"It's a good job it can't," I said with a humorous roll of my eyes. "Just because we can have kids doesn't mean we're in any rush to have one. Austin and I talked about this, and we've decided that we want to wait at least a year before we start trying for a baby." I glanced at her flat stomach, astounded that she had only given birth a matter of weeks ago.

The only reason that she was here today, and not enjoying maternity leave, was because we had an important council meeting this afternoon.

"How is the little one doing?" I asked about her Lycan pup that she and Alec had chosen us to be godparents to.

"Robert is a live wire, just like his dad," she replied with a sigh. "And he's constantly hungry. I've expressed enough milk to last him until his last feed tonight. My nipples are so sore, I feel like a milked cow."

"Ouch," I crossed my arms over my chest with sympathy. "If my baby is a rough suckler like Austin, then I'll switch to bottle feeding."

Leah's face scrunched in a humored grimace. "Ew, thanks for the mental image right before lunch. But on a brighter note, my brother, Jace, is watching Robert today. I'm pretty sure it's to impress a girl, but I'm not complaining. It gives my nipples a break."

Leah and I became good friends after we hit it off in the jailhouse. I always loved telling people that story whenever they asked how we met. Despite our different upbringings, we shared a lot in common. Neither of us knew we were shifters before we arrived here. We found out through tragic circumstances. And we were both descendants of the founding fathers of Whitehaven, which made us shifter royalty.

The two of us chatted casually as we strolled through the confederate building. I barely even noticed the four bodyguards who trailed behind us as we walked the short distance to Main Street where Leah had made a reservation at a bistro called The Beehive. The scent of honey hit me the second I stepped inside. An assortment of mead bottles lined the walls. Green vines with colored flowers decorated the wooden beams on the ceiling and framed the bar area. We were given a private table with a floral trellis screen around it, allowing us to see through the gaps, but made it hard for others to see in.

"How are you feeling about the meeting this afternoon?" Leah asked as we glanced at the menus.

I swallowed thickly, feeling my stomach flip with anxiety. It was the last Friday of the month. That was when the council opened the chambers to the public and invited them to partake in an open debate. If anyone had any issues, however big or small, like an application to obtain planning permission, a request to apply for community funding, as well as making a suggestion for us to amend our legislation or constitution, we could raise them at the meeting. Nothing was definitive. It just meant the council would consider them. Then we would discuss them amongst ourselves. We would then put it to a vote. If it came down to one vote against a majority, then that one vote would be overruled. But if two members voted in favor of an issue, the council had to consider it. My dad told me the council agreed on pretty much everything. It was easier to agree than to disagree.

"Nervous," I admitted, answering Leah's question. "I feel like everybody is expecting me to screw up."

Mainly because I was renowned for being the most disagreeable person on the face of the planet.

"Everybody is expecting you to make changes," she reassured me, and then leaned across the table to place a round speaker in the center—something Alpha Alec invented to muffle people's conversations. It emitted white noise, but it worked, thwarting any eavesdroppers. "It's your first resident meeting. You're bound to be nervous. I was when it was my first time. Things were far worse back then. Right after hunters blew up Whitevale."

The waitress sauntered over to take our order, so our conversation cut off dead until she left. Minutes passed before she returned with our drinks, then we sipped our iced teas while we waited for our food to arrive.

"Do you have any words of wisdom for me?" I asked, feeling my nerves tying knots in my stomach.

"Trust your gut instincts," she answered, making direct eye contact.

I didn't break her gaze, even though I probably should. Leah White had the power to make a person do whatever she willed them to do, but I trusted her enough as my friend not to abuse her gift. As she leaned forward to speak, I could see nothing but fierce integrity staring back at me.

"Don't fall under the whip. Voice your own opinions and do what you think is right," she advised me. "We can't begin to move forward if we're too afraid of change."

My brows formed a frown as I considered that.

"Off the record, what do you think needs to change?" I asked, studying her expression as she pondered that.

"Honestly, I think there's a gap in our security. It doesn't matter how well prepared we are, hunters have a habit of finding their way through. Then there's all the drug trafficking, arms smuggling, extortion, thefts, and financial crime. Money launderers also co-mingle illegal money with revenue made from businesses to further mask their illicit funds. There's no way we can keep track of all of that and some of the most vulnerable in our society are being exploited," Leah explained.

I didn't bat an eyelid to anything she said; such was the way of the world.

"Literally everywhere has the exact same problems. What makes you convinced we can keep it all in check here in Whitehaven?" I put my point across.

Leah flashed me a fragile smile. "I think you know the answer to that, Riley."

Did I? Maybe I do but I was still unsure.

"Look," Leah said, exhaling a sigh. "You and I both know we're walking around with targets on our heads. You've already had one assassination attempt, which almost cost you your mate." She placed her purse on the tabletop as she rummaged inside and produced a crumpled letter. She held it out for me to take. "Here, read that. This arrived three days ago."

I took the letter and unfolded it to read. The sickening message was enough to turn my blood cold.

"Fucking hell, who does this?" I blurted, horrified.

Leah's tongue darted out as she moistened her lips. "Vampires from Italy." Our eyes met across the table, and mine flared wide. "Yeah, exactly," she said.

"They're threatening to kidnap your newborn son and . . ." I couldn't even repeat the death threat they made against Leah. The things they intended to do to her were horrific.

"That's why we need the devil guarding our doorstep," Leah commented. "Sometimes you need a necessary evil to keep all the nasties in line."

"You know what?" I swallowed away the dryness in my mouth. "I like how you're thinking. Where I come from, there are plenty of reptiles who dominate the food chain, metaphorically speaking."

We returned to the USC building as the residents were arriving in droves. Leah and I were ushered in through a side door that led straight down to the council chambers. This place reminded me of a Roman amphitheater, like any moment, a gladiator would appear and end up getting mauled by a hungry lion.

I took a seat next to my father and looked out at the sea of faces who were all staring back at us. The twelve silver-haired bear shifter elders sat alongside one another at the far side of the row. Alpha Alec was sitting in the president's chair in between Leah and Beast. The Hispanic cat shifters, Rafael and Danielle, sat beside Dad. Everyone was talking amongst themselves while the last of the stragglers piled through the double doors. I spied Austin standing at the back of the room. He was wearing a dark green military uniform, embellished with medals, and the shoes he spent last night spit-shining. I knew he couldn't wave at me whilst he was on-duty, so I pressed two fingers to my lips, then ran them along my mating mark and watched him shiver delightfully. It was the same gesture as blowing a kiss to your mate, but they felt it in their genitals.

Alec slammed his gavel onto the desk, commanding silence throughout the chamber. The first fifteen minutes were dedicated to opening the meeting, reminding all in attendance about the legalities. Then he started going through the agenda, paragraph by paragraph, discussing each motion until we reached the one that I was dreading. My eyes landed on the elephant in the room. I meant the alligator. The Reaper.

It was me who submitted the request for a fair hearing, despite him not having asked since the night at the bar. Not once since he saved our lives had he approached to badger, email, or contact me in any way. I just figured all good deeds shouldn't go unnoticed.

Alec cleared his throat, clearly uncomfortable about what he had to announce next.

"Agenda number sixteen: The exoneration of Mr. Cyrus Theriot, also known as Reaper, which would permit him to exercise the right to claim his alpha status. I implore the honorable members of the council to approach this with caution. Think about what this could mean and the drastic impact this will have on our community."

CHAPTER FORTY-EIGHT

Riley

After way too much apprehensive grumbling from the bear shifter clan, my father, and the Alpha and Luna of the cat shifter community, I figured it would be dismissed point-blank.

"All those in favor of exonerating Mr. Theriot, please state whether you vote for or against," Alec commanded, his voice wavering with unease.

The chamber fell into silence as everyone waited to see how this would unfold. Reaper stood with his hands clasped casually behind his back. He was dressed smartly in a crisp white shirt, black suit trousers, and dress shoes. His hair was gelled back into a sophisticated style. He bounced his gaze around the room, then locked eyes with Leah White as he awaited the outcome of the vote.

Just as I thought, all twelve bear shifter elders voted against the proposal, with the last one hissing, "No way in Hell."

"Against," Rafael answered, then looked to his wife for support. "Against," she voted the same way as her husband.

"I vote against the proposal," Alec responded vehemently.

"I vote for the proposal," Leah voiced amidst loud grumblings from the bears.

Our earlier conversation suddenly all made sense, and I got the impression that she tried to raise this subject before but had been overruled.

"Against," Dad's words sounded final.

Then all eyes landed on me. The atmosphere in the room grew tense as if all the air had been sucked away and replaced with something noxious.

For a fleeting moment, I flicked my gaze between the man that I loved and the man that I thought deserved the benefit of the doubt. From what I could fathom, Whitehaven wasn't exactly short of heroes. How many would have to give their lives to protect this wounded state from another threat, so soon after the last? In the words of Tina Turner and her remarkable pipes, "We don't need another hero." Maybe what we really need is the opposite. An anti-hero. The right kind of wrong that would stand guard as we sleep and would scare away the boogeyman. I knew one thing: I would rather be onside with the Reaper than have him as an adversary. I had seen him in action, and I knew what he could do.

Dad's stare was practically burning holes in the side of my face as I took an intake of breath and cast my vote. "I vote in favor of exonerating Mr. Cyrus Theriot."

Cyrus's jaw hung agape as he realized what I just did. Austin blanched, and then he started breathing heavily as the sound of raucous voices filled the room. It was enough to drown out the loud hammering from Alec's gavel.

That was when Beast stood and yelled, *"Quiet!"*

The chattering died down and faded into silence. Beast sat down, and Alec slumped back in his chair, clutching his forehead.

"What the devil have you done?" My father hissed, his face ashen.

I don't think that I'd ever seen him this angry. However, the Reaper was bouncing on heels as he smirked like a fucker. I hoped I'd done the right thing because now the council had to deliberate it.

"The council is taking a thirty-minute recession," Alec finally announced before slamming down the gavel.

Leah held back as each council member got up from their seats and stormed into a room at the back of the chamber.

"Get ready for the nuclear detonator to blow," she warned me.

We were the last to enter the room, and then one of the bear elders closed the door behind us.

"What the fuck was that all about?" Alec looked between Leah and me accusingly.

Leah didn't appear the slightest bit intimidated as she glared defiantly at her husband. "Don't be such a stubborn asshole!" She jabbed her finger at his chest. "Cyrus pulled through for us once before. You know he swore an oath of loyalty to me, and I trust him with my life. I trust him with our son's life. You know you stand a better chance of finding the cure for vampire venom with him by your side. Think of your mom, and your sister." Her eyes softened. "Think of Lexi, and how Cyrus has just as much to lose as you do, if not more. We need you to cure them, Alec. And to do that, we need everyone to pull together. We're stronger when united. That includes Cyrus. Like it or not, he's part of this community too."

Alec dragged a hand through his hair, making it look wild and unruly. "But he's a criminal, Amore. We cannot justify the immoral activities he conducts in the underground."

I could see some of the others attempt to interject, but the wolf Luna didn't give them a chance. "So lay down some ground rules," she suggested, flinging her hands in the air. "Come to a compromise. Maybe organized crime is better than it being disorganized."

"No prizes for guessing who put that idea into your head," he argued, rolling his eyes dramatically. "You're starting to sound like him."

Leah's eyes narrowed into a baleful scowl.

"Hey," I cringed, cutting in. "I don't want to speak out of turn here, but I think I owe you an explanation of why I voted the way I did." I couldn't bring myself to look in my father's eyes at this point, not wanting to see the disappointment residing within them.

"Cyrus just wants someplace to call home. I

think he has the potential to contribute, but in an unorthodox way." I saw that I'd grabbed everyone's attention, even if I was being scowled at with scrutiny.

The cat shifter couple didn't appear too pleased with how this was all playing out, but they didn't give rise to the debate. The hostility was coming from the bear elders who began to growl amongst themselves about how incompetent I was. Even though my dad disagreed with me, he defended me to them, telling them they had no right to talk to me that way.

"So, let me get this straight. You're suggesting we let him conduct his business as usual? You do realize the man is a murderer?" my father reminded me, and then hissed at the grumbling bears to "shush" while I answered.

"Gangsters run most of the casinos in the human world, Dad. Cyrus is just one guy. But he's a guy all the other criminals respect. And if you can't control these guys, let him do the dirty work if that's what he wants. You'll never find perfection because it doesn't exist. People are flawed no matter if they're human or shifter," I finished with a shrug.

"Exactly," Leah reinforced. "We live in a far from perfect world. I've seen it, and I'm still seeing it every day on the news, and in my client's eyes when they come to me for help. It wasn't all that long ago that people thought of you as a monster." She looked at Alec. "What's it going to take for you to swallow your pride? I don't want it to cost us our son."

"Amore," Alec sighed remorsefully.

Leah raised a palm at him to hear her out. "Just stop. I'm getting death threats in the mail. Cyrus would lay down his life for me, and you know it. He's family. When you cure Lexi, and I know in my heart you will. She and Cyrus will mate. He's not going anywhere."

"What would you have me do?" Alec murmured. "I'm going to Italy, and I will eliminate every last one of those blood-sucking bastards myself."

As Leah wiped the tears from her eyes, an idea presented itself to me.

"Why not take the Reaper with you? No one will be expecting it," I said, making Alec consider my point. "He must know stealthy ways of sneaking around undetected. And he's fucking hard to kill. I've got to hand it to the guy, his scales are bulletproof. I've seen it with my own eyes."

"She's right. Better to stroll into Hell in cahoots

with the devil, rather than walk into an ambush blindfolded," Beast rasped as he leaned casually against the closed door.

Alec seemed to mull over the colonel's words, then turned to his wife, lifting her chin to face him. They communicated something privately, and I saw the faintest smile reach Leah's eyes.

My vote was either going to be beneficial or a contributing factor to Whitehaven's demise. That was what my dad was thinking, but I wouldn't be the daughter he raised me to be if I didn't stand up for what I believed in.

As soon as the meeting concluded, I snatched my purse from beneath my seat and power walked from the building. My head felt like it was going to explode with pressure, and I needed some air.

"Babe?" Austin said as he rushed to greet me.

"Please don't start," I began, not wanting another lecture.

He lifted me by the hips and proceeded to spin me around in circles. "You were fantastic up there!"

I grimaced as he placed me down, and the view of the street took a few seconds longer to catch up with what just happened.

"Huh? Uh?" I groaned, dizzy and disoriented.

Austin threw his arm across my shoulder while we walked to the parking lot.

"That was some risky shit, babe," he remarked. "But you can't make an omelet without breaking a few eggs."

I shot him a side glance. "Gee, thanks for the analogy. It's just the confidence boost I was looking for," I responded with sarcasm.

"What I mean is, you can't change things up without being prepared to take some risks. I'm proud of you, darlin'." His voice dropped to a husky rasp.

"Proud, huh?" Our lips met as we both leaned in for a kiss.

He pulled back with a sexy grin. "I got your text. You want us to have fiery tacos for dinner."

I laughed out loud. "What the hell?!" I wasn't talking about food, the emoji was supposed to represent my female anatomy, and the fire was supposed to mean things would get hot and heavy between us. But maybe, I should have used a winking cat face emoji instead. Right now, I was doing a great impression of the face-palm icon.

Austin glanced back through the doors and winced apologetically. "Shoot, we've got to go back inside for the hearing. And whatever happens, we've got plans for tonight."

I rolled my eyes with a smile. "Fine, we can have fiery tacos for dinner," I replied, now he'd got his heart set on that. "But you're doing the cooking."

The council returned to their seats so that Alec could address the public, and a frustrated Cyrus, who had been left on tenterhooks the entire time. Alec called for "silence" and then whacked the gavel to hush the crowd.

"The council has come to a decision about the issues raised, and we have decided by a narrow margin that Mr. Theriot shall be granted Alpha status and a provisional seat on the council," Alec announced, much to the astonishment of Cyrus. "But should he flout the laws and bend them to his will, I won't hesitate to revoke this decision." He looked Cyrus dead in the eye. "You have but one chance to prove yourself to me, Roi of the Bayou. Don't make me regret it."

Cyrus bowed his head in a mark of respect, never once breaking eye contact. "I give you my word, Alpha White."

And to a man like Cyrus, his word was more than his bond. It was his honor.

"Meeting dismissed," Alec hollered, whacking the gavel.

I released a huge sigh of relief, wishing I could sink through the chair and seep through the floorboards rather than walk through a crowd of outraged citizens and risk being stoned to death outside. Austin was waiting for me by the doors. Waiting to whisk me away to our cabin in the woods and back to the simplicity of forest life.

CHAPTER FORTY-NINE

Riley

It felt so good to be home. I took off my heels, dumped my purse on the couch and walked barefoot through the cabin. Austin bent over, plucking at his boot laces, his uniform stretched tight over his derriere. I couldn't resist tiptoeing over to him so I could smack it. We'd become one of those playful couples who couldn't last ten minutes without touching one another, affectionately teasing, or pulling pranks just for kicks. Austin was everything I never knew I wanted, and once I found him, I would rather die than live without him.

Instead of crashing out on the couch at the end of a stressful day, he removed his uniform and showered, and then got changed into cargo shorts, a shabby T-shirt, and a pair of flip-flops. Not to slob out and do nothing. No. But to light a fire in the backyard firepit and make us spicy tacos for dinner. I chopped the onions and peppers while he fried the seasoned meat, and occasionally, he would sneak a glance to watch me working in nothing but a silk robe and Luis Vuitton sliders.

"Toss them into the firepan when you're done," he instructed, eyeing my manicured nails with a smirk.

So far, I haven't chipped a single one. Unlike last time, when I helped to make gumbo and Austin almost choked on half my thumb nail.

"Yes, chef," I retort, expecting some playful teasing to follow.

I walked over to the bucket of water to wash my hands and then shook them dry. Austin put down the wooden spoon, wiped his hands on a dishtowel. We ate our fiery tacos beside the firepit, and then washed them down with some cold bottles of beer.

Austin dumped out empty plates into a pile on

the ground, and then stealthily picked something up from the nearby chopping block. The mischievous glint in his eyes usually meant I should run, and that he was planning to prank me somehow. But as he came toward me, he masked his face with innocence.

"I've got something for you," he told me, which aroused my suspicion. "Close your eyes and hold out your hand."

I took a moment to reconsider things. Maybe he planned this night to surprise me.

Okay. I'll play along.

This could be one of those sporadic cute moments, and I wouldn't want to spoil it.

I close my eyes and hold out my hand, wondering what surprise he had in store for me. Was it a gift? Perhaps a token of affection? Whatever it was, tickled my palm as he gave it to me.

"You can look now," he encouraged.

"Argh!" I opened my eyes and screamed, tossing the eight-legged monster away from me.

Austin roared with laughter as I shuddered with revulsion.

"It was only a tomato stalk." He chortled.

I glared at him and then looked for something

to throw at him, but the chopping knife was a little out of my reach.

"You're an asshole!" I yelled, slapping his bulky shoulder. "You can kiss goodbye to this," I told him, stripping out of my robe and letting it fall to the ground. "Catch your own damned pudding."

It took me three seconds to work through my shift, which was a new record for me. I found it didn't hurt as much when anger flowed through my veins. It felt a little like stretching muscles during yoga. A slight burning sensation and a little pressure. The more I got used to shifting, the less I needed to try. Austin stretched his arms as if he was going to yawn and then effortlessly transformed into a huge grizzly bear, with a growing erection. This had become a regular thing when going out for a run—a game of chase, capture, and then fuck like wild animals in the woods. But one thing I made abundantly clear to him at the start of every chase, if he could catch me, he could take me however he wanted. Including bear back. Providing we were both furry. You haven't lived unless you've seen a bear trying to run with a hard-on through the woods. Trust me. It's the clumsiest, pant-pissing hilarious thing you'll ever witness, but don't take my word for it.

Book your next vacation in Forest Hills and come and see it for yourself.

"Grrr!" Austin answered to the challenge, pushed up from the ground, fully transformed and ready for the chase.

I yelped with the thrill of it, darting into the shadowy forest with nothing but my sharp senses to guide me. There was no way in hell that Austin could catch me in this form, not with those hairy meatballs and his third leg bouncing around. Foxes are small and nimble whereas Bears are ponderous because of their size and weighty meat stick. It was fucking huge without the fur coat, but when they shifted, the sheer stretch was eye-popping. There was no way I could take Austin's bear cock while in my human form. It would split me in half. But what my Fox lacked in size, she made up for with strength and adaptability. I slowed down to let Austin catch me, and as his gigantic paws grabbed onto my body for anchorage, his thick cock stabbed eagerly at my pussy, almost entering the wrong hole a couple of times which was enough to make me yelp. People often claim they can hear screaming banshees in the woods, but they're wrong. Those are just Vixens who have well-endowed lovers. Austin kept stabbing his blunt tipped sword against my rump until he eventually found the slick pussy entrance and then he shoved it deep inside. My high-pitched cries of pleasure rang through the forest and echoed through the night. He let his bear loose so he could rut me like an animal, pogoing me off his bear cock, my eyes rolling, and my thin legs dangling off the ground. But it's not how we finish. This is just a game we like to play to appease our animal urges and keep the spark in our relationship alive. When I've had enough, a gentle nip from me is enough to tell him when to stop. He knows what I really want is for him to change back so we can wrestle for dominance amongst the fallen leaves, getting half the forest tangled in our hair. The woods don't even bother me like they did before. I love it here. It's so peaceful. I love the smell of the loam, the alpine scent, and the sound of the lazy river and the rustling leaves.

It always took me a few seconds longer to shift back because I used the methods Rebecca taught me, being mindful of every step. Things could go wrong if I rushed the process. That was not what I wanted. Not when I had a hot night of passion planned with my sexy husband. Austin held out his hand to pull me up, and then we walked back to the cabin, our naked bodies bathed in the moonlight, and lay down on an old, crumpled blanket beside the crackling fire.

"It's a nice night for trying. Just putting it out there in case you change your mind," Austin murmured as he wrapped me in a warm embrace. One side of his face was tinged orange from the fire and the dancing embers reflected in his eyes.

"Are you saying what I think you're saying?" I ask, running my hand absentmindedly over my stomach.

Austin hummed in affirmation. "Your scent has changed since this afternoon. It must've been that strong perfume overpowering my nostrils." He exhaled with a soft amused laugh as I shoved him.

"Are you serious?" I wanted to know because this was an important decision, and we agreed that we would wait. "Or are you just messing with me?"

There wasn't a flicker of mischief in his eyes as he held my gaze. "I can smell it on you." He stroked his finger down my cheek, traced the line of my throat, and then he circled it around the swell of my breast, around and around, his playful touch spiraled and then stopped at my puckered nipple. "Smells good. Well, it does on you anyway. Better than the expensive perfume you wear every day."

My lips curved into a slight smile. "Do you think

you could handle another me running around?" I arched my eyebrow, waiting for him to answer.

Austin chewed on his lip to stop from grinning. "That wouldn't be so bad," he replied. "Might even get one like me, and then what?"

"Then I would be the luckiest mom in the world because I would love to have a little you, running around the place, pranking me, and driving me crazy," I mentioned, already imagining how he or she would look, and all the cute little outfits I would dress them in, and how our kids would never want for anything.

Austin's breath caught in his throat, surprised to hear how invested I was. He leaned down to kiss me, moving over my body to take control, rubbing the calloused pad of his finger between my slick folds, delving into my molten heat, dragging it through the cleft of my pussy, and then sought my swollen nub. His strokes were electrifying, the crackling sensation bursting through every nerve ending. Short, shallow gasps escaped from my lips as he dragged me to the brink of an orgasm. And as the mounting pressure began to build, I started to tremble, my moans got louder, and my muscles coiled ready for a spasmodic release. That's when Austin stopped toying with me, and I felt the blunt heat of his cock right before he thrust deep inside. My greedy pussy shrank tightly around his length, sucking him down to the root with each grinding hip movement, the slow drag and plunge driving me to the brink of insanity.

"I love you, Riley," Austin murmured against my ear, our bodies rocking together, our limbs embroiled in a deeply sensuous act. This wasn't just about sex. It was everything. Us. Austin and me, and the family we were making from our love.

We knew what would happen if we went through with this, which made the ending so much sweeter.

"I love you too," I breathlessly reply, unable to stop myself from holding back this time.

Austin increases the speed of his thrusts; his cock head swelling to huge proportions, enabling him to lock, ejaculate a tsunami of hot, sticky cum inside me, and then keep it there. Our bodies are locked together, joined at the groin, both of us are left gasping for breath, waiting for the magic to happen. We don't say anything while we wait, too excited to speak, and both nervously waiting to see if it worked. I could shift; therefore, I should be able to conceive. But I didn't want to jinx it. Not when it was something we both wanted so badly. Austin pressed his forehead against mine to rest it there and then he held me as we waited. Moments passed, and it seemed like it was taking forever. A minute or two felt like an eternity, and it shocked me just how fragile my emotions were as my eyes welled with tears.

"Babe, look at me," Austin uttered softly.

I hadn't realized that I was looking away, staring into the glowing embers as they fizzed and popped among the charred wood. Austin cupped my face and turned me to look at him, and a hot tear rolled from the corner of my eye, and then absorbed into my hairline above my ear. I didn't need to ask him if it had worked because I could see the buoyant glimmer in his eyes. It wasn't one of his pranks. It was real. That was when I finally cracked, letting all my emotion come pouring out. Austin rocked me in his arms like a sobbing baby, which would later come in handy since we were having one of our own. I wasn't used to waiting for things, too used to getting what I wanted when I wanted, but this was a precious gift worth waiting for. Something that no amount of money could ever buy.

Austin nuzzled my neck, stamping kisses on my mating mark. "Get that cute butt of yours upstairs, Foxy Lady, and I'll fetch a jar of honey up to bed."

"Mm," I hummed, smiling. "Now you're talking."

Austin got up first and then helped me to stand. My legs were still shaking and my body ached in all the right places. I bent down to retrieve my crumpled robe, and that's when Austin spanked me on the left ass cheek to hurry me along.

"Move it, woman. I've got plans that don't include us sleeping tonight," he warned me.

Who would've thought that this guy had been a clueless virgin a few months ago? Not me, that was for sure. The way his hips swaggered as he walked, all that sex appeal, and the confidence he oozed as he smiled . . . Austin Rayne was everything I'd never dreamed about because I never knew he existed. But ever since the night I almost mowed him down on an unlit country road . . . I guess you could say that the asshole had grown on me. I fell in love with him. And now he's stuck with me forever.

EPILOGUE

Riley

I carried the huge salad bowl under the shade of the gazebo and began arranging all of the food donations. It felt so good to be outside enjoying the glorious weather, helping out at Forest Hills's neighborhood barbecue. I was thrilled to see some familiar faces here today. The folks here had always been rather tight-knit, which was a good thing because our neighbors were the eyes and ears of our community when we were away from our homes. We should be able to confide, trust, and depend on our neighbors for neighborly duties, crime prevention, and general kindness that made living in our town somewhere where we wanted to belong.

"How much longer? Some of us are starving over here," I called out as I worked, the smile never leaving my face.

"Give it two more minutes," Austin answered back.

The grass felt warm under my bare feet, and it cools the second I seek sanctuary in the shade. It's hot and humid, so I snatch a few moments of respite beneath the airy white canopy. The fact that I was a pale-skinned red-head meant that I ran the risk of being baked to a crisp. But this neighborhood was beautiful. What's not to love about enjoying a nice summer's day up in the mountains? I reached into the ice bucket and retrieved a bottle of Forest Hills spring water. I stopped and inhaled a warm breath of pollen-infused air as I twisted off the cap to take a drink. Austin was standing by the grill, flipping burgers while wearing a ridiculous chef's hat. I saw the flames licking up the meat greedily, and my stomach began growling with approval . . . or maybe it was a sign of my little fox-bear telling me that she was hungry.

For all I knew, it could be a boy. It was far too soon to tell. We hadn't formally announced anything yet. My scent had only just started to change, and people had begun asking questions. Our parents kept casting suspicious glances, which meant that we couldn't keep them in suspense any longer.

"Riley, you're looking a bit peaky," Mom said, sounding overly concerned. "Do you need to sit down?"

Whoa! Could she be any more obvious?

"Mom, I'm fine. I'm just desperate to get my hands on my husband's meat," I rushed my words, then realized what I said. "I mean, the burgers," I corrected myself.

God damned baby brain!

Mom grimaced at my comment and then skulked off to find Dad. I saw Brian putting out a fresh bowl of water for the old Labrador Retriever he'd raised from a pup. The kids were all running around playing with water pistols, some of the dads were standing around the grills like they're guarding a fresh kill, leaving the moms to rush around arranging the picnic tables.

I spotted Colonel Kian Jones, who still answered to his nickname, Beast, standing over by the children's bouncy castle, and was getting attacked by a raucous little boy and twin girls. The petite brunette standing beside him was clutching her stomach with laughter. A huge blond Viking-type guy handed Beast a cold beer, and they chortled about something private. It made a pleasant change for me to witness the community spirit after listening to a litany of complaints day after day.

Austin bestowed his father the honor of holding the spatula, and then came to greet me with a plate piled high with mouthwatering patties.

"These look divine," I said, yanking off the top of a bun and slathering ketchup onto the grilled meat.

I closed my eyes as I took the first bite, savoring the incredible taste as the juicy meatiness exploded my tastebuds to smithereens.

"Do I have the royal seal of approval from my girls?" he asked as if waiting for me to bow down and kiss his feet.

All I could offer to him is a thumbs-up because my mouth was busy tasting, and my brain wanted this precious moment to last. The smug look on his face was too cute to ignore, so I gripped his face gently and pulled him down for a peck on the lips as I swallowed. He licked his lips, tasting the same mouthful as me.

"How do you know it's a girl?" I asked.

"Because I just do," Austin answered with a shrug.

It was pointless to argue. He said he could tell for sure, so I gave him the benefit of the doubt.

"When shall we tell the folks?" His husky rasp sent delicious chills across my skin as he wrapped his arms around my waist.

It was considerate of him to wait until I'd scarfed the rest of the burger, pressing his lips against my temple while he waited. It didn't bother me that he was watching me eat like a carnivorous beast or that I'd dripped ketchup down the front of my dress. How was it possible to fall deeper in love each day? A little over a year ago, I would've scoffed at the idea and said that it was crazy.

"I thought you wanted to wait until Rebecca arrived?" I mentioned.

Austin tilted his arm so that we could get a clear view of his watch. "She's over an hour late," he muttered, and he frowned worriedly.

"Just call her," I advised, then reached out to snatch another tasty burger. "You never know, something bad might have happened," I said, with the food muffling my voice.

Austin

I fished my cell phone out of my back pocket and thumbed through the contacts. It wasn't like Becca to be late for anything, so I couldn't help but feel like something was amiss.

She picked up on the second attempt. "Hey Austin," she answered, sounding flustered as fuck. "Uh, I can't exactly talk right now. I'm kind of busy. Can I call you back later?"

"Becca, where the hell are you? Everyone is here. Your mom has made your favorite treacle tart. If you're not here in the next thirty seconds, Riley is going to eat it," I told her, noticing the indignant scowl on my wife's gorgeous face.

Rebecca's breath rattled down the line along with the sound of an injured yowl in the background.

"Dammit, I'm sorry, I'm sorry," Becca apologized, and it sounded as if she was talking to someone else.

"Oh shit! Are you that kind of busy?" I cringed, flaring my eyes with horror.

Just as I was about to hang up, thinking some guy was going balls-deep into my childhood bestie, she was quick to defend, "Eww, no! Fuck! I, uh . . . I, um . . . I did a Riley! Gotta go. I need to call a recovery truck . . . and an ambulance," she said before cutting the call.

I was left staring at the screen of my phone, mystified.

"Is she on her way?" Riley asked, placing a cold bottle of water against her forehead.

She took my baffled expression as a sign that I didn't know.

"Shall I do the honors or are you going to tell my father that you impregnated his only daughter?" she dared me to say.

I took her hand in mine and led her across the yellow patchy grass that resembled straw. My nieces and nephews darted past us as they ran around playing tag. My sisters had set up a kids' face-painting stall, which meant it was difficult to tell the fuckers apart.

Everyone seemed to be in high spirits lately. Not just here in The Hills, but across the entire state of Whitehaven. It might have something to do with the alliance our president had forged with the Reaper and how we hadn't experienced a hunter attack in months. My mate had made quite an impact during her short time on the council. The crime rate had dropped. The residents had a newfound respect for our leaders. Even I gave up my reclusive haunt in the woods and bought a nice little cabin in the suburbs. Now I had neighbors who waved at me whenever I stuck my head out of the door, or came over and chatted about the weather as I washed our car or mowed our front lawn. No, wait — that was me! Yeah, I was that guy. That irritating neighbor who could talk the tits off a turtle.

And this new me was going to become a father. I managed to persuade a woman to create a baby with me! I could just see it now; I'd be one of those dads who strapped their cub to their chest and carried a diaper bag wherever he went. Soon it'd be all juice boxes and crayon packs, and complaining about sleep deprivation to other parents in the schoolyard.

We approached our mothers who were both sitting together on the porch, swapping family stories. I dread to think about the things that my mother had confessed to Sasha. They both had watery eyes as they overcame a fit of giggles.

It better not have been about the Tripod thing!

I low-key loved that nickname, but I fucking detested how I earned it.

"Mom?" I said, grabbing her attention. "There's something I want to say to you." I flashed my eyes down at Riley.

Riley fumbled with her hands, then coughed to clear her throat. "Yeah, we wanted to wait until you were all together."

Bracken and my father and my three sisters came over to join us at this point. They looked as if they anticipated what we were about to say, but this was our special moment, and we wanted to share it together.

"Now that we've got you all here, Riley and I have something important we want to tell you," I said excitedly.

My mother looked as if she was about to burst with happiness as she placed her hand over her heart. Sasha was holding her bottom lip between her teeth. Our dads were waiting there, beers in hand, ready to drink to the good news. My sisters were practically squealing as we keep them waiting a few torturous moments longer.

"We're pregnant!" Riley said, and I pulled her tightly against me, feeling so damn proud I might explode with joy.

Celebratory cheers sounded throughout the crowd. Everybody had been listening just as anxiously and were all thrilled as we delivered our news. My chest swelled with emotion as I turned to embrace my stunning wife. I did feel like the richest man in the world right now, not that money had anything to do with it. I could see that she got it because she looked like she was thinking the same thing. The key to true happiness was counting the blessings that money couldn't buy. She'd given me her heart and her time, and those things are priceless.

AUTHOR MESSAGE

To stay up to date with my stories, check out my website and sign up to my newsletter: www.kellylord.co.uk

Printed in Great Britain
by Amazon